Lost Legacy

 Meg rose and walked toward him. "I thought I'd surprise you and have lunch with you. I got the rest of the day off. Carol told me you already ate, so I guess I'm a little late." She leaned in and kissed him. "I should go so you can get back to work."
 "I feel bad that you came all the way here for nothing."
 "How sweet," came the sound of Ellen's voice.
 Joe and Meg turned to see Ellen glaring at them from the doorway. Joe began to tremble.
 "Let me guess. You're Meg, and Joe's living with you, right?"
 Meg glanced at Joe, then nodded.
 Ellen glared at Joe. "No wonder you were so uncomfortable when I asked you for your phone number, you lying son of a bitch!"
 "You must be Ellen," Meg said innocently.
 "Very good. You're younger than I expected, but as long as you're out of high school, I'm sure Joe doesn't mind. I didn't mean to interfere. I just came back for my hat."
 As Ellen stomped passed them, Joe said, "Ellen, let me explain."
 She turned back toward him. "You can explain to my lawyer."

What They Are Saying About
Lost Legacy

Joe Hillery, a happily married man with a lovely wife and a young family, finds himself in desperate need to pay the mortgage on his refurbished ancestral home. He becomes enthralled by the generous sum offered him by the local Pagan high priest, Marcus Phillips, to recount to the Coven his time-travel adventures. The three coven witches, determined to be the one with Joe when he locates the mystical ring, cast love spells over him. Can Joe prove himself strong enough against their love spells to save his marriage?

I highly recommend Ralph Horner's most recent release, the suspenseful witches' tale, *Lost Legacy*. It artfully depicts the wickedness of three coven witches warring against one another, determined to be the one with Joe, whom it has been predicted will locate the Wiccan Ring of Power, missing for centuries.

JoEllen Conger
Conger Book Reviews

Other Works from the Pen of
Ralph Horner

Tandem Tryst - Jeff has a second chance with his late wife when he finds her in a previous life at the 1893 World Columbian Exposition. But a mysterious woman tries to steal the ring that sends him back in time.

Witch's Moon - Joe travels back in time three-hundred years, where he has only two days to find someone who will touch the ring on a witch's finger.

Midnight Mist - An enchanted ring sends Melody ahead one hundred years in time to reunite with her true love, Jeff. But Alice, Melody's mentally disturbed sister, has time-traveled to the present with her, vowing to kill Melody.

*To Helen,
Keep Writing your
mysteries. Best Wishes*

Lost Legacy

Ralph E Horner

Ralph Horner

A Wings ePress, Inc.

Paranormal Suspense Novel

Wings ePress, Inc.

Edited by: Terri Joyce
Copy Edited by: Jeanne Smith
Executive Editor: Jeanne Smith
Cover Artist: Richard Stroud

All rights reserved

Names, characters and incidents depicted in this book are products of the author's imagination or are used fictitiously. Any resemblance to actual events, locales, organizations, or persons, living or dead, is entirely coincidental and beyond the intent of the author or the publisher.

No part of this book may be reproduced or transmitted in any form or by any means, electronic or mechanical, including photocopying, recording, or by any information storage and retrieval system, without permission in writing from the publisher.

Wings ePress Books
www.books-by-wings-epress.com

Copyright © 2017 by Ralph Horner
ISBN 978-1-61309-672-7

Published In the United States Of America

Wings ePress Inc.
3000 N. Rock Road
Newton, KS 67114

Dedication

To my daughter, Angela Knispel.

Prologue

Medea's Curse 1707

Medea rung her hands as her dark eyes glanced about the room desperately seeking some way to escape. The young woman scurried to the window at the other end of the small bedroom. Steel bars blocked the open window. They were too close together for anyone fit through.

In a banquet room on the other end of the mansion, several men sat at a long table smoking, playing cards, and drinking ale. Four young women were among them while a belly dancer gyrated about the table with a large snake draped around her neck. A blaze crackled in a great fireplace at the back of the room.

Three men wearing tricorns and waist coats entered, stopping just short of the table.

"Nathon, Medea is here. She's locked in a spare room," one of the men announced.

"Which room?" asked a tall, thin, dark-haired man who sat at the front of the table holding a mug.

The dancer stopped.

"In the guest room."

Nathon sneered. "Well, since she is in the guest room, she must be our guest. Bring her here, and I'll show her a little Cyrus hospitality."

Some of the people laughed.

"On second thought," Nathon rose from the table. "I'll fetch her myself."

A portly man with a brush-like beard leaned forward. "You're quite certain you don't need assistance?"

"Assistance?"

"Aye. She's a high-spirited lass."

Nathon smiled. "I would hope that I am still in good enough health that I might be able to contain the wench."

Some of the men snickered.

"But very well, Edward, come with me if you must."

Edward and Nathon left the smoke filled room. Nathon almost sprinted down the long hallway while Edward waddled behind. When they reached the last room on the left, Nathon searched through an assortment of keys on a large ring. He unlocked the door and slowly pushed it open. The men hung back, not knowing if the maid would be retreating or attacking. No sound came from inside. Nathon forced the door open wider. They stepped inside, but the room appeared to be empty.

The stout man peered in behind Nathon. "Where did she go?"

Nathon put a finger to his lips with a smirk. He knelt next to the bed and saw Medea cowering under it.

"Come out from under this bed, witch!"

The girl screamed as the tall man grabbed her arm and pulled, twisting it in pain. Medea yelled as she tried to break free of his grip, but Nathon dragged her out. He grasped her narrow wrists and yanked her to her feet.

"Come with me, girl."

Medea fearfully gazed into Nathon's determined eyes. "Master Cyrus, let me go. I've done nothing to you."

The two men ignored her pleas and forced her out of the room, each grasping one of her wrists. They marched her down the hall and turned into the banquet room. Edward released her and stepped back.

With Nathon still holding Medea's arm, one of the guests yelled, "Don't they make a splendid couple? I pronounce thee man and witch."

Everyone in the room roared.

"We're in luck," Nathon said. "She hasn't escaped on her broomstick, as I had feared."

Chuckles were heard among the men.

"This shall be a night we will all remember because of what I shall obtain from this despicable creature."

Nathon turned to Medea, raising the palm of his free hand. "Wench, if you value your life, give me your ring."

Her blank expression caused Nathon to examine the fingers on both of her hands but he didn't see a ring.

"I wear no ring," Medea said quickly.

Grating his teeth, he looked into her pale face and growled, "You do wear a ring! That blasted pentagram ring of yours. Where is it?"

Medea was wide eyed with fear. "I have no such ring, sir."

He shook her entire body. "'Tis the same pentagram ring that Diehla Thorne wore before you. The ring that all ye devil ridden witches use for your black magic."

"Master Cyrus, I have heard of the ring of which you speak, but I truly know not where it be." Her voice trembled.

"Damn you! Damn you, girl!" he yelled in her face. He wrenched her wrist and looked toward the men who had brought her to the house. "Did any of you see the ring she wears?"

"No, I saw it not," one man said.

Another apologized. "I regret to say I was not looking for a ring."

"I saw it!" Edward replied.

Nathon stared at him. "Are you quite certain?"

"Quite."

"Which finger?"

"Her index finger. Her right one, I'm sure."

"He lies!" Medea yelled and tried to jerk away from her captor.

"Nay, he doth not." Nathon looked toward his guests. "You see, 'tis a man's ring, so she and the other sorceresses are forced to wear it on their index fingers." Peering at Medea, Nathon growled, "For the final time, witch, where is the ring?"

The young woman sank to her knees, folding her hands. "Master Cyrus, I possess no such ring as you say. I can't give you a thing that I do not possess!" Her cheeks reddened as she cried in despair.

Nathon's eyes turned to slits. "You're trying to make a fool of me in front of my guests. I'll see you burn in hell for this, witch!"

He threw her down on her face. The terrified girl raised herself up on one elbow and pushed back the black hair from her eyes to look at him.

"Your punishment for this act of deceit is death!" Nathon whispered sharply, gazing down at her.

"Nay! I'm innocent! Please spare me, sir." Medea's sobs filled the room.

"Don't kill her, Nathon," one of the women said. "You put a fearful scare into the wench, isn't that enough?"

He turned toward the woman. "Nay, I say she dies!"

"She may cast a spell on you," a man holding a mug quipped.

"Silence! If one other person questions my decision here tonight, he shall join the witch in death!" A hush fell over the room. "Now Jonathon, Edward and Joshua, assist me with what needs to be done."

As the three men came toward her, she stared up at Nathon, sobbing. "Please, Master Cyrus, have mercy, I beg you!"

"Take her to the hearth." Nathon pointed.

The men grabbed Medea and dragged her across the room. There she was forced to kneel upon the stone hearth before the fire.

Nathon crept toward her. Medea's demeanor changed from fear to anger. She glared up into Nathon's face and hissed, "Beware Nathon Cyrus, in another time, centuries from now, I will return to live again through one of my descendants who will bear my face. When your descendant seeks the ring again, he will be murdered by my descendant. This act of revenge will end the Cyrus line. My curse is on you, Nathon Cyrus!"

Nathon pulled a thin leather strap from under his waist coat. "You'll not return, you miserable witch!"

While the men held the struggling woman in place, Nathon forced her face away from him, toward the fire. He looped the strap around her neck.

"Now die in silence!" He tightened the strap. "You're finally getting what you deserved years ago, you evil temptress!" The veins protruded from his neck.

Despite Medea's gasps and flailing arms, Nathon continued to strangle the girl on the hearth. While she choked and gagged, some of the guests watched in horror. Others laughed and joked about the killing. Medea soon became silent then lifeless. Nathon dropped her limp body on the floor in front of the hearth.

He turned to face the others. "If anyone tells of what has transpired here tonight, he shall receive the same as she. Now William and Peter, I want you to search her body thoroughly."

The men went to Medea's body on the floor and defiled her but found nothing.

"Philip and Edward," Nathon shouted, "go to the guest room and find that ring. It must be in that room somewhere. It surely has to be!"

One

The Deal

    With a single candle burning in the center of the small table, the black-haired woman spoke. "Will everyone please join hands?"
    She and the other three people at the table took the hand of the person next to them.
    The young woman closed her dark eyes. "We are gathered here tonight to contact the spirit of Abigail Jennings, daughter of Matthew the Blacksmith, from late seventeenth century Willstown. I call you, Abigail, from the spirit world. Hear me. Appear before us now."
    The woman repeated the words several times. Abruptly, a gust of wind whipped through the room, followed by the sound of glass shattering on the floor nearby.
    Joe's heartbeat quickened and his grip tightened on the people who held his hands.
    "She is here!" The clairvoyant's eyes remained closed. "Abigail is asking me who I am. I am Luna LaBrock, a clairvoyant from Manchester. The year is 1992. I'm calling you on behalf of Joseph Hillery." Luna went silent, then opened her eyes. "Abigail said she does know you, Joseph." Luna paused as if listening to the spirit. "She wants to hear you. Say something to her."

"Abigail." Joe wondered if she would recognize his voice. It had been twelve years since he had gone to her time. "It's me, Joseph. I'm trying to find out what happened to you after I came back to the twentieth century. There are no records here that tell me about your life, only that you returned home the day after I was sent to my time. Did you have any other encounters with Diehla's witches?"

"Nay, Joseph," Luna said in another voice. "Thank the Lord I was spared."

Joe frowned at Luna's change in speech, which sounded startlingly familiar. *It's Abigail! She's speaking through Luna.*

"Joseph, I had a very good life. I married three years after you left me. I had four children. I owe thee my life for saving me from that giant in the witch house."

"That's the least I could do for you after you risked your life for me trying to touch Diehla's ring."

"And how has thy life been, Joseph, three hundred years hence?" Her voice was gentle.

"After we defeated Diehla, I married Ellen, the love of my life. We have two children and I have a business here in Willstown."

"I am so happy that you found happiness, too. My time is nearly gone, but 'tis wonderful to have heard thee again, Joseph, bless thee."

Luna opened her eyes and let go of Joe's hand. "The trance is broken. Abigail has returned to the spirit world." From a button under the table she turned the lights on.

"Luna," Joe said, "You spoke in Abigail's voice."

Luna smiled at him, then took a couple of deep breaths. "Well, as you two have seen, Joe has spoken the truth, as incredible as it seems. I believe I have learned more from this experience than he has." Luna looked at the man with short brown hair sitting across from her. "Well, Barry, is your skepticism satisfied?"

"I still can't believe it! I mean how—"

"I've never lied to you," Luna interrupted. "At least not about my psychic powers." She smirked at him. "Yes, Joe was actually with Diehla in 1680 as he claims."

"Although I've been a witch all my adult life," Sayde said, a hand to her chest. She took a deep breath. "This revelation proves the witches of old had unimaginable powers."

Joe noticed that besides Luna's large disc earrings and rings on almost every finger, she also wore a silver star around her neck. He hadn't realized when he made the appointment that this psychic was a witch.

"To think you met Diehla Thorne herself, actually spoke to her," Luna said, gazing at Joe, a look of awe in her beady dark eyes.

Luna's interest in Diehla made him uncomfortable.

Luna glanced at the woman with short blonde hair who looked to be in her mid-thirties. "How about you, Sayde? Have you any doubt about Joe's traveling back in time?"

Sayde shook her head. "No, not if you insist, but I still don't see how it was possible."

Luna squinted. "Joe went back to Diehla's time because she sent him there. She must have had even more power than we ever imagined because of her ring."

Barry hit the table with his fist. "If this is true, as you claim, it's the most incredible story I've ever heard."

Joe glanced at Luna. "If you're able to contact the dead, why couldn't you have contacted Diehla yourself?"

"Because I can only contact the dead if at least one person in the circle knew the deceased. Obviously this is the first time I've been able to reach a spirit so long dead."

"Thank you, Luna. I found the information I was looking for." Some of Joe's guilt washed away upon hearing that Abigail had a safe and happy life after putting herself in danger for him. "What do I owe you?"

"Maybe we can make a deal." Luna folded her hands on the table. "When you were in Diehla's home, did they show you any of their magic secrets?"

"Yeah, I learned a couple of things when—" Joe stopped, noticing how intently all three stared at him. *No deals with witches.* "Well, I was only in that house for one day. I mean, I didn't actually learn how they performed their magic. So I have nothing to barter with."

"Even if you don't know how they did their magic, you did see them perform some. Perhaps we can still swap my fee for that information."

"Thanks, but I'd rather just pay you." Joe forced a smile.

Luna sighed. "That'll be thirty-five dollars."

When Joe laid the money on the table, Luna said, "We will keep your secret to ourselves and not sell your story to the tabloids."

"Thanks." Joe smiled and turned away, leaving the room and Luna's small house.

~ * ~

When Joe returned home, he explained his ghostly experience at the séance to his wife, Ellen.

She shook her head. "Thank God you finally got that over with. I'll call Nancy later and tell her how things went."

"Thank her for giving us Luna's name."

Joe decided he should wait to tell Ellen that Luna and the others were witches and that they even tried to barter for his fee.

In the time Joe and Ellen lived in Hillery mansion, they only changed a couple of little things and made the necessary repairs. Joe wanted the house to remain historic. Even the portrait gallery with its display of the ill-fated Hillerys, cursed by Diehla, hung on the wall in the same place near the hearth.

~ * ~

Two nights later while Ellen was doing the dishes, the phone rang. She wiped her soapy hands on a towel before answering. Stepping toward the living room she called, "Joe, it's for you."

"Who is it?"

Ellen shrugged as Joe picked up the phone. A woman's voice said, "Hi Joe, this is Luna LaBrock, the psychic you saw Tuesday night."

Joe felt uneasy. The witch had tracked him down. "How did you get my number?"

"From the phone book, of course. Joe, our coven has a proposition for you. If you share your entire time-travel story with us and any information you picked up from Diehla's coven, we'll pay you a considerable sum of money."

Joe didn't want to get mixed up with witches, considering it was Diehla herself who had cursed his ancestor, Judge Jeremiah Hillery, after he passed sentence on her. For three hundred years, every male Hillery descendant died before reaching the age of forty. If it weren't for his time-travel victory over Diehla, he would be worrying about his own early death right now.

"I didn't see or hear enough to be paid," Joe replied.

"Our coven leader, Marcus Phillips, is wealthy and would be willing to pay you for any information you have."

Joe's video production business was failing and he was behind on his mortgage payments. He needed time to think about this. He wondered why these witches were so interested in what he saw in the past, but he knew Luna wouldn't tell him the truth if he asked.

"I'll think it over, Luna."

"Wonderful. You still have my phone number, right?"

"Yes. I'll call you in a couple of days if I change my mind."

When Joe hung up, Ellen asked, "Who was that?"

Not wanting to tell her he had witches calling him at home Joe answered, "Just some business I had to finish."

~ * ~

Back at the office on Monday, Joe had almost forgotten about the call from Luna when his receptionist, Carol, put through a panicked call from Ellen. His wife sobbed out the words, "Joe, in the mail we got…" She began to cry.

"Ellen, calm down. What came in the mail?"

"A foreclosure notice on our home." She sniffed. "Hillery mansion has been in your family for centuries, and now we're going to lose it."

An adrenalin rush of panic went through Joe, but he knew he had to stay calm for his wife. "Ellen, take it easy. I might have a way to get the money for the payment. Just calm down. I'll talk to you about it when I get home."

Ellen sniffled. "All right, Joe."

When he got off the phone, he squeezed the bridge of his nose and closed his eyes. Joe wished he hadn't refinanced his home to keep his failing business going. He knew what he had to do. He found Luna's phone number in his wallet then dialed, praying she hadn't changed her mind about the offer. As the phone rang, he started to perspire, knowing this was his only hope of keeping Hillery mansion. *I wish I hadn't played down what knowledge I did learn.*

The phone was finally answered. "Hello?"

"Is Luna there?"

"I'm sorry but she's doing a reading right now. Can I take a message?"

"No, I'll try her back later. Is this Sayde?"

"No, this is Paula. If you give me your name and number, I'll have Luna call you."

Joe didn't want to give her his business phone. "Thanks, but I'll call her later." He hung up.

Two hours later he called her again. "Luna LaBrock speaking."

"Luna, this is Joe Hillery. I've decided to take you up on your offer, if it's still good."

"Yes, yes. You sure changed your mind in a hurry. Marcus will be thrilled."

Joe breathed a sigh of relief.

"Marcus would like you to meet with him and Sayde twice a week from seven until nine in the evening until they've heard your entire time-travel story. They want to learn as much as you can give them. Marcus will pay you for each session."

"Do you know how much that will be?"

"No. You'll have to take that up with him."

"What nights do they want me there?"

"Marcus would like to see you on Tuesdays and Fridays, if that's convenient."

I'd meet them in the middle of the night if they'd asked me, but with knowing little about Diehla's ancient magic, how can I stretch the meetings long enough to pay our mortgage?

"Since tomorrow is Tuesday," Luna said, "we'd like you to start then. I'll be there for your first meeting."

"Fine, I'll see you tomorrow night at seven."

"You'll be coming to our parish on Hall Street." She gave him the address. "When you get into Manchester, take Maple south to Bridge Street. Go left then make a right onto Hall. It's a couple of blocks down on the left. Ask for Marcus Phillips when you arrive."

Joe didn't like the fact he was meeting the head witch at their parish. It still didn't add up that they were paying him a lot of money for his stories. What choice did he have but to go?

~ * ~

At the dinner table that evening, Joe looked at Ellen. "I'll have the money we need to make the mortgage payment soon."

Ellen smiled and reached for Joe's hand. "How did you manage it?"

Because their eight-year-old son, Tommy, and five-year-old daughter, Amy, were at the table, Joe hesitated. "I'll explain later."

Ellen nodded and smiled at him again.

With Tommy's dark brown hair and eyes, he favored his father. Amy looked like a small version of her mother with light brown hair, blue eyes and petite frame.

In the living room after the kids were in bed, Ellen asked, "So tell me where all this money is coming from."

Joe and Ellen had a good marriage and an honest relationship, but Joe thought for now he should keep the true nature of his business to himself. Ellen had enough on her mind without worrying about who he was dealing with.

"This is a new account that I decided to do business with."

"How did you get it so suddenly?"

"The customer is an eccentric millionaire. He approached me recently with his unusual business practices. I didn't want his account, but with our house on the line, I called him to confirm that I'd do business with him."

Ellen snuggled up to Joe on the couch. "The timing couldn't have been better. I think he must have been sent from above. Someone is looking out for us, Joe."

Ellen's statement made him feel even more ashamed of his secret dealings.

"He wants to meet with me twice a week in the evening. Our first meeting will be tomorrow night at seven."

She turned to look at Joe. "You have to do business with him at night?"

Joe nodded. "I told you he was eccentric. Now you know why I didn't want his account. He's got some kind of superstition about doing business at certain times of the day."

"Maybe he's into astrology, but that's a small inconvenience for saving our home."

~ * ~

Joe found the parish, which looked like any other church. The area was so highly populated he had trouble finding a parking place and had to park two blocks away. When he got to the parish, he knocked on the heavy, white, wooden door. He grew tense, waiting for one of the witches to answer. The door was opened by a short woman with flaming red hair wearing a black robe. It made Joe think of the witches he'd seen in Diehla's coven home.

"Can I help you?" she asked.

"Yes, I'm Joe Hillery here to see Marcus Phillips."

She smiled. "Of course. Come right in." She held the door for him.

"Hi, Joe, I'm Trish Spencer." She smiled and shook his hand. "Marcus is in the parish hall. Follow me."

She led Joe to the back of the building and into a large, smoky, incense-filled room. A huge black pentagram was painted in the middle of the white floor. People in black robes congregated around the room. Strange discordant music, which seemed appropriate for the gothic surroundings, filled the air.

Creepy. I feel like I don't belong here.

Heads turned as they passed three women and a single man standing near a large smoking cauldron.

When they got to the back of the room, a dark-haired, bearded man who looked about forty sat enthroned in a large chair. Joe spotted Luna LaBrock among three young women who sat on the floor in front of him. Another young woman stood behind the man massaging his shoulders.

Luna was wearing black lipstick and nail polish, the Gothic look. Joe thought she looked sinister, unlike her appearance the night he was at her home. Luna smiled at Joe and waved.

The man's dark eyes were brooding. Like the others he wore a black robe and a silver five pointed star on a chain around his neck. Trish introduced Joe to the man. "This is Marcus Phillips, our high coven priest."

Two

The Explanation

Marcus slowly stood as the girl behind him stopped her massage. He looked directly at Joe. A slight smile formed on his face. He extended his hand and Joe shook it.

"Luna told me about your fantastic experience. Please tell me more." Marcus's smile broadened. "Diehla Thorne returned from the dead and sent you back to her time?"

Joe nodded.

"Our moon Mass tonight will begin at eight o'clock. Please join us."

Joe shook his head. "Sorry, not tonight."

"I'll take less than an hour of your time tonight," Marcus said. "First let me introduce you to some of our coven before we go to the study. I believe you already met Barry."

"Yeah, last week at the séance," Joe said.

Barry was the only person wearing a green robe. The young man turned from the woman he was talking to and raised his hand in a mock wave.

Marcus pointed to the young woman who had been massaging his shoulders. "And this is our masseuse, Megan O'Leary."

With her dark-brown pixie haircut and little turned up nose, Joe thought Megan looked like a pixie herself as she smiled at him. Her pale complexion made her brown eyes look almost black.

"Your sign?" She raised her palm. "No, let me guess." Megan squinted at Joe's face for a moment. "Leo. You're a Leo, right?"

Joe nodded. "That's very good."

"I'm good at a lot of things." She flashed him an impish grin. "My friends call me Meg. If you ever need a good massage, it'll be my pleasure."

"I'll keep it in mind, Meg."

Marcus continued the introductions, pointing to an Asian woman. "This is Circe Tiiu."

The young woman had the Goth look: heavy black liner around her almond eyes, black lipstick and nail polish. She smiled. "Hi, Joe."

"Circe is our coven psychologist," Marcus said. "She does remarkable things with hypnotism."

Joe had no intentions of using this sinister looking woman's talents.

Marcus turned to a statuesque woman who looked to be in her late twenties. "And this young lady is Paula Rulavich."

Joe judged her to be almost six feet tall as she was at least two inches taller than he.

Paula extended her long fingers with a smile. "My pleasure, Joe. I spoke with you on the phone the other day."

Joe shook her hand. "Right."

Like Luna and Circe, Paula wore the Gothic look. Joe thought she was by far the most attractive woman in the coven, with her medium-brown hair cut in a pageboy, high cheek bones and slightly pointed nose.

"Paula's a model," Marcus continued.

"What kind of modeling do you do?" Joe asked, forcing a conversation.

"Runway, fashion shows, that sort of thing."

"Excuse us now, people," Marcus interrupted. "Luna, are you coming with us?"

She nodded and followed Joe and Marcus out of the parish hall and down to the study. Sayde was waiting with four glasses of wine on a desk. After everyone was seated, she handed each a glass.

"Thank you, my dear," Marcus said to Sayde. He glanced at Joe. "Luna and Sayde both told me about your time-travel experience. I can't even think of an adjective to describe my interest." Marcus took a sip of wine, watching Joe the entire time. "In the visits you'll be making here, we want all the information you can give us about Diehla Thorne, her coven members and, of course, the magic they used, no matter how trivial it may seem to you."

"I know how interested you are, but before I agree to this, what will my fee be?"

"Five hundred dollars a visit. A one thousand dollar check each week."

Unbelievable! I've got to play up what I know and even embellish if necessary. "Why is this knowledge so important to you?"

"We have always revered the name of Diehla Thorne not that we agree with everything she did, of course, but her magic might have been unchallenged by any other witch or wizard."

"Some say Victor Zabno was her equal," Sayde said.

"Joe, with you, we have found a person who has actually met Diehla Thorne and even been in her home. It's too wonderful to be real!" Marcus laughed with joy.

"We don't have time for a session tonight," Sayde said.

"When I spoke with you on the phone, it slipped my mind that we were having our moon ritual this evening," Luna said. "But as long as you're here, why don't you join us?"

Joe shook his head. "I'm sorry. I really can't stay this evening."

Sayde smiled. "You'll be paid just for coming tonight."

"Thank you." *Five hundred dollars for this chat? What's the catch?*

"We do insist that you attend our next ritual," Marcus said. "Next Tuesday night is our Autumn Equinox Sabbat."

"I appreciate the invitation, but I have my own religion."

Marcus raised his voice. "Joe, we insist that you attend. You'll be paid for coming, even though we won't be seeking information from you that night. Instead of being here from seven to nine, you'll be coming one hour later, from eight to ten. And we still do need you here this Friday at seven to begin the information process."

"Of course," Joe said, not understanding why Marcus was so insistent on his taking part in their Tuesday night ritual.

"Everyone in the coven knows about your time-travel experience," Sayde said. "However, don't give any of your information to anyone else in the coven other than Marcus, Luna and myself, understood?"

"Yes." Joe obediently nodded, feeling uneasy.

~ * ~

When Joe returned home, Ellen asked him how it went.

"The new client is very wealthy but the drawback is he insisted I meet with him personally every Tuesday and Friday night."

"How long must you meet with this mister, what was his name?"

"Marcus Phillips. I'm not sure how long."

"Why can't he meet you during normal business hours?"

"Remember, he's eccentric."

Ellen nodded. "Yes, of course. What kind of videos is he producing?"

Joe tried to deflect the question. "He's just getting started in this business. After he does his shooting, we'll be editing and marketing his videos. Right now I'm explaining to him how this process works."

"But what type of video is he making?"

"The occult."

Ellen frowned. "You mean horror films?"

"Yeah, and new age documentaries."

"He's not dangerous, is he?"

Joe shook his head. "No, I don't think so."

Ellen took in a deep breath. "Like I said, it's a small price to pay for keeping our home."

I don't like lying to Ellen, but I'll level with her after my dealings with Marcus are over.

~ * ~

Joe met with Marcus, Sayde and Luna in the parish study again on Friday. Joe explained to them how witches were able to fly.

"The lard material is from unbaptized children?" Sayde asked with a grimace.

"Yes. It wasn't the staff or rod that permitted them to fly, but the ointment they applied to it."

"Joe's not making that up," Luna said. "I read that in a book on witch folklore, but without knowing the author, I wasn't sure if it was true." She peered at Joe with her dark beady eyes. "Why would they show you something so sacred to them?"

"Three members of Diehla's coven took me to see an old psychic witch. She told Ludmilla, Diehla's half sister, that I traveled through time to get there. I convinced Ludmilla that I was a powerful wizard, using my pen, photos and a cigarette lighter to help my story." Joe smiled. "She gave me the flying ointment recipe."

Sayde set her glass down. "We're aware of Ludmilla and a few of the others who lived with Diehla. We know that Ludmilla's father was Victor Zabno, known as the black magician. He trained the young Diehla in his craft, gave her his pentagram ring and was her lover."

"Did you also know Ludmilla died in the fire that destroyed Diehla's house?" Joe asked.

"How do you know that?" Marcus asked.

"A book I read said one of the two bodies found in the ashes had an amulet around its neck. Ludmilla showed me the amulet her father had given her."

"Ludmilla did wear an amulet." Marcus looked at the two women. "Joe couldn't have known that unless he actually met her."

"So you have that information about her amulet in a book somewhere?" Joe asked.

Marcus ignored the question. "Do you remember Diehla's lover, Yves Laughton?"

"Yes." *What a creepy guy he was.*

"We have in our parish an old parchment with information written by his daughter, Medea Laughton, from the year 1704. You won't find that in any library book. We even know that the other victim of the house fire was Beldameth Rollins."

Joe cringed just hearing the name of that evil, hideous crone. She was his biggest adversary in Diehla's house. She even sliced his arm when she sent flying daggers at him.

"We feel we are the descendants of Medea's coven," Luna said.

"Why's that?" Joe asked, uneasy with that fact.

"Because Victoria Sidedrop, the founder of this coven," Luna continued, "is the descendant of Yves Laughton. Medea was Victoria's fifth great-grandmother. We have her family tree on record."

"This is one of the reasons we're paying you," Marcus said. "We need information to verify stories passed down from Victoria's grandmother."

Luna took a sip of wine. "Since she was a small child, Vickie's grandma bragged to her that they were descended from a great sorcerer and sorceress."

Joe raised his glass. "So it was Victoria's grandmother that you got those papers from?"

"Yes," Sayde said, "but it wasn't until 1929 when Vickie was sixteen that she really became interested in those old stories of her granny's. It was then that she read the writings of Medea Laughton."

"What's in the papers?" Joe asked.

"Some history about Diehla's coven told to Medea by her father, Yves," Sayde said. "Medea's memoirs of her coven life and of her father's tragic death."

"And these papers still exist?" Joe took a sip of wine.

Sayde smiled. "They're brown and withered, but still readable."

"Then you know what happened to Diehla's coven members who escaped the fire?"

"It seems everyone assumes that after Diehla's house was burned, it was the end of her coven," Luna said. "But only two died, so ten were still left."

Joe frowned. "Where did they go?"

"They migrated to Portsmouth," Luna said. "And soon they became thirteen members again. One of their new members was Gabrielle Lasaunt, Medea's mother. Yves and Gabrielle came here to Manchester ten years later with a few others to form a new coven. When Medea was in her twenties, she became high priestess and was almost as powerful a witch as Diehla, making us believe the coven must have found and possessed the magic ring after Diehla was burned."

"So what happened to Medea and the ring?" Joe asked.

Luna set her empty glass down. "In 1707 it was illegal to kill a witch, so a ruthless man named Nathon Cyrus took the law into his own hands. He strangled her to death in his home. He was never arrested or even questioned for Medea's murder."

Joe cringed. "Why did he kill her?"

"We believe Cyrus wanted the magic pentagram ring," Sayde said.

"Medea was wearing it?" Joe asked.

"Again, we're not sure, because Medea was dead and couldn't continue her writing," Luna said.

"You're certain Nathon Cyrus and his friends killed her?"

"Some of Medea's coven recognized the three men that dragged her from her yard as Cyrus's friends," Sayde said. "They weren't surprised when her body was found the next day in an open field just south of Cyrus's home. He had great influence in Manchester back in the early eighteenth century."

"So this Cyrus got the pentagram ring?"

"No." Sayde shook her head. "If he had, he would have really wreaked havoc. As you know, the ring had great powers. Medea would never have let her enemies gain possession of that jewel."

"What happened to it then?"

Sayde took in a breath. "That's the hundred thousand dollar question. Medea wrote that she owned a special ring, but she never mentioned how it looked or how she obtained it or that it had once been Diehla's. So it's possible it could have been another magic ring, but we assume it was the Diehla ring. No witch has ever again had the power of Diehla or Medea."

"How old was Medea when they murdered her?"

"Only twenty-five. She left behind a son and a daughter. It was her son that Victoria is descended from. That's how she got the old papers."

Marcus peered at Joe. "Did you actually see the ring on Diehla's finger?"

"I did." Joe nodded. "There were five gem stones marking the five points of a star on a yellow gold band. It changed colors with the movement of her hand. As I told Luna last week, the ring was the key to Diehla's and my wager. She sent me back to her time giving me only two days and one night to find someone brave enough to touch the ring on her finger. A young man named Seth Penrod lost his head trying, and Abigail, the girl we contacted in our séance, also failed. Thank God I was there to save Abigail's life the night Diehla was arrested."

"If you won the wager with Diehla, who touched the ring for you?" Marcus asked.

"Her sister, Ludmilla. As I mentioned, she thought I had magical time-travel powers," Joe raised his hands and wiggled his fingers.

"And wanted me to help her become the coven leader. She felt betrayed that her father had given the ring to Diehla."

Marcus smiled. "That doesn't surprise me since Ludmilla was the daughter of Zabno."

Joe looked at Marcus. "When did Victoria start this coven?"

"When she was in her teens, she began to study witchcraft, then joined a coven here in Manchester." Luna poured Marcus another glass of wine. "In 1940, at the age of twenty-seven, she started her own coven."

"So this coven's been around for over fifty years? Is Victoria still living?"

"She is," Marcus said. "But she left us about three years ago because of poor health. She still practices the old religion at her home here in Manchester. She has a granddaughter in our coven, Megan O'Leary."

"She's the masseuse?"

Marcus nodded as he opened a drawer next to the desk where he sat. "Joe, we really won't start the real questioning until next Friday. Tonight we just wanted to talk and get to know each other a little." He pulled out a check book and began to write. "When you join us in our Autumn Equinox ritual on Tuesday, you'll understand us better." He tore out a check and handed it to Joe. It was made out for one thousand dollars.

Yes!

"Next Friday night, I'll give you another thousand and every Friday until your services are no longer needed."

Joe nodded. *This is too good to be true. There has to be a catch.* Joe was going to ask Marcus why the insistence on his joining their ritual, but kept quiet, knowing the longer he stalled them the more money he would make.

"I might be on the wrong track, but don't witches pray to the devil?" Joe asked.

Marcus laughed. Sayde and Luna said nothing, but Luna glared at him.

"Absolutely not!" Luna's voice raised a few decibels. "We're witches, not Satanists. For us to pray to Satan would be buying into Christianity. Satan was invented by Christians as the Antichrist. Our religion predates Christianity. Our primary god is female." She ran her multi-ringed fingers through her black hair and shook her head in frustration. "Are you Christian?"

"Yes," Joe said.

"That figures," Luna said with a sigh. "In Diehla's time, witches referred to the goddess as Diana, the moon goddess. Now she is called simply the Mother Goddess." Luna raised her hands and glanced toward the ceiling. "She is the mother of the entire universe. We believe everything is part of her, even our own bodies."

"But when I was in Diehla's time, I saw what appeared to be a statue of Satan on their altar," Joe said, trying to explain his questions.

"What you saw was Pan," Luna barked, "the half-goat, half–man god. He's the hunter also referred to as the horned god. He's the male side of our religion. Through the years Christians have used his likeness to represent the devil, but the Bible never describes Satan physically."

"Luna, relax," Marcus said as if afraid she might offend Joe.

"Christians have always been out to make our lives miserable." She hit her palm on the table.

"It sounds like you've got quite an animosity for Christians," Joe said.

"I don't like any religion that tries to wipe out anyone who's different," Luna said. "We've been torched, hanged, decapitated, crushed and persecuted for centuries!"

Wow. I'd better keep my mouth shut. I might blow this deal.

Sayde looked at Joe then at Luna. "I'm sure Joe didn't mean anything derogatory by his questions, Luna."

Marcus laughed, as if trying to defuse an uncomfortable situation. "Joe, since we pray to a goddess instead of the usual male god, we've attracted many women to our religion, especially feminists."

"For every male wizard there are estimated to be ten female witches," Luna added. "Some covens are all women. We keep a low profile, but among women, witchcraft is the fastest growing religion in this country."

"I'm sure we're boring Joe with these statistics," Sayde said.

"You paid me until nine o'clock and I've got five minutes. What kind of magic does your coven practice?"

"It's much more natural in origin." Sayde attempted to pour Joe more wine. He put his hand over the glass and shook his head. "We learn how to use the psychic powers from our minds." She set the bottle down. "Unlike the magic of old, which was often from forces beyond."

"Unfortunately, none of the ancient magic secrets were passed down to us," Luna said.

"Why is that?" Joe asked.

"Witches didn't want their enemies to find out how to use their secret magic and they were afraid of being executed, so their secrets were passed by word of mouth. When Medea was murdered, her knowledge of maleficia was buried with her."

Marcus glanced at his watch. "It's after nine, Joe. I'll show you out."

"Thank you, but I'll see myself out."

"We'll see you on Tuesday night," Marcus said. "Come a few minutes before eight, please. Our rituals begin promptly on the hour."

Driving home, Joe was still bothered by the fact he was being forced to attend their pagan ritual. *Five hundred dollars just for attending and they aren't planning to learn one thing from me that evening? What's going on?*

~ * ~

After Sayde had gone, Marcus and Luna sat alone in the study. Marcus gazed intently at Luna. "Joe must never learn the true reason we're paying him."

"Or Sayde either," Luna returned.

"But I think it's time the rest of our allies know the truth."

Luna laughed. "Yes, before they think you've gone off your rocker paying Joe a thousand dollars every week for his stories."

"Tomorrow is Saturday. I'll call an afternoon meeting with our allies at my home. I'll phone them in the morning."

"I hope our group believes you, Marcus."

"If not, you'll have to convince them. This is the biggest thing that's happened to witches in our time, and it's happening to us, Luna." Marcus clapped his hands together in a grand gesture.

Luna smirked at the thought.

Three

The Conspiracy

Ellen was overjoyed when Joe showed her the thousand dollar check. She hugged and kissed him. "This is a godsend!" She started to cry.

Joe's son, Tommy, asked, "Daddy, are we going to have to move?"

Joe was stunned. He hadn't realized Tommy knew about their money problems.

"Of course not." Joe patted his son on the head.

~ * ~

Joe thought it might be a good idea to be more prepared for his next visit to the coven. He decided his first move would be to do some research at the library. When he visited the next day, the librarian showed him a book on local history. He found the name Laughton. Yves was born in the year 1643 and died in 1696 from a farmer's gunshot blast. Yves was believed to be a sorcerer who had once lived with Diehla Thorne, and his only known child was his sorceress daughter, Medea.

Under Medea, Joe found more information. "MEDEA LAUGHTON 1682-1707. Daughter of feared sorcerer, Yves Laughton. It was said that by the age of thirteen, Medea was already displaying her talent for the black arts. By the time Medea was in her early twenties, her name was infamous in the colonies. Strikingly attractive, she had numerous affairs, even with outsiders. It is unknown how many children she bore, but all were illegitimate.

Medea lived in and around Manchester, New Hampshire until her mysterious death on October 7, 1707. Her body was found in an open field just south of Manchester. Her death was caused by strangulation, but there were no suspects or arrests for her murder."

After Joe read that information, he decided to tell Ellen where he really got the money. It would be a relief to share his Wiccan dilemma.

~ * ~

While Joe was busy at the library, Luna, Megan, Circe, Paula, Trish and Ken, one of the coven's few men, gathered in Marcus's large den. Seated behind his desk, Marcus cleared his throat. "I have called you here today to reveal the most important upcoming event in all of our lives as witches."

With everyone's eyes fixed on him, Marcus paused.

"Well, tell us," Megan demanded.

Marcus raised both hands and looked at Luna. "Tell them, my dear."

Luna took a deep breath. "I had a psychic vision on September eighth after I took Joe Hillery's hand at the séance. I didn't know what to make of it because at first I didn't believe his story. But after it was revealed he had gone back to Diehla's time, I knew my vision was something that will eventually happened to him. On the sixteenth, the morning after Joe visited the parish, I had another vision, this time in a dream. It verified my original vision."

"Get to the point." Paula said, folding her long arms.

Luna closed her eyes as if her news were too awesome for her to speak. "Through Joe Hillery we will find *the* ring!"

"You mean Medea's ring?" Megan asked.

"Yes! Yes! Medea's ring, Diehla's ring, Zabno's ring. The magic ring we've all waited so long to find!"

After a moment of silence, everyone began to talk at the same time.

Marcus clenched his hands into fists in front of him. "It seems too good to be true, but we will find the ring soon."

"Luna," Ken said, "I'm not trying to question your psychic powers, but you and Marcus are celebrating as if we've already found the ring. What if you're wrong? The ring has been missing for almost three hundred years."

"Luna has never been wrong about one of her premonitions," Marcus said. "And in this case she had two. That's never happened to her."

Ken, in his early thirties, was short and thin with shaggy, sandy hair. His brown horned rim glasses gave him the look of the intellectual he was.

"Both visions happened after I saw Joe," Luna said. "I'd stake my life on the fact he finds the ring soon."

"What exactly did you see?" Megan asked.

"Joe was standing in the dark holding the ring while someone was shining a flashlight on it. The light reflected back from the diamonds like a brilliant rainbow. It was breathtaking."

"Could you be tuning into another century?" Trish asked. "Joe saw the ring in Diehla's time."

"No. They didn't have flashlights in 1680, and Joe never had possession of the ring."

"This is the reason I'm paying Joe for his visits," Marcus said. "Not so that he can spin his yarns, amazing as they may be."

"But what if Joe isn't meant to find the ring for a year or even three?" Paula asked. "How are you going to continue paying him this exorbitant amount until he locates it?"

"You're right, Paula," Marcus said. "We have no way of knowing when Joe will find the ring. I only used the money as bait until I could find a more permanent means of keeping him with us. I have chosen you six as possible allies for a plan I have devised. If it works and we find the ring, the seven of us will have unlimited power."

"What's the plan?" Paula asked.

"Use your imagination. Instead of money to motivate Joe, you ladies will lure him with your feminine wiles. I *can* call you ladies?"

"We've been called other things," Megan quipped.

Everyone chuckled.

"Wait a minute, Marcus," Trish said. "What about Sayde and the others?"

"Sayde and the others have been against everything I've tried to do since I became coven high priest. Besides, Sayde despises Diehla and Medea. So why should we include her in our plan to find their ring? I'm only asking my most trusted coven friends."

Trish folded her arms with a scowl. "What happens to the other coven members who aren't included in this plan?"

"Sayde and the others will be out."

"Out of our coven?" Trish gasped.

Marcus nodded.

Trish glared at Marcus. "If you're going to do this behind Sayde's and the others' backs, I don't want any part of it. May I be excused?"

"Do you realize if you leave we are the minority? With you, we are seven. Without you, only six of thirteen."

Trish searched for words to satisfy Marcus. "But you won't need me. You'll have the power."

Marcus was silent for a moment then said, "If Sayde or any of the others gets wind of my plan, we'll all know where it came from."

Trish began to tremble. Avoiding his glare she looked toward the door. "Don't worry, Marcus, your secret is safe with me."

As she headed out of the room, Luna warned, "Watch yourself, Trish."

The young red-headed woman continued out of the room without another word.

With a stern expression, Marcus looked at the others. "Consider Trish a traitor. I want everyone to watch her."

"But what can we do about her?" Ken asked.

"I have a plan for traitors that I'll discuss with all of you later. I'll be damned if she's going to spoil our legacy."

~ * ~

Trish strolled out into the cool, humid afternoon. The overcast sky reflected her mood. She was the only swing person in the coven. She was friends with some of Marcus's clique and also best friends with Sayde, the high priestess. Trish felt certain Marcus and his allies would obtain the ring and she worried how they'd use its magic. She knew the group in that house would stop at nothing for power, regardless of the consequences. As Trish got into her car and backed out of the long driveway, she also worried about what they might do to her, even if she didn't tell a soul about the plan. Marcus and his friends were worried she might not keep quiet and that was dangerous for her. She contemplated talking to Sayde in confidence and maybe getting Joe involved. She wondered if she should leave town, but then her family and her friends in the coven would worry about her. She cried as she drove home.

~ * ~

"I need two of you ladies to seduce Joe Hillery." Watching the women's faces, Marcus slowly grinned as the girls glanced at one another. "If all of you come on to him, he'll get suspicious. Who wants to volunteer for this mission?"

The young women looked at each other again. No one raised a hand, as if waiting to see who would volunteer first.

"Come on, ladies. Joe's not bad looking. Perhaps I should explain your benefit for succeeding. The one who can lure Joe away from the money will be high priestess of our new coven."

"And you'll be legendary," Luna added. "Because the woman who accomplishes this for us will most likely be the person who is with

Joe when he discovers the ring. Your name will go down in witch history."

"Now with that said, who wants to volunteer?" Marcus asked again.

Megan's, Paula's and Circe's hands sprang up. The Asian witch, Circe, dropped her hand when she saw the statuesque model raise hers.

"We have two, splendid. I don't care how you accomplish your task, but make Joe fall in love with you so we have control over his every move. If one of you succeeds, we'll be in contact with him when he finds that ring."

"I agree, Marcus," Paula said, "but Joe strikes me as the loyal husband type. This may be more difficult than you think."

Marcus threw his head back and laughed. "I'm sure one of you ladies can change that."

"What are you going to tell Sayde when she finds out you stopped paying Joe?" Ken asked. "Joe may tell Sayde himself."

"It's a chance we'll have to take." Luna gazed at Ken with her beady eyes. "But in my vision, Joe hadn't aged, and my instincts tell me the ring will be found soon and with one of us holding that flashlight."

"When do we start?" Megan asked.

"At the Autumn Equinox ritual," Marcus said. "I've seen to it that Joe will attend. You'll get your chance during our orgy."

"Joe agreed to participate in our orgy?" Megan frowned.

"Of course not." Marcus shook his head. "Joe has no idea."

Megan scrunched up her face. "I knew that was too good to be true."

"He only thinks he's coming to observe our ritual for which I have agreed to pay him his usual fee." Marcus took a deep breath. "I'll call you back here for a follow up meeting in a few more days. As far as Trish is concerned, I'll deal with her soon. Very soon. Good luck to you, Meg, and to you, Paula, and may the best witch win."

Everyone left the house except Luna and Marcus, who sat in the dining room with two glasses of wine.

"If the others knew that it's you who will likely win Joe's affection, they might feel betrayed." Marcus laughed.

"I still don't think you need volunteers to back up my plan." Luna raised her glass. "With witchcraft I won't even need my feminine wiles."

"But this way all the ladies will believe we have given them a fair chance to be our new high priestess. When you receive the honor, they won't object." Marcus smiled with a nod.

Luna took a sip of wine. "Marcus, if any of the others are smart, they may use spells on Joe as well."

"Don't sell yourself short. You're our most powerful witch, my sweet." Marcus leaned in and kissed her.

~ * ~

That evening while Joe ate dinner with his family, Ellen went on about how relieved she was thanks to the extra money.

"The bank is finally off our back. I'm so proud of you, Joe." She smiled at him. "I feel as if I can depend on you no matter what trouble comes along."

She's so happy. I can't tell her about my true dealings now. I'll wait a couple more days.

~ * ~

When Joe arrived at the Wiccan parish on Tuesday, Sayde escorted him into the smoky candle-lit ritual room. The coven members were assembled in their black robes standing in small groups murmuring. A different sickening, sweet, incense smell billowed from an altar in the center of the room. Autumn fruit, flowers and grain sat on top. To the right was a flaming cauldron. Luna made her way toward Joe and greeted him with a smile, taking his hand with a squeeze. Having started a spell, she hoped that the more time she spent with Joe, the more effective her spell would be.

As Luna engaged Joe in casual chit chat, he spotted Marcus sitting in the back of the room surrounded by three women. Megan again rubbed his shoulders.

He reminds me of a sheik with his harem.

Sayde strolled out to the middle of the room next to the altar. She counted heads with her finger, then stopped as if thinking. "Does anyone know why Trish is late?"

No one answered. A couple of people shook their heads.

"We'll have to begin without her." In a raised voice Sayde said, "People, let's all form our magic circle now. It's time to begin the Mabon ritual on this Autumn Equinox celebration."

Everyone headed for the altar and surrounded it.

"Officers, take your places," Marcus said.

Sayde, Megan and Luna walked to small tables evenly spaced in the witch's circle. Each table held a black pot billowing with incense. Joe found himself between Sayde and a middle-aged, heavy-set woman.

Sayde whispered, "Joe, take your shoes off, please. Place them outside of the circle."

As he turned to step away from the others, he noticed everyone else was barefoot. The only exception was Barry, who stood in stocking feet. Feeling uncomfortable, Joe left his socks on and tossed his shoes under a table next to the wall.

Marcus asked Circe to cast the circle. One of the young women began to play tom-toms as Circe laid down a red rope on the circular boundaries. When she joined the circle, the drumming stopped. Everyone pulled their hoods over their heads and the lights went out. A flaming cauldron inside the circle shed the only light.

Looking at the others around him in the dim candle lit room, Joe felt like he was in a horror film. *I wish I didn't need the money so badly.* He was nervous that harm might come to him.

"Hail guardians of the watchtowers of the east, power of air," Luna said, in her low whispering tone. "We invoke you and call you, golden eagle of dawn, star-seeker, whirlwind, rising sun, come. By the air that is her breath, send forth your light, be here now. The door to the east is open."

"Hail guardians of the watchtowers of the south, power of fire." Sayde's voice was loud and clear. "We invoke you and call you, red lion of the noon heat, flaming one. Summer's warmth, spark of life, come. By the fire that is her spirit, send forth your flame, be here now. The door to the south is open."

Megan spoke next in a high voice, "Hail guardians of the watchtowers of the west, powers of water. We invoke you and call you, serpent of the watery abyss, rainmaker, gray-robed twilight, evening star, come. By the water of her living womb, send forth your flow, be here now. The door to the west is open."

Marcus in his loud deep voice in theatrical fashion said, "Hail guardians of the watchtowers of the north, powers of Earth, cornerstone of all power. We invoke you and call you. Lady of the outer darkness, black bull of midnight, North Star, center of the whirling sky. Stone Mountain, fertile field, come. By the Earth that is her body, send forth your strength, be here now. The door to the north is open. The circle is cast. We are between the worlds, beyond the bounds of time, where night and day, birth and death, joy and sorrow meet as one."

Marcus and Sayde walked to the cauldron.

Sayde whispered, "This is the time of harvest, of thanksgiving and joy, of leave taking and sorrow. Now day and night are equal in perfect balance and we give thought to the balance and flow with our own lives."

Marcus raised a sheaf of wheat and tossed it into the fire.

"Thank you, Mother Goddess, for my independence as well as all of my sisters," Sayde replied.

Marcus poured a libation of wine into a metal cup and took a drink. He passed it to Sayde. She took a sip and passed the cup around to everyone in the circle. As they drank, each person asked the goddess for something that was spiritual in nature. Without a word, Joe took a sip and passed the cup.

Marcus asked everyone to sit. Circe placed a large black hat littered with silver stars and gold moons on her head. In a sing-song voice, she led the coven through a series of breathing exercises over the rapture of the cauldron flames.

"We are now in a trance state," she finally said.

I don't know about the others, but I don't feel I've passed into a trance.

Glancing at the coven, he found their eyes were closed. Some moaned as they breathed. Megan and Paula breathed with a more vocal, mystic hum which sounded as if they were trying to harmonize together in different pitches.

With a counting method, Circe brought everyone out of the trance. Sayde said a prayer of fertility. Then the coven drank from the silver cup once more. The tom-toms sounded and six young women disrobed, exposing their shadowy nude bodies in the firelight.

What the hell is going on?

While the others sat on the outskirts of the circle, the young women erotically pranced around the cauldron. The longer they danced, the wilder they became, each performing a different routine. A couple of the girls waved their arms in the air.

Luna turned and took Marcus's hand and brought him into the inner circle to dance. Then Sayde took Barry in and Circe grabbed Ken's hand. A girl with long blonde hair selected the heavy-set woman. Paula came toward Joe. Not wanting any part of this, he shook his head, but she pulled him in anyway. People began jumping over the flames of the cauldron. Joe felt light headed. He wished he hadn't taken the second drink of wine.

Before long everyone was dancing around the cauldron, snarling, snorting and hissing like wild animals. Joe stood in disbelief as the rest of the men and women disrobed then pawed and fondled one another. Joe moved back to the outside of the circle, hoping he was exempt from the orgy. In the dim cauldron light, Paula and Megan danced around him.

His head was spinning from the drink, the stench of incense and the dancing girls' pale nude bodies.

With her hands behind her head, Megan swayed her hips from side to side while she shook her firm, rounded breasts near his face. Her naked figure was breathtaking, much shapelier and more developed than the taller, thinner model. Thinking of Ellen, Joe turned away from Megan and bumped into Paula's naked body. Megan swung her pelvis back and forth. Her ebony lips parted in a smirk as she moved to Joe's side. He jerked away from the girls, but Paula grabbed him and rubbed her firm, bare breasts against his chest. The way her green eyes searched his, Joe knew he wasn't exempt.

Some of the others lay on the floor making love: Barry with Sayde, Ken was on a young woman, and Luna was on Marcus with Circe kissing his chest. The young blonde girl snuggled with the heavy-set woman while another woman massaged her breasts from behind.

I've got to get out of here.

Then Joe remembered that no one was allowed out of the witch's circle until it was uncast. He couldn't afford to lose the money they were paying him but he decided to resist any sexual advances. No matter which way he turned, one of the two women was there. Paula grabbed his crotch. Joe pulled away.

I don't care about their damn circle; I'm leaving.

As soon as he started away, Megan clutched his neck from behind and Paula grasped his feet at the same time, sending him down on his rear end.

"You're not going anywhere." Megan slid her naked body across his chest. Before he could move, Paula sat on his legs. Circe joined the girls, holding Joe's shoulders down. He struggled, but the three women kept him subdued. Megan lay on his chest with her face next to his. She gave him a burning kiss.

Four

A New Plan

While Megan forced her lips on Joe's, Paula unzipped and removed his pants. Circe knelt on his shoulders from behind. Megan pivoted her body so she could unbutton his shirt while partially laying on him.

"Stop!" Joe squirmed and shoved but couldn't get free. "I'm a happily married man!"

"You still will be." Megan laughed. "Only now we'll make you happier."

Paula licked his ear.

The three women were all over Joe, massaging and kissing him. Megan met his lips again, then his face and throat. Circe licked his midsection while Paula tongued his thighs. Joe felt guilty as he became aroused. In his dizzy state of mind, the incense smell worked as an aphrodisiac and intensified the thrilling sensations. Hearing the strange snarls mixed with assorted lovemaking around him, Joe's sensual feelings continued to build. He felt Paula's warm, moist mouth engulf him. When it was over, he lay limp and relaxed on the floor with the three women next to him. Others were heard panting and gasping.

Soon it became quiet. Joe heard only a few whispers. As he lay on the floor he was angry and confused.

Why did these three women force me into an orgy? Is this why Marcus insisted I attend? But how did this benefit Marcus?

"All rise and be robed." Marcus's voice boomed.

Everyone rose and threw their robes back on. Outraged, Joe zipped his pants and buttoned his shirt. *I'll have to hide my anger if I want to keep my home.*

"Now, everyone gather around the cauldron for prayer," Marcus said.

Paula sat on Joe's right and Megan on his left as Marcus said a short prayer to the goddess.

Sayde turned to face the cauldron, her whispering barely audible over the crackling flames. "Oh great Mother Goddess, tonight we pray thanks for bringing to us this very special man, Joseph Hillery. The knowledge of our ancestors, which we thought was lost centuries ago, is now partly restored to us. Help us to use this knowledge wisely. Madam of the harvest, we, your children, although we continue to be persecuted, have overcome as we are gathered here tonight to worship you and the old religion." Sayde turned and faced the coven, glancing at each person. "Now everyone put your arms around the person next to you."

Paula and Megan each placed an arm around Joe. He cringed at their touch. Sayde started a chant as everyone but Joe joined in, arm in arm. They swayed from side to side for several minutes before the circle was uncast. The lights went on and Joe could see his watch. To his surprise it was almost eleven o'clock. He had told Ellen he'd be home shortly after ten. The late hour would surely raise her worry and suspicions.

Refreshments were set out on the tables. Angrily, Joe decided to leave.

"Joe," Sayde called to him. "Please stay for snacks."

"It's late, and I don't want my wife to worry."

"Joe, dear," Sayde returned, trying to keep up with him, "Please don't be angry or misunderstand about what happened during the orgy."

Joe continued to walk away from her.

"Please give me a chance to explain."

Joe stopped. "Look, the only reason I didn't leave before the ritual was over was out of respect for your magic circle. I wasn't told I'd be in an orgy!"

"Joe, sex during our orgies doesn't mean the same thing as when you're with your wife. It's only a spiritual thing and brings pleasure to us. Outsiders have a hard time understanding this. I had no idea myself that you were going to be involved personally, I swear."

Not knowing whom to believe, Joe turned away and walked to the door.

Just before he was out of the ritual room, Sayde yelled, "Joe, can we count on you for Friday night?"

He stopped, turned and nodded to her then left the room.

It was after eleven-thirty when Joe got home. As he expected, Ellen had questions as to why he was so late. It seemed to him that she was suspicious of another woman, but she didn't hint at it.

"Joe, you smell of incense." Ellen sniffed his hair. "You reek of it!"

"I told you Marcus was strange. He burned incense tonight," Joe said. "What am I supposed to do? Tell him he can't?" Joe turned and headed for the bathroom. Ellen stood silent.

Joe was relieved that she hadn't followed him into the shower as the black lipstick stains were all over his body and ran off pooling into the drain. The lyrics from a song, "Old Black Water Keep on Rolling" went through his mind. When Joe climbed into bed, Ellen turned away from him without even saying good night.

Because of these witch bitches, my marriage is being destroyed. Why do I feel guilty when I'm only going along with these pagans to keep my ancestral home?

Joe decided to get to the bottom of why he was included in the orgy.

~ * ~

Marcus called another meeting at his home the following evening. "Well, I don't have to tell any of you that last night's plan was a disaster. And now Sayde is asking me questions as to why Joe was included in the orgy. Because you three ladies angered Joe, Sayde's afraid he may not return. I tremble just thinking that we might have lost Joe and the ring!" Marcus closed his eyes and lowered his head. "I can't let that happen."

"Let me try to hypnotize Joe into cooperating." Circe, always looking Gothic, was the only person wearing black at this meeting.

Megan eyed the young Asian woman and sneered. "And how are you going to get him to cooperate for that?"

Circe blinked a couple of times. "I'll come up with a plan."

The tallest witch, Paula, said, "Let me work on Joe a little more. I'll bring him around. I don't believe there's a man alive who can resist me."

Megan glared at her. "Joe did last night."

"The sexual experience I gave him will prey on his mind." She smiled. "But I might need to be alone with him to really be effective."

Marcus let out a breath. "Maybe seduction wasn't the best plan. Joe could be one of the rare men who really *is* loyal to his wife."

"Give me another try," Megan said. "A more subtle approach may be needed rather than attacking Joe like we did last night."

"Something's got to be done and soon." Marcus squeezed the bridge of his nose. "If we're lucky enough that Joe returns, it will cost me five hundred dollars a visit."

"We need another strategy," Luna said. "Circe's idea might be the way to go."

"Marcus, give Paula and me one more try before we use hypnotism," Meg said.

"All right. This Friday night at around nine you can approach Joe as he leaves the parish after our next meeting. If both of you fail again, its Circe's turn. We'll meet here on Saturday afternoon to review the situation." Marcus looked at Meg then Paula. "And may the best witch win."

"By the way, does anyone know where Trish is?" Megan asked.

Everyone shrugged.

Megan worried that Marcus or one of the others may have done something to her.

Is she dead or just in hiding?

On the way home, Meg thought of a new plan to secure Joe's affection.

How could I have been so stupid? I'm a witch, descended from Medea, the very sorceress who last owned the ring. Why seduce Joe with my charms when I can have him with witchcraft. I'll be damned if I'm going to let one of the others be high priestess when it's my legacy.

When Megan got to her second floor apartment, she sat in the living room among seven flaming colored candles and visualized a full moon in her mind's eye. Using the moon's energy, she said, "As I draw down the moon I ask in the name of the goddess that Joseph Hillery falls in love with me, so let it be."

She rose and took the glowing red candle and placed it into a bowl of water. "Just as this candle burns, so shall his love for me. Joe, you will be irresistibly drawn to me, so let it be."

Megan removed the candle wax from the water, set it in a green satin bag and put it to her heart. She faced the moon. "I bind thee to me."

That night she slept with the green bag under her pillow to complete the spell.

~ * ~

Marcus sat with Luna in her living room, drinking a glass of wine. "Thank you for the invite, my sweet."

"With Paula out of the house tonight, I thought this would be a good time to see each other."

Marcus smiled. "Since your love spell on me works so well, how's your spell going with Joe?"

"I didn't notice any change in him at the ritual, but tomorrow night at our meeting I'll give him the eye. I'll know if the spell worked by the end of the night." She leaned toward Marcus and closed her eyes, then kissed him.

~ * ~

The following night at the parish, Sayde again apologized to Joe. "Marcus can verify that I knew nothing about what happened Tuesday night."

"She's right, Joe. It was a big misunderstanding," Marcus said. "You weren't supposed to be involved in the orgy, but the girls didn't know it. Several of the women are attracted to you because of your unique experience."

"That's not a good enough explanation for me. Now my wife suspects I'm having an affair."

"You're right; it's no excuse," Sayde said. "But I tried to explain to you after it happened. Our orgies aren't personal like an experience with a loved one. They're more spiritual in nature.

"For that terrible misunderstanding and all the trouble we caused you, I'm going to put a little extra in your check tonight," Marcus said. "It's the least I can do."

"Thank you," Joe said, not convinced of Marcus's sincerity. He felt Marcus was up to something.

"Joe, you haven't heard from Trish, have you?" Sayde asked.

"No, why?"

"She's been missing since Sunday."

"Are the police looking into it?"

"Yes, but they haven't found any clues."

There's something going on they're not telling me. "Is Trish's car missing?"

"Yes," Sayde said. "But if she went someplace without telling anyone, why did she leave everything behind in her apartment?"

"Well, let's get on with our meeting," Marcus interrupted. "What else may be of interest to us?"

"Imps. The witches' familiars." Joe eyed all three to see if he'd piqued anyone's interest.

"You actually saw their imps?" Luna asked.

Joe nodded. While Sayde and Marcus looked at each other, Luna gave Joe the eye to see if he was afflicted, but he didn't respond like a person under a love spell. No gazing back at her, no admiration in his eyes.

"Diehla's imp was called Grichwick," Joe said. "He was a shape-shifter. The imp took on the form of a toad, a mouse and a fly. Do witches have familiars today?"

"No," Sayde said. "Although some writings from the past did mention familiars, there was never anything written about them from reliable sources like Medea."

When Joe filled them in on other familiars he'd seen, he noticed Luna's beady eyes searching him again. *What is she up to? Is she casting a spell or reading my mind?*

My spell's not working for some reason. Damn! Luna looked away.

At the close of the meeting, Sayde opened a safe. She took out a few brown withered papers and laid them on the table in front of Joe. "These are the twenty or so pages written by Medea Laughton from somewhere around 1700 until her death in 1707."

As Joe examined the writings, he noticed they were laminated in clear plastic. Although the documents were badly faded, he was able to read them.

"It's hard to believe that this was written back in the early seventeen hundreds. You must treasure these papers." Joe continued going through them as he spoke.

"Yes, they're the backbone of this coven," Sayde said.

"We even have them Xeroxed in case they were stolen or destroyed," Luna added.

Before Joe left, Marcus handed him his check. Marcus had added an extra two hundred dollars. Twelve hundred dollars just for those two nights. He didn't know what to say.

Sayde left the parish conference room right after Joe.

Luna looked at Marcus. "My love spell failed."

"How could it?" Marcus leaned forward with a frown. "If Paula or Megan succeeds, one of them will be high priestess over you."

"Yes, but what would be worse is if none of us succeeds."

Marcus closed his eyes and shook his head.

~ * ~

As Joe made his way down the hall toward the front door, he heard his name being called. He turned to see Megan and Paula coming toward him from an adjacent hallway. Joe stopped short of the front door as they approached. Both women were dressed more conservatively; no black lipstick or nail polish. Paula wore a skirt and Megan a black windbreaker and shorts.

"We're here to apologize," Paula said.

"Sorry about what happened Tuesday night," Megan said.

Paula shook her head. "We thought you were supposed to participate in the orgy."

"If anyone's to blame, it's Marcus for not communicating with us." Megan laid a hand on Joe's arm, making him uncomfortable.

"Are we forgiven?" Paula asked.

Joe wasn't convinced they were sincere. "Yeah, you're forgiven." He started for the door.

Megan stepped in front of him.

"What is it now?" he asked.

"I can tell you're still upset," Megan said.

"I've got to get home to my wife."

"If he has to leave," Paula said, "let him go."

"With the way you faced off with the infamous Diehla Thorne and traveled through time, you're almost like a god to me. Please, please don't hate me."

"Oh, please, Meg." Paula rolled her eyes.

Joe smiled at the girl with the pixie hair cut. "No, Megan, I don't hate you."

"Please call me Meg. All my friends do."

"Okay, Meg."

"Goodbye and I hope to see you around here soon," Meg said.

"I hope you'll continue to attend our rituals," Paula added.

By the front door, Meg turned to Paula. "Can you give me a ride home?"

"I'm not going that way. Take the bus like you always do."

"It's just that it's so late." Meg glanced from Paula to Joe.

"How far from here do you live?" Joe asked gazing into her squinting brown eyes.

"About two miles. But I don't want to put you out."

Joe wanted to get home, but felt obligated because of the money he was receiving from their coven. "Come on. I'll take you home."

"Thank you so much, Joe," Meg said as if surprised. "Isn't he sweet?"

As they turned to leave, Joe caught a glimpse of Meg grinning at Paula.

"If you take Meg home, who's going to protect you?" Paula asked.

Five

The Love Spell

As Joe drove, Meg gave him directions. "I have my own place." Joe glanced at her sitting on the other side of the seat. "Do you live alone?"

"Yes, but my grandmother lives below me. She owns the building."

"She's Victoria Sidedrop, the founder of your coven, right?"

"They told you about her?"

"No. I'm a psychic, too." Joe smiled. "Marcus and Sayde told me you and your grandmother are descendants of Yves and Medea Laughton."

"You know more about me than I know about you."

"But you should know about me; you're a clairvoyant. Remember you knew my sign?"

She smiled at him. "I did."

Soon they were in a residential area with older homes.

"Here it is, on the right." Meg pointed to a large white two story house. The front porch's light was on. Joe pulled over to the curb.

"Come in for a minute and I'll make you a hot cup of chocolate," Meg said.

Joe shook his head.

"That's the least I can do for you after giving me a ride home."

"I appreciate the offer, but it's late." Joe glanced at his watch. She pouted, then playfully said, "You're not afraid of me because I'm a witch, are you?"

"Meg, I have to get home. My wife worries." Looking at her pretty face, Joe forced the image of her naked body lying across him out of his mind.

"You're uncomfortable because I'm descended from Diehla Thorne's lover?"

Joe shook his head.

"I just want to make you a cup of cocoa. I'm not going to turn you into a frog."

Joe laughed. "All right, but I can only stay for a minute."

She flashed him a big smile. "I totally understand."

They got out of the car and Joe followed her to the back of the house, up the outside stairs to her second floor apartment.

"Why are we going in through the back?" Joe asked.

"My apartment is only the back part of the second floor. This is the only way in from the outside." She put the key into the door. "The second floor front apartment is sometimes rented out, but there's no one living there now." She unlocked the door, they stepped in and she turned on the living room light.

"Make yourself comfortable. I'll be right back with your chocolate."

Joe sat on the couch as Meg went into the kitchen. While he waited he noticed everything in the room was black and white with a variety of candles sitting on shelves and mounted on the walls. A small incense candle sat on an end table. Joe also spotted a framed prayer to the mother goddess on the wall with a black pentagram just above it.

In the kitchen, Meg poured two cups of hot water. *I have to remember not to be physical with him until the second potion starts to work. I don't know if my first love spell had any effect. I had to talk him into giving me a ride. I'll have to keep him here with my dynamic personality until this potion takes effect.* Meg dropped a couple of small wax pellets into the cup with the cocoa and stirred.

Soon she entered the living room with the drinks. She smiled, sat on the couch next to Joe and set the cups on the coffee table in front of them. Out of nowhere, a black cat jumped up on her lap.

"Nice looking cat," Joe said. "What's its name?"

"Her name is Shyebony." Meg handed Joe a steaming cup. She sipped her drink with one hand and stroked the cat with the other. "I hear you have your own business. What kind of work do you do?"

"I'm a distributor for various series and programs on video tapes."

Meg nodded. "That sounds interesting."

Joe cautiously took his first sip. "This is really good. What's in it?"

"The usual; cocoa powder, milk, water, and a secret witches' ingredient." Meg held back a snicker.

"What about you. Where do you work?"

"At the Bell, Book and Candle."

Joe frowned.

"It's the occult book store here in Manchester."

"What do you do there?" Joe glanced at his watch and took a quick drink of his cocoa.

"I do a little of everything." She flashed him a smile. "I'm the assistant manager."

"I'm impressed."

"Don't be. The position doesn't pay much more than what the clerks make and the job has a lot of responsibility."

"How about your social life?" *Why in the hell did I ask her that?* Joe took a final swig and set his empty cup down on the coffee table.

Yes! The spell is working! Meg forced herself not to smile.

"I'm sorry, that's none of my business," Joe said.

"I'm flattered that you asked, but I'm so involved with witchcraft and busy at the book store that it takes all of my free time. And it's hard to stay in a relationship with a guy who's an outsider when he finds out what I am."

Why am I happy she's available? I love Ellen.

For some reason Joe felt like a teenager with a crush. "But isn't there anyone in your religion you could date?"

"Witches are almost all women, and of the few guys I know, they're either in a relationship, gay, or just not my type." Meg sipped her chocolate.

"Why are there so many more women in witchcraft?"

"From its beginning, witchcraft has been predominantly female. Through magic, women have been able to climb to power in a male dominated society. Many witch killings of the past were done to keep women in their place."

"So witches were sort of the first women's movement?"

Meg nodded with a smile as she set her cup down on the coffee table next to Joe's. "Let me get you another cup of chocolate."

"No thanks." Joe glanced at his watch again. "I've got to get going."

"Before you leave, I wanted to tell you how much I admire your bravery and cunning in dealing with the spirit of Diehla Thorne. Just being in the same room with you makes me feel tingly." Meg arched her shoulders.

"Tingly?" Joe smiled.

"How did it feel going back to 1680 and matching wits with the great Diehla Thorne?"

"Well, they don't come any braver than me." Joe playfully threw his shoulders back.

Meg laughed. "You've got a sense of humor, too. I love that in a man."

"Actually, I was scared to death because of the witches' magic and being in an unfamiliar time." He gave her a hard look.

"Who wouldn't be?" Meg leaned forward to peer at him.

"But it's strange when you're faced with a life and death situation. Even though you're terrified, you still do what you have to."

"What was my ancestor Yves Laughton like?"

How can I tell her the truth? He was evil to the core and would have killed me if he could have gotten away with it. "Let's say we didn't get along too well."

"Oh, sorry." *I think he's ready for some touching now.* Meg reached over and began massaging Joe's shoulders.

"Meg, I don't have time for a massage." Even though Joe felt he'd enjoy it, he wanted to get home to Ellen. Strangely, the reason was because of his wife's suspicions of his late activities rather than any guilt he'd feel.

"Turn away. This will only take a minute or two. I just want to relieve some of your tension. It'll help you sleep."

Joe faced the other way as Meg rubbed and squeezed his shoulders and back. "I was right. Your muscles are tight. Try to relax, Joe."

"Meg, I really have to go."

Her firm massage gave him goose bumps.

"I was the top student in my massage class."

"I believe you were." Joe grunted with his eyes closed, feeling glued to the spot.

Meg rubbed her fingers firmly down his spine. The sensations tingled down his arms and legs.

"How long have you been doing this?"

"About four years. I'm a registered massage therapist. I only do this for my friends, but eventually I'd like to open my own shop and do it for a living."

While Meg continued with her massage, Joe wondered why this beautiful young woman was coming on to him. Was she really in awe of his dealings with Diehla or was there some other darker reason connected to the three women forcing him into sex. If so, Joe couldn't determine what it might be. He checked the time once more. What would he tell Ellen for being late again? Why couldn't he make himself leave?

Meg massaged deeper, going from Joe's ribs to his chest.

Joe became physically aroused. "Meg, you've been working on me for over fifteen minutes. I have to leave."

"But your muscles are still so tense. Joe, you're perspiring," Meg said with a childish gasp. "I hope I'm not making you excited." She peered over his shoulder, down to his lap. "I am. How embarrassing." She removed her hands from him. "I didn't mean to turn you on. I still feel bad about what happened at the orgy. I think you'd better go. I shouldn't have kept you here this long."

Joe wanted to stay but forced himself in check by thinking of his love for Ellen. The thought of taking advantage of this opportunity overwhelmed him. He gazed at his watch again. "Boy, I've got to go. Don't want to worry the missus."

"I hope you don't get in any trouble because of me."

"At the end of your massage, I thought you were coming on to me."

A look of surprise crossed her face. "But you're married!"

Joe got up to leave. He turned to look at Meg who innocently sat on the couch holding her cat. With an uncontrollable urge, he bent down and kissed her lips. The cat jumped down as she put her arms around Joe and kissed him back. He knew he should stop but he couldn't. Goose bumps skittered down his back as she left his lips and kissed him all over his neck and throat before meeting his lips again. Running her fingers over his shoulders to the back of his head she kissed him passionately. Meg broke free of their long embrace and lay on her back. Smiling up at him, she unbuttoned his shirt.

That action gave him a sudden rush of guilt. Joe pulled away and stood. "Meg, this was a huge mistake. I don't know what came over me." He buttoned his shirt.

"I don't think we should fight our feelings." She reached up for him.

"Even if I were single, I'm old enough to be your," Joe paused, "your older brother. I'm thirty-seven and you look like you're barely twenty."

"I'm twenty-three. But what difference does age make? You don't look your age."

Joe headed for the door.

"Just because a person is married doesn't mean they can't have secret desires."

Joe opened the door and turned toward her. "Goodbye, Meg." With that, he left the apartment.

Meg stood, folded her arms and glared at the door. "You'll be back, Joe Hillery. I'll make damn sure of that!"

On his way home, Joe was confused not knowing why he had such strong feelings for Meg. He had never been unfaithful to Ellen, never even dreamed of it. He felt like he was in a strange fog and none of this had actually happened.

When Joe arrived home, Ellen stood in the living room, hands on her hips, and glared at him. "Joe, where have you been? I want the truth!"

"The client wanted to go out for a drink with me."

"And there were no phones where you were?"

Joe wished he would have thought to call her. The lump in his throat became so large he felt as if he were choking on his own words. "I'm sorry, hon. I just didn't think of it."

"I guess I was the last thing on your mind."

Joe reached for her, but she pulled away.

"I was worried. You've become so mysterious since you began meeting with this Mr. Phillips, if that's who you're really seeing."

Joe scowled. "What does that mean?"

"You didn't even give me a phone number where I could reach you and you apparently didn't think about me tonight." Ellen started to cry.

"Why are you so upset?" Joe tried to give her a hug.

She pulled away again. "I think you're seeing another woman."

Joe's heart pounded, knowing he had a real problem. Then he remembered he had the extra two hundred dollars in his check. He took out his wallet and held up the check. "If you think I'm having an affair, why did Marcus Phillips give me a check for two hundred dollars overtime tonight?"

Ellen took it and looked at the amount. Her crying subsided and she wiped the tears from her eyes and gave Joe a hug. "I'm sorry. I don't know what's come over me."

Joe hugged her back and she collapsed in his arms. He felt if he hadn't thought of the extra money Marcus had given him, his marriage might have suffered further from the incident. Joe knew he'd have to do some soul searching.

~ * ~

Marcus called another meeting at his home.

Marcus stared at Meg. "From what Paula tells me, she had no luck with Joe last night, but he gave you a ride home."

Why should I cooperate with Marcus just to be his second banana when I can have the ring for myself? "He took me home, but I didn't get anywhere with him. I couldn't even get him into my apartment for a cup of hot chocolate. He must be a very loyal husband."

Marcus leaned forward with a frown. "Joe gave you no sign he might be interested in you?"

My grandmother was the coven founder and Medea was my ancestor, not his. The ring is my birthright. "No." Meg shook her head.

"Don't give up yet, Marcus." Paula ran her fingers through her medium-brown hair, throwing her head back. "Let me get him alone."

"Well, you'd better succeed, Paula, and quickly. If you fail, it's Circe's turn with mesmerizing."

Meg smiled to herself. *I'll see to it their plans fail.*

~ * ~

While Luna and Paula ate Sunday dinner at their home, Luna said, "I've got a plan for Joe that can't miss."

Paula's hand froze in front of her face with her fork full of Chinese food as she waited to hear more.

"Rather than trying to seduce Joe, why don't we use a love spell on him?"

"I don't have a love spell. With my looks, I've never needed one, although I've often thought of developing one to get rid of some guys." Paula smiled.

"It will be you who enchants him because of my love potion that you'll be wearing." Luna took a sip of wine. "By tomorrow night, Joe won't be able to resist you, no matter how loyal he is to his frumpy wife." Luna laughed.

Paula frowned. "You've bruised my ego, but with the ring at stake, we can't leave anything to chance."

"But if you succeed, we share the high priestess honor, agreed?"

Paula extended her hand and Luna shook it.

~ * ~

Later that evening, Marcus got a phone call from Luna. "My witch's instincts tell me that Meg is a liar. I think she used a love spell on Joe."

"Why do you think that?"

"I had a dream that Joe was in her apartment drinking cocoa and the two of them were getting along just fine."

"I'll find out, and if your instincts are right, Meg is also a traitor."

~ * ~

When Joe arrived at the parish for their next meeting, Marcus asked, "So, Joe, what did you think of Meg's apartment when you were there?"

Joe was surprised that Meg told him about last Friday night. "She's got a nice place. I just stayed for a cup of cocoa."

"Meg said you stayed a bit longer."

Joe felt betrayed. "What did she tell you?"

Marcus smiled. "Your secret is safe with me, but don't mention any of this to Sayde."

Why is he keeping this from her?

"We're having a new moon Mass Friday night. You're not required to attend, but we'd be more than happy to have you."

"I'm sorry, but my wife and I have plans."

"Meg said she hoped to see you there."

Like the others, Sayde entered the office in street clothes.

Marcus turned toward her. "I was trying to convince Joe to attend our new moon ritual this Friday."

She smiled at him. "Yes, we'd love to have you."

Joe was still having trouble getting Meg out of his mind, but didn't know why. Was it because she'd seduced him? Just hearing that she wanted to see him made him determined to attend the ritual even if it made Ellen more suspicious. At the end of the meeting, Joe told them he would be there.

When Joe entered the parking lot, Paula climbed out of her car. "Joe," she called. "Do you know anything about cars?"

"Not much."

"My car won't start. Could you at least look at it for me?"

Joe opened the hood and looked into the dark engine. "Do you have a flashlight?"

"Yes, I carry a small one in my purse." She pulled it out and handed it to him.

He turned it on and shined the light around the engine. He spotted the problem right away. The center wire was disconnected from the distributor. He plugged it in. "Try it now, Paula."

She turned the ignition on and the car started. "Thank you, Joe."

He looked at her. "Paula, someone must have intentionally pulled that distributor wire out. They don't just fall out."

"I don't know anything about cars." She jumped out of the car. "For your help let me buy you dinner tomorrow." She made certain she was close enough to him that he would smell her tainted perfume.

"Thanks, Paula, but what I did was nothing. I'll see you later." Joe went to his car.

That's Luna's strongest love spell and Joe's walking away from me? Aaaahhhhh! She clenched her fists in frustration. When the tall woman got back into her car, she slammed the heel of her hand against the steering wheel. "He's not even attracted to me with a damn love spell? Damn it! Damn it! I've lost my chance of being high priestess. I hope Circe hypnotizes him into a zombie."

~ * ~

The next day Luna called Marcus to give him the terrible news.

"How could your perfumed love spell fail?" Marcus asked.

"There is only one way. If Joe's already enchanted."

"Meg?"

"Of course it's Meg. When Joe took her home, she probably used a love spell on him."

"If that was your strongest love spell, why didn't you use it to begin with?"

"Because it only works if the man has a casual interest in the woman. Joe knows I belong to you and Paula is, let's say, every guy's type. We didn't think she'd need a spell."

"If what you're saying is true, Meg is lying to me again. I'll call her tonight."

~ * ~

Marcus called Meg at her apartment. "I know about your little game, Meg."

"What are you talking about?"

"You put a love spell on Joe, and it seems to have worked very well. You lied about Joe going to your apartment on Friday night. I know because I just had a conversation with him."

"All right, so he came in for cocoa."

"Why are you trying to double-cross us?"

"Well, Marcus, I have my plan and you have yours, and may the best wiccan win."

"If you were the one to deliver the ring, then you would be our high priestess. Why are you doing this to me?"

"I'd be high priestess, but you said nothing about coven leader. Why should I settle for number two?" *Egotistical jerk!*

"But if your plan fails, you won't even be in this coven," Marcus said. "I have others with me."

"Let's just see what happens, okay?"

"You'll destroy our coven!" Marcus yelled into the phone. "Some may even want revenge against you."

"You mean I may end up like Trish? And what do you know about her disappearance, Marcus?"

"Nothing, I swear. Perhaps she's in hiding. Please don't betray me, Meg."

"Oooh, you said please. You are worried, Marcus."

"For the sake of your grandmother, we have to stay united."

"My grandmother, of all people, would be happy if I became her coven's leader."

"This is your final decision? You're going against us?"

"Yes."

"Then you leave me no choice," Marcus said. "I'll show Joe the portrait."

"You can't! You swore to my grandmother and the coven that the portrait was never to be revealed to an outsider. You took an oath to wicca itself."

"Joe's not really an outsider. He works for me. I pay him enough, and he knows more about our ancient magic than we do. I think this is a special case. Think about it, Meg. If you change your mind, I'll do the same. But you'd better call me before my meeting with Joe."

"Marcus, I'll see you thrown out of the coven."

~ * ~

Meg still hadn't phoned Marcus by Thursday, so he called Joe at his office.

"Joe, we won't be meeting with you tomorrow night, but when you're finished at work today could you please stop by the parish? I have something important I want to show you."

I guess I'm losing that day's pay this week. "Sure, but I can't stay long."

"It'll only take a minute. We're having a ritual tonight so come to the back door, please, and I'll be there to let you in."

At five Joe called Ellen to tell her he had to work late and not to hold supper for him.

~ * ~

"I feel like I'm sneaking in," Joe said, arriving at the parish at six o'clock.

"I have something of interest that I wanted to show you before we begin our ritual," Marcus said. "Follow me."

"Sounds mysterious." Joe followed Marcus down the hall to a small room.

Inside Marcus walked to a vault. He opened it and pulled out a large frame. Wrapped in brown paper, its picture was hidden. Joe curiously watched Marcus remove the wrapper. When it was off, Marcus's body blocked his view. He turned to face Joe then held the picture up. Joe saw a portrait of Meg, but her hair was long and flowing, not the pixie cut she wore now. Strangely, she was wearing a long ruffled dress from another time.

"Why are you showing me this portrait of Meg?" Joe asked.

"Read the inscription on the bottom."

On the lower right hand corner was printed 'Medea Laughton' and under it was the date, 'June 1705.'

"This is Medea Laughton?" Joe asked as if confused.

Marcus nodded with a smile.

Joe continued to examine the painting. Medea had the same squinty eyes, little turned up nose and smirking facial expression. "The resemblance is unbelievable."

"You're the first non-wiccan to have seen the portrait of Medea Laughton. Meg is a throwback to her ancestor. For your own sake, I'd keep away from her, Joe."

"Why?"

"Meg is cursed, really. I didn't mention this before, but like Medea, the people around her become the victims of her sorcery. Meg's very dangerous."

"What has she done?"

"Recently she and Trish had an argument, and Trish hasn't been seen since."

"Yeah, I heard about Trish."

Marcus gave him a stern look. "I hope she hasn't cast a spell on you already."

Though Joe was deeply attracted to Meg, the fear that she may use magic on him terrified him.

"We'd better be going to the ritual now." Marcus wrapped the painting up and put it back in the vault.

Joe was bothered by the portrait and what Marcus had told him.

Sayde popped her head into the room. "I thought I heard voices. Joe, what are you doing here?" She entered the room.

"Joe wanted to see me about something."

Meg entered the room behind Sayde. "Well, look who's here." She flashed Joe a smile.

Seeing Meg's face filled him with dread and also desire.

Meg smiled. "Joe, are you going to join us for the ritual?"

"No. Marcus and I had some business to discuss. My wife has dinner waiting."

"We won't be meeting tomorrow," Marcus said to Joe. "But I'll see you on Tuesday at seven."

Joe headed for the back door.

"Joe, wait," Meg called.

Marcus laughed as she ran after him, catching him at the door.

"Marcus showed you the portrait, didn't he?"

"Yeah, but I really do have to leave."

"Right!" Meg angrily folded her arms and glared at him.

Gazing into her beautiful brown eyes, lust grew in Joe's heart, but he fought his desire and exited the parish.

Meg returned to the ritual room with Marcus and some of the others. She scowled at him. "Damn you, Marcus. I swear I'll get you for this!"

"But you won't have the ring. I will," Marcus whispered with a smirk.

When Joe arrived home his head was swimming but he pulled himself together to act as normal as possible.

Tommy gave him a hug when he walked in. "Daddy, can you play with me?"

"Not tonight, Tom. Daddy's got a headache."

Ellen walked into the living room. "Hi, Joe. I didn't expect to see you this early. We just finished eating. I'll heat your dinner for you."

"Thanks, it was a rough day."

Joe collapsed on the couch in front of the TV. Watching his children playing with toys in front of him, he wondered how he could have been so attracted to a woman who was so dangerous. Even his family could be at risk. He still couldn't believe how much Meg and Medea resembled each other. *Like Marcus said, Meg's a throwback and possibly Medea's reincarnation. And what did happen to Trish?* He was happy that he had no intentions of even talking to Meg again. His fear outweighed his attraction for her.

Later, Meg gave her love spell a powerful booster. She stood in her front yard holding a red and a green candle.

She closed her eyes. "Just as these candles burn, so shall Joe Hillery's desire for me. Joe, you will be drawn to me."

Then she yelled, "You must come to me! I bind thee to me. So let it be."

She raised the candles up over her head. The wind gust whistled around her and blew out the flames. The breeze carried the smoke north toward Joe. It sailed down the street, around bushes as if the smoke possessed a mind. While Joe slept, desire grew in his heart. He dreamed Meg was making love to him on a cloud while his lust grew. He woke up panting.

Ellen woke. "Joe, what's wrong?"

"I just had a terrible nightmare."

"You're sweating."

"I'll be all right." Joe patted her shoulder. "Just go back to sleep, honey."

Joe got comfortable, but was surprised that he was obsessed by the thought of Meg again. When he fell asleep, he dreamed he was making love with her the rest of the night.

Six

A Victory for Meg

The next morning at the office, Joe sat at his desk unable to concentrate on his work because Meg was on his mind. He decided to pay her a visit at the bookstore but he couldn't remember the name.
It sounded like a spell--oh, the Bell, Book and Candle!
He pulled a Manchester directory out of his desk drawer and found the phone number.
A man answered.
"Hi, is Megan working today?" Joe asked.
"Yes, but she's with a customer. Can you hold?"
"No. I'll talk to her later." Joe checked the address in the book and left the office.
As he drove south he couldn't understand why he had to see Meg. He was in love with his wife. Joe decided to turn back, but just before he did, the need to see Meg overpowered him again.
When he got into the Manchester business district, he soon saw the store. BELL BOOK AND CANDLE was printed in black across the large front window. Under it were the words "Occult Bookstore." Joe parked his car, fed the meter, and crossed the street. As he approached the store, he noticed the sign on the front door: "Occult Books-Supplies-and Tarot Card Readings by Appointment."

It was warm inside the store, but the lighting was dim. Joe smelled incense similar to the witches' parish. Books filled the aisles and walls. A thin, balding, middle-aged man stood behind the rectangular counter which contained incense, candles and other occult supplies. Beads, charms and an assortment of curiosities hung over the counter. Joe searched the store for Meg. He saw her talking to a female customer in the back. He looked at some of the book titles while he waited. The man at the front said softly in an effeminate voice, "Can I help you with something, sir?"

"No, I came to see Megan, but I see she's with a customer."

When the woman customer headed for the register with her purchase, Joe walked to the back of the store. Meg was kneeling, as she rearranged some books between two center aisles. He stood next to her.

"Can I help you?" she asked, still looking at her work. She gazed up to see Joe. A smile crossed her face as she rose, clutching a book. "Joe! What are you doing here?"

"I just had to see you."

"Really? You mean you didn't come to purchase one of these books on oriental philosophy?" She held up the book in her hand.

Joe smiled and shook his head. "Have you had lunch yet?"

"No."

"Could I take you out for a sandwich?"

"You seemed so terrified of me at the parish last night I didn't think you wanted to see me again."

"I was acting childish."

A heavy, middle-aged man approached them. "Miss, do you have any books on out-of body?"

"Yes. They would be two aisles down on the left."

"Thank you." The man walked away.

"Let's get out of here so we can talk." Joe's head swiveled as if expecting more interruptions. "Can you take your lunch now?"

Meg glanced at her watch. "It's not even noon, but sure." She smiled at him. "I'll tell Sherman. Have you ever been in an occult bookstore?"

Joe remembered he had once, twelve years ago when he and parapsychologist Brad Heins searched for information on ring magic just before Diehla Thorn's return. "Only once."

"Look around, and I'll let you know when I'm ready."

Meg walked away while Joe browsed the books. He watched her leave the counter and go into a store room. She returned with a box and set it on the counter. She and Sherman opened it and pulled out some charms. Breathing in the incense, Joe strolled up and down aisles glancing at books on witchcraft, Satanism, tarot cards, demonology, astrology, spells and psychic energy.

Why am I in an unholy place like this, and trying to cheat on Ellen? I should leave.

"Let's go, Joe," Meg said coming out from behind the front counter with her purse. Just hearing her voice Joe was under her enchantment once more. He met her at the door.

"Enjoy your lunch," Sherman said.

Joe held the door as they passed through the musty store into the fresh sunny autumn air.

"What a beautiful day." Meg smiled at him.

Joe melted, gazing into her enchanting, pixie-like face.

As they crossed the street walking to Joe's car, she asked, "Did you find any interesting books?"

"Nothing that I'd care to buy."

Meg stopped next to the passenger door. "I was really surprised to see you."

"Pleasantly, I hope." Joe unlocked her door then got in on the driver's side. He turned to her. "Do you drive to work?"

"I don't own a car. I take the bus. In fact, I don't even have a driver's license. The bus takes me right to the corner of the book store."

Joe pulled away from the curb.

"You know this part of the city better than I do. Where's a good place to have lunch?"

"Go up to the next light and turn left. That's Oak Street. Take that to Sagamore. At the intersection there's a nice coffee shop called Janie's."

When they arrived they sat in the front, near a window.

Looking over the menu, Joe reached for Meg's hand. "I don't know why but I had to see you."

"I'm flattered." *Yes, my booster spell is working!*

Joe looked into Meg's squinting brown eyes and his heart beat with joy. "I can't get you out of my mind."

She smiled at him. "If I didn't know better, I'd say you were falling in love with me."

"I'm not sure, but I want to keep seeing you."

The waitress approached with her pen and tablet. "Ready to order?"

Meg nodded. "Yes. I'll have the garden salad, oil and vinegar, and a glass of mineral water, please."

The waitress glanced at Joe.

"Give me the hamburger deluxe and a coke."

"It comes with fries. Cheese on the burger?"

"No cheese." Joe closed his menu.

When the waitress left, Meg said, "You're a real health nut; a cheese-less burger."

Joe laughed. "Why did you tell Marcus I went into your apartment last Friday?"

"I didn't tell him anything. I thought you told him."

"No, but how did he know?"

"Marcus is trying to keep us apart, that's why he showed you the portrait of Medea."

Joe shook his head. "I don't understand."

"He's afraid if we get close you'll start giving me the information he's paying you for."

"Are you trying to gain secrets from my time travel?"

Meg shook her head. "Of course not. But I am attracted to you." She smiled. "Joe, I would like to continue seeing you too, but on one condition."

Joe frowned.

"That you stop meeting with Marcus and Sayde."

"Why?"

"I'm afraid of what Marcus will do with any knowledge you give him. Trish is missing because of him."

Marcus told me Trish was missing because of Meg and now she's telling me it's because of Marcus. Who's telling the truth? "He told me she was missing because you were practicing black magic on people."

Meg squinted at him. "Bull. They had a falling out a couple of weeks back. I was there when it happened."

Joe still wasn't sure she was telling the truth. "I want to continue seeing you, but I really need the money. My business is at stake."

"It's your choice, Joe, but if you meet with Marcus again we're through. I feel my own safety is at stake if Marcus learns anything more. He'll continue telling you lies about me because he knows I don't want him to learn any new magic."

"If he's that dangerous, why don't you join another coven?"

"This coven is the one my dear grandmother started. If I had been twenty-one before she became ill and left us, she would have made me coven leader. Since Marcus has become our high priest, he has gotten power hungry. I wish I could get him out."

"You can't?"

"He's got powerful and loyal followers like Luna, Circe, Paula and Ken."

Meg was right there with them rubbing Marcus's shoulders. She's either lying or their feud is a new one, perhaps having something to do with me.

Meg wrapped her fingers around Joe's left hand. "Please promise me you won't give Marcus more information."

Joe gazed at her without comment then asked, "Is Sayde dangerous, too?"

"No, she and the others in the coven are okay, but anything she learns, so does Marcus. He only tells his closest friends what his dirty plans are." Meg glanced out the window. "I'll understand if you can't give up the money." She looked back at Joe. "But this is the last time we can meet. I'm sorry, Joe."

He had to keep seeing her, but without the money he'd lose his family, his home, and his business. Joe felt spellbound, gazing into Meg's entrancing eyes. *I'm going to do what she wants. I can't lose her.* "I will stop meeting with Marcus for you." Joe reached over to grasp her hand. "I need you." Joe couldn't believe his own words.

She clutched his hand back with a smile. "Do you mean it, Joe?"

He nodded. Meg leaned across the table and kissed him. The waitress came with their food. "Enjoy your meal."

Meg smiled at him. "Joe, you're going to have to call Marcus tonight so he knows you're not meeting with him and Sayde on Tuesday." She took a bite of her salad and watched him.

Joe signed. "I'll call him as soon as I get back to the office."

"I'll try to help you monetarily any way I can. Since you took me to lunch, I'll take you to dinner tomorrow night."

"Tomorrow night?" Joe asked. "Where?" He took a bite of his burger.

"That'll be my little surprise." She grinned. "Where we're going there will even be entertainment. You'll love it."

The couple finished their lunch gazing into each other's eyes.

Joe pulled up in front of the book store. Meg turned to him with a smile. "Don't forget to be at my apartment tomorrow at seven."

"I wouldn't miss it for the world."

She kissed him hard then climbed out of the car. She leaned in through the passenger's window. "Before we go, I'll introduce you to my grandmother."

Joe nodded with a smile. Meg went into the store as he pulled away.

When Joe got back to the office, he was in turmoil. If he phoned Marcus and called the deal off, he could lose his business, his home and his family as well, but the thought of losing Meg overwhelmed him. Joe put a hand to his forehead and rubbed his brow with a sigh.

Why am I so in love with Meg? And why am I going to destroy my life with this phone call?

After wrestling with the problem, he finally called Marcus at his home. There was no answer the first time, but he finally reached him.

"Marcus, I wanted to let you know I won't be coming to the parish to meet with you and Sayde on Tuesday."

"Is there a problem?"

"I'm finished doing business with you."

"But Joe, we had an agreement. You don't need the money anymore?"

"There are some personal reasons for my decision. I'm sorry."

"There's nothing I can do to make you reconsider?"

Am I making a mistake? Joe took a deep breath. "I'm afraid not."

"Sayde is going to be terribly disappointed." Marcus paused. "Tell Meg Marcus says hello." With that, he hung up.

Meg was right. Marcus knows she's behind my decision. Could Meg have used a spell on me? That's ridiculous.

~ * ~

"Why is Mr. Phillips meeting with you on a Saturday night instead of the usual Friday?" Ellen stood with her hands on her hips as she peered at Joe. He had helped her finish cleaning the supper dishes before putting on his jacket to leave for Meg's. "Who are you really seeing, Joe?"

"Don't do this in front of the kids. We've been through this before."

Ellen turned. "Tommy, take Amy into your bedroom and put something on the TV for her."

"Okay, Mommy," Tommy looked at his mom then his dad. "Come on, Amy."

Joe felt his son knew there was trouble. "You've seen the checks, Ellen. Why are you asking me this?"

"No real client would request evening hours, especially on a weekend! How do I know when you received those checks?"

Joe's throat was dry and his heart pounded. "Knock it off, Ellen." He acted the part of a misunderstood husband, but even at the risk of losing his family, he had to see Meg.

"You could be getting the money during business hours then going out with some woman at night that has nothing to do with the client." Ellen glared at her husband then looked as though she might cry.

What's wrong with me? I'm cheating on the love of my life? Joe flopped down on the couch.

Suddenly, the desire for Meg overwhelmed him again. "If you want me to stay home and watch TV, then you worry about the mortgage and the bills."

Ellen closed her eyes. "No, Joe, you have to go."

"If you want me to stay here, that's what I'll do." Joe glared at the television.

"I don't know what's wrong with me." Ellen shook her head. "You've never been unfaithful. Go before you're late for your meeting with Mr. Phillips."

Joe stood without a word, walked to Ellen and kissed her. She didn't kiss him back. He went into Tommy's room and told the kids goodbye.

On the drive to Manchester, guilt consumed Joe again, but the thought of Megan's pixie-like face entered his mind and the guilt washed away.

When he arrived at Meg's apartment, she greeted him at the back door with a smile. She twice squeezed her eyes closed.

"What was that?" Joe laughed.

"My witch's greeting." Her violet-red lips parted into a coy smirk. She was dressed in a tight black top, short black skirt and heels. She also wore eye-makeup without looking Goth.

She glanced at her watch, tapped it with her finger and teased, "You're five minutes late, Mister."

Joe smiled. "Meg, you look great!"

"Why, thank you, Joe. You don't look so bad yourself." She leaned in and kissed him. "I'll get my jacket."

Joe couldn't help eyeing her as she walked ahead of him into the kitchen. He was thrilled that this ravishing young woman was interested in him.

She turned and waved for him to enter, then lifted her black jacket off the back of the kitchen chair and threw it over her shoulders. "I almost forgot that I want to introduce you to my grandmother."

Meg took Joe through the kitchen door of the apartment into the hardwood hallway. He followed her down the worn wooden stairway to the first floor apartment.

"How old is your grandmother?"

"Seventy-eight, but because of her poor health she looks older."

Once inside Meg's grandmother's apartment, Joe saw the side door and porch. Meg led him through the laundry room and kitchen then into the spacious living room.

In a wheelchair and surrounded by several cats, a withered, white-haired woman peered at the television. She looked as if she were ninety.

"Grandma, there's someone I'd like you to meet."

The old woman glanced up as if surprised. She wore a sweater and her gnarled hands rested on a blanket on her lap.

"Grandma, this is Joe Hillery. Joe, Victoria Sidedrop."

"Nice to meet you, Ms. Sidedrop." Joe nodded with a smile.

"I'm told you met Diehla Thorne's ghost and she sent you to her time, 1680. Is that true?" The old woman leaned forward with a scowl.

Joe took a deep breath wondering if she believed it. "It is."

Victoria shook her head. "You must take us for fools."

Seven

The Chessie Cat Club

Meg's jaw slackened. "Grandma, it's not polite to say a thing like that."

Joe smiled at Meg. "It's okay. I know my time-travel story's hard to believe."

The old woman looked at Meg. "Is Joe your new boyfriend?"

"Grandma, you're really blunt tonight. We just started dating. I'm taking Joe to the club for dinner."

"Has he ever been there?"

"No, but he'll love it."

Victoria frowned and shook her head. "He's an outsider. The last two you dated were outsiders. Why don't you date one of your own?"

"Grandma, I wanted you to make a good impression on Joe. This is the kind of behavior that makes outsiders dislike us. You're acting like an old crone."

The old woman frowned. "Megan, show some respect."

Joe tried to change the subject. "I heard you started the coven that Meg's in."

"How old are you?" Victoria peered at Joe.

"Grandma!" Meg glared at her grandmother. *I'll have a good lecture for her when this fiasco is over. I'll not have her destroy this relationship now that I have Joe right where I want him.*

"It's okay." Joe held up his hands to calm her down then looked at Victoria. "I'm thirty-seven."

"My granddaughter is only twenty-three. You're too old for her."

Meg placed her hands on her hips. "Grandma, I am going to continue seeing him with or without your approval."

"It'll have to be without it then."

"Let's go, Joe." Meg stomped toward the front door. She opened it and turned. "I'll talk to you tomorrow, Grandma."

They exited the house into the chilly night air. Making their way across the porch and down the steps, Joe said, "I made a great impression on your grandmother."

"Don't worry, she'll come around."

Joe opened the passenger door for Meg. As soon as he got into the driver's seat, she slid against him and slowly crossed her right leg over her left knee. Laying her left hand on his leg, he glanced down at her shapely calf then back at her face. She gave him another quick impish blink.

"Since I'm driving, I think it would help if I knew where we were going?"

She smiled. "Of course. Turn left at the end of the street."

Joe pulled away and they were soon in the heart of downtown Manchester. While he followed Meg's direction, her closeness and exotic perfume intruded on his concentration. He was so infatuated with her, he felt as if he were in a dream. Joe couldn't help laying his hand on her knee.

I'm getting to him. She gazed at him with a child-like expression. "I hope I'm not distracting you."

"It's just that you're so close I feel like we're Siamese twins."

Meg threw her head back and laughed. Joe fondled her calf and smiled at her. She beamed back at him. As he looked back at the road, the car in front of him stopped suddenly. Joe jammed on the breaks pitching Meg forward and narrowly missed hitting the car.

Meg put a hand to her chest. "Joe, that was close! I am distracting you." She removed her leg from his lap.

Joe's heart pounded and his hands shook. He started on his way again then glanced at her. "Are you all right?"

"I'm fine." She forced a smile and nodded.

"I don't think I'd pass the breathalyzer test right now."

Meg squinted at him. "Have you been drinking?"

"No, but you intoxicate me." He glanced at her.

Meg laughed again.

Before long, Meg said, "Here it is, on the right." She pointed to a place with a marquee, 'Chessie Cat Club' Fine Dining - Entertainment. Just above it was the illuminated face of a grinning cat. Alternating light bulbs gave the appearance of the cat glancing from left to right while smiling.

Joe pulled into the parking lot.

"You'll love this place." Meg got out of the car.

Joe came around the car to meet her. "Is this some kind of witches' hangout?"

Meg smiled and nodded as she took his arm. "You'll meet others in our community here."

They passed through the glass front doors to the hostess who greeted Meg by name. The smell of incense filled the air. Joe noticed shrunken heads hanging over the front counter and pentagrams on the walls. The hostess led them into the large dining room. At the front of the dimly lit room a spotlight shone on a young woman singing and snapping her fingers to "Fever."

Meg and Joe were seated at one of the smaller tables in the back of the room. Each table had a potted candle for light. Meg removed her jacket and placed it on the back of her chair. Joe did the same. A jazz band played from a short platform to the right of the singer.

The waitress brought menus.

"Choose anything you like," Meg said. "This night is my treat. It's my way of thanking you for what you've sacrificed for me. What did Marcus say when you told him you were through meeting with him?"

Joe scanned the menu. "He wasn't very happy, and before he hung up he said to tell you hello." Joe looked at Meg.

"That's his way of letting you know that he's wise that I'm behind your decision."

Still going over the menu, Joe saw the main section was called FELINE DINNERS. Names with puns appeared: Salmon Steak: it's the cat's meow, New Zealand Lamb, grilled to purr-fection. The other two sections were called FAMILIAR FAVORITES, a play on words for witches' familiars. A smaller category, SPECIALTIES OF OUR ILK, listed seaweed salad, roast eel, toad stew, octo-pie and even bat-soufflé among other oddities.

The waitress returned. "You ready to order, Meg?"

"Yes. Can I have the toad stew and a garden salad, no dressing please?"

The girl looked at Joe.

"Diane, this is Joe."

The waitress smiled with a nod.

Gazing at the menu Joe said, "I'll have the New Zealand lamb with baked potato and the salad with French dressing."

They ordered their drinks and the waitress left.

"Toad stew?" Joe grimaced.

"Don't knock it till you've tried it. If you're nice I may give you a taste." Her smile widened as she watched his expression.

"I hope this dinner isn't costing you too much."

"It'll cost me everything I have in the bank, but you're worth it." Watching Joe's concerned look, she laughed. "Gotcha. Joe! Will you relax?"

The singer finished her number, and everyone gave her a round of applause while hipper customers snapped their fingers.

"She's a witch, too?" Joe whispered.

"Yeah. Some of the people eating here think this place is only a gimmick. They don't realize it's owned and run by witches. The employees and even the entertainers are wiccan."

The band started to play "That Old Black Magic" as a magician appeared in the spotlight at the front of the room. He announced himself as Albert the Great.

"This man doesn't do tricks. He does real magic," Meg whispered.

Joe frowned in disbelief.

At first the magician did the usual tricks, pulling a rabbit out of a hat and making flowers appear. But at the end of his act, he pulled out a black silk scarf from his top pocket. He unfolded it and threw it up in the air. It floated just over his head. The magician's eyes never left the scarf. Then in dramatic fashion, he pointed at it. Joe watched in surprise as it suddenly turned into a bat and flew over the tables. Some people shrieked while others laughed as it dive bombed a few customers. It finally flew back to its master. The magician held his hands together palms up. The bat landed there then dissolved back into the black scarf which fell limp in his hands. Everyone applauded. The magician bowed and left the spotlight.

"I don't believe my eyes," Joe said. "Usually an animal trick appears in a hat or a dove pan. But that bat was a piece of cloth!"

"I told you Albert the Great did real magic."

Next, a thin young woman with short dark hair dressed in a black body suit took the magician's place and swayed to "Moon Dance."

The waitress returned with their drinks. Just as they took a sip, Luna and Paula walked up to their table. "Well, well, if it isn't the wicked witch of the west," Luna said.

Paula nodded. "Hi, Meg. Hello, Joe."

"Meg, can we speak with you for a moment in private?" Luna motioned toward the corner of the room.

Meg nodded and squinted at Joe which he took for '*I know what they want.*'

"I'll be right back, Joe." She left the table and all three women walked to the remote area.

While Joe sat alone watching the dancer moving her hips and snapping her fingers to the sound of jazz trumpets, he missed Ellen and his kids and wondered what they were doing. He wasn't sure why he'd come to this strange place with Meg. Had he simply fallen out of love with Ellen and into love with Meg? Could it be that simple? Even in his confused state of mind, he sensed something was wrong. He wondered what was being said as he watched the three women engaged in intense conversation using manic hand gestures.

Luna frowned at Meg. "So, Black Widow, we see you brought your victim with you tonight."

Meg smirked. "How did Marcus take it when Joe told him he wasn't going to meet with him anymore?"

"Not too well." Paula glared at Meg.

Luna interrupted, "But Marcus doesn't want the coven split up over this. He actually admires you. He told me he underestimated you as a witch and will give in to your demands."

"Then tell him my demands are great. I want to be high priestess and coven leader."

"You're making a lot of enemies, Meg," Paula said.

Meg smiled at her showing she wasn't afraid.

"And what are you going to do with Joe after he finds the ring for you?" Luna asked.

"Dump him. He believes I'm as madly in love with him as he is with me." Meg laughed.

"Joe might be harder to get rid of than you think," Paula said.

"Do you believe I'd use a spell like that without an antidote? He'll be running back to his wife faster than you can say Ellen Hillery."

"And what if his wife won't take him back after what you've done?" Luna asked.

Meg shrugged. "That's his problem."

"That's really heartless, Meg," Paula said.

"If either one of your love spells had worked, you'd have done the same thing." Meg smiled at them. "You thought I didn't know." She turned and walked away.

As the two women watched her stroll back to her table, Luna said, "I'll see that bitch dead before I let that poor excuse for a sorceress take possession of the ring and become our leader."

Paula ended her glare at Meg to look at Luna with a nod in agreement.

When Meg returned to her seat, their dinners were on the table. Just seeing her face eroded Joe's dwindling feelings for Ellen.

"Trouble?" he asked.

"They don't like the fact that you're not meeting with Marcus." Meg peered at Joe. "They'll lie about me just to break us up."

Joe nodded and cut into his lamb. *I'll change the subject.* "What's with the black lipstick and nail polish you women wear at your ceremonies?"

"It's called the Goth look. Most of us only wear it for our rituals. Before a sabbat meeting one time I was all Gothed up and I went into this grocery store. A little boy started to cry. He pointed at me and said, 'Mommy, she's a vampire.'" Meg started to chuckle, then took a sip of her drink.

"You're real funny, Meg; scaring kids." Joe smiled.

She gazed at him with a grin while she chewed.

As they were finishing their dinner, Sayde and Barry joined them.

As Sayde sat down next to her, Meg leaned forward. "Hi, Sayde. I've been meaning to ask you if the police found anything out about Trish."

Sayde shook her head. "No. Nothing. I'm worried sick about her. The police suspect foul play." Sayde looked at Joe. "I'm sorry you decided to discontinue our meetings."

As Joe stopped to swallow and clear his throat, Meg slipped off one shoe and leaned back in her seat. Reaching across under the table with her foot, she tapped Joe on the shin to keep him quiet. With

Sayde and Barry not included in Marcus's plan, Meg wanted to keep Joe from talking.

"Well, you see..." He stopped as he felt Meg's foot tap his shin again. He glanced at her, not sure what she wanted him to say.

"And?" Sayde asked.

"As I was saying…" Meg nudged him again and he stopped.

"What happened between you and Marcus?" Barry asked.

Meg moved her foot up on Joe's chair next to his thigh.

"Well, it's because..." Meg nudged his thigh. Joe stopped again and glanced at her. She looked down at her plate so the other two wouldn't know she was signaling him.

"What was I saying?" Joe flashed them an embarrassed smile.

"You were starting to tell us why you're not going to meet with us anymore." Sayde looked at Barry in disbelief.

Having trouble concentrating, Joe tried again. "See, Marcus—"

Meg gave him a quick thrust to the groin and he jumped out of his seat.

"I see Joe's ready to leave, so I guess we'd better be going." Meg slipped on her shoe and rose from the table. "It was nice talking to you."

Joe was unsure what was going on, but he put on his jacket. "It was nice seeing both of you again."

Sayde and Barry frowned at each other.

Meg paid the check and they left the restaurant.

"What was all that foot tapping about?" Joe asked.

"Sayde's nosy and this is none of her business. Let Marcus tell her why you quit him."

Joe unlocked Meg's door. "But we didn't even order dessert."

"We'll have that at my place." Meg raised an eyebrow.

On the ride back, Meg sat close to Joe again. As he drove she laid her head on his shoulder and played with his mustache. She softly kissed his throat then stuck her tongue in his ear.

Joe flinched. "Not while I'm driving. You're going to get us killed."

Meg snickered and kissed his lips.

It was almost eleven o'clock when they arrived at the apartment. Meg sat on the couch, took her shoes off and put her feet on the coffee table. Joe sat next to her. Shyebony jumped up on her lap. She stroked her cat. "So, what did you think of the club?"

"It was different. I thought the food and entertainment were pretty good. As nice as it was, I'll admit I was anxious to be alone with you."

Meg frowned. "I hope you didn't mean tonight, Joe."

Joe's jaw dropped. "Well, I was under the impression…"

"I have to get up very early for work tomorrow. There's this shipment I have to receive."

What's going on? "But I thought…"

"Gotcha!" Meg threw her head back and giggled. She looked at him and laughed again.

Joe made a mock pout. "That's not nice. You had me going there. I thought I had my signals crossed. You should have been an actress."

"I should have been." Meg smirked at him.

Joe took her chin in his hand and gazed into her brown eyes. "You've got the most enchanting little face I've ever seen."

"Joe, that's so sweet."

The way she said that, he thought she was touched by his comment.

She put her arms around his neck, peered into his eyes and gave him a burning kiss.

Eight

The Breakup

Joe and Meg lay on the floor in an embrace. *She looks as happy as I feel.* Joe touched her face with a finger. "That was unbelievable, young lady."

She smiled at him. "You just needed the right woman."

Joe realized how late it was. He glanced at his watch. His heart started to pound. "Oh my God, it's after midnight!"

Meg sat up. "You'd better go."

Joe stood, pulling his pants up. "What am I going to tell Ellen?"

"I hope you've got a story."

"I told her I was seeing Marcus. She thinks he's a video customer."

Meg stood next to him with no expression. "When will I see you again?"

"I don't know." He slipped his shoes on. "I'll call you tomorrow." He kissed her then left through the back door.

~ * ~

When Joe arrived home he found Ellen on the couch watching TV. She turned and glared at him as he entered. *She's furious. How can I get through this?* He noticed the clock said one a.m.

"Sorry I'm late. You didn't have to wait up for me."

"Don't flatter yourself." Her angry eyes were locked on him.

Joe slowly walked toward her. "Marcus insisted I go out for a drink with him. Some place called the Chessie Cat Club."

"And again you didn't think to call me?" Ellen rose from the couch.

"Is it a federal offense that I forgot to call?"

"Stop the charade, Joe. I know you're seeing another woman." Her eyes were slits. Her speech was rushed.

"Not this again." Joe closed his eyes and shook his head.

"Let me see your check."

"What?"

"Let me see the check Marcus gave you." She held out her hand.

"I won't get it until Tuesday."

"Tonight is when your check is due." Ellen approached him. She examined his collar for lipstick. With none there, she sniffed at his shirt. Tears came to her eyes. "You reek like your whore. Who is she, Joe? Anyone I know?"

Joe gazed down at the floor waiting for the slap that didn't come. He'd have felt better if it had.

Ellen's eyes were livid with rage. "I asked you who she is. I have a right to know, damn it!"

Joe met her teary, angry eyes. "I'll leave in the morning."

"You son of a bitch!" she yelled, then turned and scurried down to the bedroom, crying.

That night while Joe slept on the couch, he was occasionally awakened by Ellen's sobbing, making him feel like a heel.

~ * ~

While Ellen made breakfast for the kids, Joe packed his possessions.

"Why are you crying, Mommy?" Tommy asked.

"Mommy just has a cold, honey." Ellen put a tissue to her nose.

When Joe walked into the kitchen with his suitcase, he said, "I'll call you when I want to see the kids."

"Where are you going, Daddy?" Tommy asked.

"Daddy's going away for a while."

"A long while." Ellen turned from the stove to glare at him.

Joe forced a smile. "I'll see you kids later, all right?" He kissed Tommy and Amy on the cheeks.

"I don't want you to go, Daddy." Amy said.

Joe held back tears and left through the kitchen door without looking back.

Driving to his sister's home, Joe was overwhelmed with being separated from his wife and kids.

When he arrived, his sister Beverly said, "Joe, what a surprise!"

"Bev, could I spend a couple of nights at your place until I find an apartment?"

"What's going on with you and Ellen?"

"It's a long story."

"Are you okay?"

Joe paused to take a breath. "Yeah, just peachy."

"Of course you can stay with us."

"I really appreciate it, Bev. I'll explain everything to you later."

In Bev's living room that evening, Joe was embarrassed and felt he was intruding on his sister's family. With her husband listening, Joe admitted he was seeing someone else, but he was vague about the circumstances.

After he explained his situation, he said, "I feel like I'm putting you two out."

Bev's face showed sympathy. "Not at all. You're welcome to stay as long as you want. Isn't he, Marty?" She looked at her husband.

"Yeah, sure," The blond, round faced man said with a nod.

Joe and Bev had a family resemblance with the same slim build, wavy dark brown hair and moody brown eyes.

"It's nice having my big brother staying here." Bev rubbed the back of Joe's hand. "We don't see enough of each other."

Joe nodded.

"I'm not sure what it is, but you seem like a different person." There was concern in Bev's voice.

"It's not just that I've lost Ellen, but I have changed."

"Maybe you're going through a mid-life crisis." Bev leaned forward. "You and Ellen are the last couple I ever expected to split up."

Bev fixed up the bed in her spare room. Joe retired early. Looking at pictures of his kids, his thoughts drifted to Meg. He wanted to call her, but couldn't from his sister's phone.

~ * ~

Joe sat at his desk the next day trying to concentrate on work. His receptionist buzzed to tell him he had a call from Megan O'Leary.

"Put it through, Carol."

"Joe?" came the sound of Meg's high voice.

"What's up, Meg?"

"Why didn't you call me last night?"

"Ellen and I broke up."

"Last night?"

"No, Saturday night, after I got back from your place."

"I'm sorry, Joe, really. I feel like it's partly my fault. What can I do for you?"

"Nothing."

"You sound really down. But maybe it's for the best. I mean, I couldn't continue seeing you if you were going to stay with your wife. And I sure don't want to end our relationship. Where are you living now?"

"With my sister in Lowell."

"Isn't that where you grew up?"

"Yeah." Although Joe was happy to hear Meg's voice, he didn't feel like having a conversation.

"That's quite a drive to work for you. Joe, I've got it! Why don't you stay at my place for a while?"

"I don't think that would be a good idea." Joe looked to the floor.

"It's a great idea, and I'd love having you here."

Joe's breathing increased. *This is a dream come true. There's nothing I'd like better.* "Are you sure about this?"

"Yes. When can you move in?"

"Not for a couple of days." Joe smiled. "I don't want my sister to know where I'm going."

"Move in tomorrow night, please?"

Joe laughed. "If you insist. I'll give you a ride home from work."

"When we get back to my place, I'll give you a full body massage," Meg said.

Joe smiled at the thought, then Ellen's face entered his mind.

"I have to get back to work. Sherman's giving me looks. See you tomorrow before five."

That night at supper, Joe told Bev he had found an apartment in Willstown and he'd be moving out in the morning.

"Boy, that was quick," Bev said.

"One of my employees gave me the tip."

The following afternoon at four o'clock, Joe drove to the occult book store. Meg was at the cash register when he entered. She gave him her impish blink. "It's so cool that you're coming home with me." She turned. "Sherman, I'm leaving now. I have to get Joe moved in to my apartment."

Joe heard the manager's voice. "Go ahead, Meg. I'll see you tomorrow."

The temperature was about seventy degrees as they left the store. Meg put her arm around him then kissed him on the way to the car. "This is the first time I ever lived with a guy."

Joe opened the door for her. "I feel honored." As he got in the car and she scooted next to him with a smile, his depression washed away. He felt like he was in an enchanted world. He was happy he and Ellen had split up. For some reason, Meg was the woman he loved. When they arrived at her apartment, it didn't take them long to get him settled.

"You realize you'll be sleeping on the couch while you live here," Meg said matter-of-factly.
Did I miss something? Why is she being so moral now? "Wherever you say is fine."
"I mean we're not married, and you're still legally married to Ellen."
Joe nodded as Meg started to laugh. "I had you going there again, Joe."
He grabbed her and kissed her.
With a seductive look, she said in a breathy whisper, "Come into my room. I'm going to make a new man out of you."
Meg lit two incense candles on the nightstand. Joe removed his shirt and let his pants fall on the floor. He pulled down the comforter and lay on his back. When she disappeared into the bathroom, he noticed strange paintings all over the walls and even on the ceiling: nude witches next to a cauldron, praying to the moon; young witches riding on broomsticks.
Meg entered the room. "Slide over to the edge and roll onto your stomach."
She stood next to him, rubbed some lotion into her hands and massaged his neck. He shut his eyes in pleasure as she worked her way down to his shoulders.
"This feels great," he whispered.
"You've had so much stress the past couple of days I've decided to give you a full body massage." Meg dug her fingers into Joe's shoulders and back. "As I told you, eventually I want to do this for a living."
"You'd quit the book store?"
"No, just do some massage on the side. I'm already certified."
Joe flinched.
"I'm sorry. Did I hurt you?"
I'm surprised at how strong her hands are. "No, I think you just applied too much pressure to a sore area."

"You're not ready for deep tissue work yet. This is your first massage."

"This isn't your firmest massage?"

"No, this is only medium work I'm doing."

Joe was surprised that this petite young woman had so much strength in her hands. He shut his eyes in ecstasy as she continued her way down either side of his spine.

"Are you still awake?" Meg whispered.

"Barely."

"Roll on your back now.

She massaged his chest.

"Does your grandmother know about me staying here?"

Meg wrinkled her little nose. "No, not yet. I didn't want to upset her."

Massaging his ribs, Meg asked, "Could you give me a ride to work in the morning?"

"I'm at your beck and call. Are you finished?"

"Not quite. I told you this was a *full* body massage." She rubbed his pelvis and soon was on the inside of his thighs. She slowly worked her way up to his groin.

When the erotic massage was over, Meg jumped onto the bed next to him and put her arms around him with a kiss on his cheek.

"Did I relax you?"

"I'm so relaxed, I can't remember my name."

She laughed. "Did I make a new man out of you?"

"I'll change my name in the morning." Joe smiled at her and touched her nose with his index finger.

"See how nice it is not having to worry about time and what Ellen will say when you get home?"

Joe nodded in agreement. *But why do I still miss her?*

~ * ~

That evening at Hillery mansion while Ellen watched TV with the children, her thoughts were on Joe. Holding back tears, she left the kids and went into the bedroom. Lying on the bed, she cried softly into her pillow so the kids wouldn't hear her. Had she lost Joe for good? After she got herself under control, she decided to call their old friend Brad Heins, remembering he was the one who helped them defeat Diehla's spirit, breaking the three hundred year family curse. But how could a parapsychologist help her with this problem? Brad answered the phone. Ellen started to weep again as she explained their break up.

"But why would Joe be interested in another woman? Are you sure he's seeing someone else?"

"Yes, but for some reason I still love him, Brad."

"That doesn't sound like Joe. He adores you."

"You've been such a good friend of ours and helped us in the past. I was hoping you might help us one more time."

"Do you know where he's staying?"

"No." Ellen shook her head and held back more tears. "I haven't spoken to him since he left on Sunday morning."

"I'll give Joe a call at his office this week."

"Thank you." Ellen lowered her eyes, placing a tissue to her nose.

"I'll tell you what. Maybe I'll fly in to see him."

"You'd come in all the way from Chicago on such short notice?"

"I was meaning to pay you two a visit soon anyway."

"Oh, Brad, you're wonderful." Ellen sniffed with joy. "When would you get here?"

"Probably not until next Monday."

"I'll pick you up at Logan."

"No. I'll rent a car and contact you when I arrive."

"Joe has changed so much and he's secretive," Ellen said. "I just hope your trip won't be in vain."

"I'll find out what I can for you. I'll stop and see him at his business before coming to see you at the mansion."

"I can't tell you how much I appreciate this," Ellen said with a sniffle.

When Brad hung up the phone, a woman sitting next to him asked, "Who was that?"

"The wife of a close friend. They've got marital problems all of a sudden. I'll be taking a trip to New England on Sunday night."

Brad, now in his early fifties, had salt-and-pepper hair, but with his broad shoulders and trim physique, he still maintained his distinguished good looks.

"You're going all the way to the east coast just because your friend's wife asked you to?"

Brad nodded. "I hope to be back here by the end of next week."

"I'll miss you." She leaned close and they kissed.

~ * ~

The rest of that week Meg nightly made love to Joe. They spent Friday and Saturday evening at the Chessie Cat Club and took in a movie on Sunday. After the show, Meg asked Joe to stop in to see her grandmother.

When they arrived the old woman was pleasant. "Joe," she said, "I'm glad you're dating Megan. I've never seen her so happy." She patted Meg's hand.

Because of his Hillery ancestor being a legendary witch killing judge, Joe was not totally convinced of the old woman's sincerity.

"I've never been happier either." Joe smiled. *Meg must have had a talk with the old lady.*

Meg grinned. "See, Joe, I knew you two would get along."

"Megan, I've baked a blueberry pie." Victoria pointed. "Would you please get it from the kitchen?"

~ * ~

Brad landed at Logan International in Boston at noon. Renting a car, he headed north. Just before getting into downtown Willstown, he found Joe's long, red brick warehouse which had once been a junior high school. The sign said 'Willstown Video Industries.' He parked the car and entered through the double-glass doors into the small lobby stopping at the receptionist station where a young woman sat wearing a telephone headset.

"May I help you, sir?" she asked.

"Yes, I'm here to see Joe Hillery."

She leaned forward. "May I tell him who's calling?"

"Brad Heins."

"Have a seat, Mr. Heins. I'll let Mr. Hillery know you're here."

Brad sat in a cushioned chair next to a table piled with magazines in the brightly lit room.

"Mr. Hillery will be with you shortly," the receptionist said.

"Thank you." Brad paged absently through a magazine.

Soon, Joe entered the lobby. "Brad," he smiled, strolling toward him. Joe shook his hand. "It's good to see you again. Come into my office."

Brad followed him to the first door on the left. *I feel like a spy. This may not be easy.*

Inside, Joe sat behind his desk. "Have a seat."

Brad took a chair directly across from him.

I'm happy to see my old friend, but this sudden visit must be because of my breakup with Ellen. "What brings you to Willstown?" Joe leaned back in his chair.

"Well, I haven't been here for a couple of years, and Ellen called me Tuesday night."

Joe hung his head. *Here it comes.*

"She was in tears. It's none of my business, but over the last twelve years you two have become my friends."

Joe clicked his pen over and over. "What did she tell you?"

"That you're seeing another woman and you moved out last Sunday."

"If you were anyone else but the man who helped save my life, I'd say it's none of your business." Joe leaned forward. "How much time do you have?"

"As much time as you've got. That's why I came here all the way from Illinois."

Joe buzzed his receptionist. "Carol, I'm not seeing anyone for the rest of the afternoon. Only put through phone calls."

Joe told Brad everything from the séance to selling his knowledge to the coven.

"It started as a legitimate business venture, but then I met Meg."

"That's who you're seeing?"

"Yes." Joe's speech now rushed. "And in a short period of time I fell in love with her."

"And Meg is a witch?"

"She is. Brad, you'd be surprised how many witches live in this area. They've even got a hangout in downtown Manchester called the Chessie Cat Club."

"How could you get mixed up with witches after all you and your family have been through in the past?"

"I needed the money to save this business and I was behind on the mortgage payment. I had no choice."

"But you gave up that money just because Meg asked you to?" Brad shook his head in disbelief. "May I ask you what Meg's last name is?"

"You're not going to tell Ellen?"

"Of course not."

"It's O'Leary. She's an ancestor of Yves Laughton, Diehla's lover."

Brad pursed his lips in frustration. "A perfect match for you, Joe." Brad let out a breath. "And where are you staying now?"

"With Meg."

"If you really are in love with Meg, you should do the decent thing and file for divorce so Ellen can go on with her life. I'd better be going."

"I was going to give you the grand tour of the warehouse and I thought maybe we could go out for a sandwich or a drink."

"No, I'm not in the mood." Brad stood.

"You're angry."

"Joe, I don't think I know you anymore. I'd better leave before I say something I'll regret."

Joe glared at him. "If that's the way you feel, go ahead and leave."

Brad rushed out of the office, slamming the door behind him. Joe stood with a scowl.

On the way to Hillery Mansion to see Ellen, it entered Brad's mind that with Meg being a witch, maybe she put a love spell on Joe. *I've read about that kind of thing.*

~ * ~

Luna descended into the dimly-lit basement. Several smoky incense candles were used for light. She found Marcus and Circe sitting at a small table with a huge candle in front of them.

"Thanks for joining us, my dear," Marcus said.

"I hope this is important." Luna sat in the chair next to him.

"I wanted you to be here in person to hear our plan and pray with us to the goddess that it works. It's time to settle a score with Meg."

Nine

Brad Investigates

Ellen greeted Brad at the door with a hug. "Thank you again for coming. Come in and have a seat on the couch. I'll get you something to drink."

He entered the living room as Ellen headed to the kitchen. She returned with two glasses of wine. She handed one to Brad and sat in a chair next to him.

"Did you see Joe?" She peered at him.

"Yes, and I don't want to betray Joe's trust," Brad said. "I won't reveal the name of the woman he's seeing, but it's no one you know. And she's a practicing witch."

"Joe's seeing a witch?" Ellen's voice raised a pitch.

"Joe became mixed up with her through his dealings with Marcus Phillips. Have you heard of him?"

"Yes, that's Joe's new client. His name was on the checks Joe was receiving."

"Joe told me you didn't know the true nature of his business dealings. Apparently this Marcus is the head of a coven in north Manchester. He was paying Joe for some knowledge of magic."

Ellen set her wine glass down on the end table. "So that's where Joe's been getting the money. He told me Marcus was a strange video business client who kept odd hours."

"Joe met Marcus through a clairvoyant named Luna LaBrock." Brad took a sip of wine.

"Luna LaBrock is the psychic my friend recommended. Joe used her to get information about the colonial girl, Abigail Jennings." Ellen paused with a reflective look. "That's how Joe met this woman? She's part of Luna's coven?"

Brad gazed into his wine glass, then at Ellen. "Yes, but please don't make any trouble right now. I think there's more to this than we know. Joe told me he'd given up the money from Marcus just because this woman asked him to."

"So that's why Joe didn't have a check last Saturday when he came home at one in the morning. Do you know why Joe became interested in her?"

"No, but I'll tell you what I believe. Promise you won't think I'm crazy?"

Ellen sipped her wine. "I promise."

"I think Joe may be the victim of witchcraft."

"Witchcraft?" Ellen raised her eyebrows.

"It fits the scenario. Joe got mixed up with witches, then suddenly for the first time he's unfaithful to you and gives up money he desperately needs all because this woman he doesn't know asks him to. It's as if he has no will of his own. I've seen this kind of thing before."

Ellen held her wine glass in front of her face. "Isn't that reaching a little to make me feel better? But if this is true, then Joe's just a victim." Ellen looked away as if considering the idea.

"A love spell is the only logical explanation."

"Brad, you might be right. Joe adores his kids, but he hasn't even called to see them, and he's been gone for over a week."

Brad finished his wine and set his glass down on the end table. "I'm going to do some investigating, but I don't know where this Marcus lives. His phone number is unlisted, probably because of who he is."

"I've still got Luna's number," Ellen said.

"Great. I'll make an appointment to see her for a psychic reading. Afterwards I'll ask her a couple of questions about a certain witch."

"But all this investigating may keep you here longer than you planned." Ellen frowned with concern.

"I have to get to the bottom of this." Brad landed a fist into his thigh.

"Please stay here with me and the kids."

He shook his head. "I don't want to impose."

"Nonsense, you're staying. I insist." Ellen smiled.

"Thanks Ellen." Brad smiled back at her. "Let me have Luna's number and I'll call her now."

~ * ~

Two nights later Brad had his fortune told by Luna LaBrock. He was surprised how much she knew about him. She told him his profession, knew he was from the Midwest and even tied him to Joe. Because of this, Brad didn't want to ask her about love spells for fear she may be in on Meg's plan. He knew he'd have to get his information from Meg directly.

After the session, Brad said, "Joe asked me to give Meg a package, since I'm here in Manchester. I can't remember the name of the place where she works. The Chessie Cat Club keeps going through my mind."

"That's where Meg hangs out. She works at the Bell, Book and Candle."

"Yeah, that's right." Looking into those psychic beady brown eyes, Brad felt as if she were looking into his mind. It made him feel uncomfortable wondering how much else she knew about him.

"It's the occult book store here in Manchester. You could give me the package. I'm in that store all the time."

"Joe asked me to deliver this personally."

Brad noticed Luna gazing at something behind him.

"I'm afraid my pet python has gotten out of her aquarium."

Brad turned to see a large empty rectangular glass tank on a shelf at the other side of the room.

His eyes widened. "I'd better be going."

~ * ~

Brad called the Bell, Book and Candle from Hillery mansion the next morning. He was told Meg would be there until five.

The sun was shining but the air was cool and windy as Brad parked in front of the occult book store. Inside the incense-filled shop, he tried to locate Meg. Acting like a customer, he browsed through the books, trying to determine the sales people from the customers. Besides the man behind the counter, it looked as if there were two other employees. One was a young girl about eighteen and the other a young woman in her early twenties with short dark hair, wearing a black top and skirt. Brad watched her as she walked to the front counter to talk to the man. Brad assumed this was Meg. He didn't want to ask for her by name for fear it might tip her off that he was spying, but he didn't want to speak to the wrong person. As she straightened books along the wall, Brad approached her.

"Miss, could you help me?"

She turned with her brown eyes squinting at him.

"I'm looking for a book on love spells. Where would they be?"

"Follow me." She smiled at him and headed for the back of the store. "There are a lot of books on that subject right here."

She pointed then started to walk away.

Brad forced a conversation. "Is there any one book you'd recommend? This is all new to me."

"Is there one particular woman you're trying to attract or women in general?"

"It's someone I know."

She bent over searching the titles. Brad couldn't help notice her shapely figure.

"There are a couple of good books here." She stood with two books in her hands. "One of these two would probably be your best bet."

Although Meg was attractive, Brad sensed strangeness about her. Besides her pale complexion, her eyes squinted as if sensitive to light, yet they were piercing at the same time.

"Have you ever used a love spell?" Brad asked. "From either book?"

"No."

"Love spells." Brad looked at the books with a smile. "This is probably nonsense."

"Love spells do work. I know from personal experience."

"Which one have you used?"

"I've used several but not from any books. But these two books are good. I know both of the authors. Just look for the spell that fits your needs. Is there anything else you need today?"

"No, I think these will do. Thanks for your help, miss."

She smiled, turned away and walked to another part of the store. Brad went to the register and Sherman rang up Brad's purchases.

"That young woman was very helpful. What was her name?"

"That's Meg. I don't think I could run this store without her. She has a great knowledge of the occult."

I got the knowledge I was looking for.

As Brad left the book store greeted by the chilly breeze, he passed Paula walking in the other direction toward the store.

Meg was straightening books toward the back when she noticed the tall model enter the shop. Meg couldn't hear Paula's conversation with Sherman. Keeping out of sight, Meg crept closer to the front to eavesdrop.

Sherman went into the stockroom then returned with two books. "These are probably the best books on voodoo in the store."

Voodoo? Is Paula trying to send me a message?

"Paula, are you sure you want to learn such dark magic?" Sherman asked in his high voice.

"Yes. I'll take them both. I have to teach someone a lesson." Paula turned and gazed in Meg's general direction.

Meg straightened books pretending not to notice in case Paula had spotted her. *So Marcus is playing hardball. I'd better get home soon and place a protective spell around me.*

~ * ~

That afternoon at Hillery Mansion, Brad said, "I'm going to call a friend who lives nearby. He's an expert on magic."

Ellen smiled. "When I called you last week, it was as a friend. I didn't realize you'd be using your skills and acquaintances to help."

"See." Brad winked. "It comes in handy having a parapsychologist as a friend."

They both laughed.

Brad went to the phone on the desk and called his friend's home.

"Brad, it's good to hear from you again."

"Fenton, I need some information about love spells."

"What kind of spell was used and who's the victim?"

"I know who used it, but I'm not sure what type of love spell she used."

Ellen stepped closer to listen, as Brad explained the situation to Fenton.

"What makes you believe a love spell was used?"

"The woman Joe fell in love with is a practicing witch."

"That does sound suspicious."

"When I spoke to her at the occult book store where she works, she told me she has used love spells."

"What coven does she belong to?"

"A coven in Manchester called the coven of Laughton."

"That's headed by Marcus Phillips."

"Yes, that's the one." *I'm happy he knows about these people.*

"One of the girls who belongs to that coven has recently disappeared. I heard Marcus himself was questioned by the police. He's dangerous. Some in that coven are black witches. Your friend would be wise to stay away from those people."

Brad closed his eyes. "I agree, but what can you do for my friend Joe?"

"If you knew the exact spell, it would be much easier to remove and cheaper. However, I have a cover-all antidote I can use on him. It takes a little longer and is much more expensive, but it'll do the job. You'll have to get your friend to come here in person."

"I just hope I can."

Later that evening after the kids went to bed, Brad explained his plan to Ellen.

"You've got to get Joe to agree to go," Ellen said.

"I'll call him at his office tomorrow. I hope he's still speaking to me."

Ellen folded her hands and lowered her head. "I pray that Fenton can cure him, but I'm worried about his price."

Brad nodded. "I'll do what I can."

~ * ~

Brad called Joe at work. "Can I see you for a couple of minutes today? It's important, Joe."

"All right. Be here at one and I'll see you." With that, Joe hung up the phone.

"Boy, that was quick," Ellen said.

"He'll give me the honor of seeing me at one. If Joe's not under a spell, I want nothing more to do with him. Right now, I'm giving him the benefit of the doubt."

In Joe's office that afternoon, Brad tried to convince him to visit Fenton. "Maybe you've forgotten, but twelve years ago it was you who was desperate for me to do something about Diehla's spirit which was returning to destroy you. And now I'm asking for your cooperation."

Joe lowered his head. "No, I haven't forgotten that you saved my life, but you have to accept that I've fallen in love with another woman and I've never been happier."

"You're happy, Joe?" Brad leaned on his desk, peering at him. "You're willing to lose your wife, kids, ancestral home, and because of the money Meg talked you out of, you're going to lose your business as well. All you have is Meg, and if she has used a love spell on you, she'll dump you as soon as she gets whatever it is she's after."

Joe closed his eyes. Brad felt like he'd finally made contact with him.

"Just see Fenton. If the antidote doesn't work, then you really are in love with Meg. But if it does change your feelings for her, you still may be able to save your marriage and family."

Joe shook his head. "This is stupid."

"Joe, do this for Ellen. You owe her that much."

Joe blew out a breath. "All right." He raised his hands to show surrender. "When do I see this witch doctor of yours?"

"Since tomorrow is Saturday, I made the appointment for two o'clock. Where should I pick you up?"

"Meet me here in the parking lot at one-thirty."

That evening when Joe arrived at Meg's place, he wondered for the first time if he only had these strong feelings for her because he was under her spell. When she made love to him that evening, it still felt real to him.

As Joe and Meg ate breakfast the following morning, Meg asked, "Are you all right?"

"Yeah, why?" *She's noticed a difference in me.*

She crunched on toast and gave him a thoughtful look. "You seem like you're somewhere else this morning."

"I'm just worried about bills and my business."

She took his hand. "I'm so sorry about your financial problems, but it's better to lose your business and get a job than to have any dealings with Marcus. Trust me."

I don't know who to trust anymore.

"Since you're having lunch with your friend, let's have dinner at the club tonight."

Joe forced a smile. "Okay."

~ * ~

On the way to Fenton's home the following afternoon, Joe said to Brad, "I never knew we had a witch expert in this area."

"He's one of the world's leading authorities on the occult."

"Fenton? First or last name?"

Brad glanced at Joe. "It's his first name. His last name is Cyrus."

"Cyrus? That was the name of the guy who killed Meg's ancestor, Medea."

"Was it Nathon Cyrus?" Brad asked.

"Yeah, that was it."

"He was an ancestor of Fenton's. Nathon lived in Fenton's house in the early seventeen hundreds, I believe."

"That means Medea was probably killed in his house." Joe was anxious to see the infamous home.

When Brad pulled up into the long driveway Joe could tell that, like his own home, Hillery Mansion, the large Cyrus house was built centuries ago. It was a gray-sided, two-story house with a sharply peaked, black roof.

Brad rang the doorbell. A man about fifty wearing a suit answered the door. They followed him into the lavish living room with a spiral staircase on the opposite end.

The man walked around to the front of the couch. "Mr. Cyrus, Brad Heins and a Mr. Hillery are here to see you, sir."

A white haired man entered with a book in his hand. He turned toward Brad and Joe. Smiling he walked to Brad and pumped his hand. "Brad, it's so good to see you again." The tall, thin man looked to be about seventy. With his curly white hair sticking out from the sides of his head and his thick glasses, he looked like a mad scientist.

"It's good to see you again, Fenton," Brad said. "And this is Joe Hillery, my friend that I told you about."

"Nice to meet you, Fenton." Joe shook the older man's hand.

"Brad told me how you ended your family curse," Fenton said. "If I weren't an occult expert, I wouldn't have believed how it actually happened. I know all about Diehla Thorne. With her spirit returning from the dead, I believe she was the most powerful witch of all time, but partly because of that ring she wore. When you have more time, please give me all the details so I can record your incredible experience in my journal."

"Sure." Joe nodded. "Brad told me your ancestor Nathon once lived in this house."

Fenton nodded with a grimace. "I'm sorry to say he did."

"Did he murder a woman named Medea Laughton here?" Joe asked.

"Yes, you know your local history. May I ask where you heard that?"

"From Marcus Phillips and Sayde Anderson. They're witches from Manchester."

"I'm well aware of who they are. And I'm sure I'm not one of their favorite people." Fenton strolled to a portrait gallery on the wall opposite the staircase. "This, my friends, is the portrait of Nathon Cyrus." Fenton pointed to a portrait of a thin man with short dark hair and cruel eyes. "I wish this devil had never been born. You mentioned Medea's murder. Let me show you something before we begin."

Fenton led them out of the living room into a large adjoining room which looked like a banquet hall. There was a single long table in the center of the room. To the right was a large fire place.

"This is the room where Nathon brutally murdered Medea Laughton in front of his sadistic friends back in 1707."

"Wasn't she interrogated here about a ring she owned?" Joe asked.

"That's right," Fenton said. "It was said she wore the very ring once owned by Diehla Thorne. Have either of you heard of the Hell Fire Club?"

"Yes." Brad nodded. "It took place in the early to mid-eighteenth century in Ireland and England. A group of rowdy men gathered for sinful pleasures and manly amusements."

"You're partly right." Fenton smiled. "I don't know about rowdy, but they were usually wealthy, influential men of the community. And there were chapters here in the colonies. Benjamin Franklin was a member of a later more refined chapter. In the early eighteenth century, Nathon was the leader of a Hell Fire Club here in this house. Members met on moonlit nights in this very room."

"Didn't assorted ladies of the evening attend meetings?" Brad asked.

"Yes, but by no means were they the only women who attended. There were young local girls looking for excitement and even some high society ladies whose identities were kept secret. Lady Mary Wortly Montagu was one of the notable women who joined a club in England."

"What was a meeting night like?" Joe asked.

"I can only tell you what a meeting would have been like here; lots of general gaiety, with music and belly dancers, while members drank ale at this table and smoked. They amused themselves with feats of skill, wrestling, fencing and even sexual encounters on the floor, to name just a few." Instead of looking at Joe and Brad, Fenton glanced about the room as if he were seeing visions of the past. "Because of the club's satanic affiliations, they would do things like pour liquor on a cat and light the poor thing on fire. Other animals were sacrificed on an altar."

Joe grimaced.

"I'm sorry if I'm upsetting you. Just trying to give you a feel for the experience. On meeting nights, people found spying on the premises would be dragged in and tortured or killed. This room has seen more ungodly acts than I care to know." Fenton stopped to shake his head. "With the ring's power, Nathon thought he could rule the world, or at least raise demons to punish his enemies."

Brad let out a breath. "I never realized all the dark activities that went on at a meeting."

Fenton looked at Brad with a nod. "On the evening of October seventh 1707, Medea was kidnapped and brought here. No one but Nathon knew she wore a magic ring, not until Nathon's men forced her into this room, that is. However, Nathon's plan went amiss when he found the ring missing from the girl's finger. She claimed she never heard of the ring. After much interrogation and threats, he threw her to the floor over there." Fenton pointed to the floor just in front of the fire place. "Nathon became so angry that he decided to murder her himself. Two of his friends forced her to kneel on the hearth. It was there Medea cursed him as he crept towards her with a leather strap."

"What was the curse?" Joe asked.

"She vowed that in a distant time she would return through a descendant to avenge her death on one of Nathon's descendants, who would again seek the ring. She claimed her avenger would bear her own face. This would also end the Cyrus line, and gentlemen, I am the last Cyrus descended from Nathon."

Suddenly, the portrait of Medea appeared in Joe's mind. *Meg is her twin and maybe her avenger!*

"It always bothered me that Medea's curse was placed right there on the stone hearth. After her curse, Nathon strangled her with his strap."

Joe and Brad could almost see the murder.

"When she died, her body fell on the floor over there." Fenton pointed again. "Just to the right of the hearth."

"How do you know all this with such detail?" Brad asked.

"Like Joe's family curse, ours was also recorded. This event was written by Nathon's younger brother, Jonathon, shortly after Nathon's death. Jonathon was an eyewitness to Medea's killing. That document has been kept in this house from generation to generation so that no one other than our family would know the shameful truth. Apparently some of Medea's descendants also recorded the murder."

"What about Medea's curse?" Brad asked. "Have the Cyruses put any credence in it?"

"Some have. My father and I were among those that did since there is a coven in Manchester that dedicated itself to Yves and Medea Laughton. The one we thought might be Medea's deliverer is a woman by the name of Victoria Sidedrop. She not only founded that coven but is an ancestor of Medea's. Without knowing what Medea looked like, we were never sure. With me having no children, I guess I could still be her target of revenge, but she's getting on in years and I'm told she's in a wheelchair, so the probability is diminishing."

"It could be another witch," Joe said.

Fenton scrunched his face in surprise. "Who?"

"Victoria has a granddaughter, Megan O'Leary. She's the woman who Brad thinks may have bewitched me. She's also a descendant of Medea's."

"Oh no! I didn't realize there was a younger descendant. I thought when Victoria's daughter died it was the end of her line."

I don't want to upset him anymore by telling him I saw Medea's portrait and Meg does have her face. Joe felt a common bond with the old man. Just as Joe was the final target of his family curse, Fenton was likely Medea's target and Meg had to be her avenger. "What about the ring? Were there any clues as to what happened to it?"

"No. Nathon was certain she was wearing the ring when she was forced here. One of the men who kidnapped her swore he'd seen her wearing it."

"Is it possible she hid the ring somewhere in the house before she was taken to this room?" Joe asked.

"That was what Nathon thought. She was locked in the guest room until they dragged her in here with the others. Nathon and his friends searched that room for years after the murder. Even his descendants looked in vain."

"Where is the guest room?" Brad asked.

"It's in the closed off section of the house. It hasn't been used for many years."

"May we see it?" Joe asked.

"Very well. Wait here. I'll have to get the keys for that section." Soon, Fenton returned. "Follow me." He headed toward the door at the other end of the large room. He unlocked it with one of the keys. Joe and Brad followed him halfway down a long hall to a door on their left. Fenton turned to them. "This is the room where Medea was held prisoner. My family has searched this room for that ring for generations." Fenton put a key into the lock and turned the knob, pushing the door open.

Inside, they found a musty smelling place shrouded in dust and cobwebs. There was a piano, some lamps, a lounge chair and several boxes on the floor. On the other end of the brown colored room was a single window.

"Couldn't Medea have escaped this room out that window?" Brad asked.

"At that time, the window was nailed shut with iron bars."

"Have you ever tried to find the ring?" Brad asked.

"No. The last person in my family that did was my father when I was a small boy. He almost destroyed the room. I felt if he and the others couldn't find it after all that time, it was useless. I've never been tempted."

Eyeing the room, Joe couldn't help wanting to search it like a young boy seeking buried treasure.

"Were things like the walls and boards in the floor checked thoroughly?" Joe asked.

"Yes. There were no loose boards or holes in the walls where a ring could have been hidden. All of that was checked centuries ago. Even though everyone who's ever been in this room knows how long it's been searched, they always feel they could find the ring if given the chance."

"You must have read my mind," Brad said.

"In 1707, there was a bed on this wall where they found Medea hiding." Fenton pointed to a dusty dresser and mirror. "That was the most often searched area. Well, if you're ready, we can go back and proceed with the antidote."

Ten

The Antidote

Fenton led them out of the room and locked the door. As they walked back down the hall, Joe said, "Brad tells me you're a witch expert."

"Well, I've studied everything from spells and curses to demonology. I've also been following witch activities here in New England for quite some time. Although I do consider myself an expert on the subject, I don't practice witchcraft. In fact, I vehemently oppose it. I've devoted my life to helping those afflicted by black magic."

They made their way through the banquet room into the living room.

"Have a seat, gentlemen. Joe, let me explain more about my services. If you knew the exact love spell that was used, it would be simple to cure you, and the price would be very reasonable. However, Brad told me you don't know what spell was used, so I'll have to give you the general antidote. It removes all love spells, but the treatment is more involved and costs much more."

Joe bit his bottom lip in frustration. "If someone puts a love spell on you, they're not going to tell you which one they've used. I don't even know if there is a love spell on me, that's Brad's theory. And how much is this going to cost me?"

"Well, being that you're a friend of Brad's, I'll make the price reasonable. Because of the expensive ingredients I use, the usual fee is one thousand dollars."

Joe scowled. "A thousand dollars?"

"For you, I'll make it three hundred dollars."

Joe stood silent considering the situation. "Fenton, I'll make you a deal. You want me to give you information about my experience in Diehla Thorne's time. If you want details, it'll be a long process."

Fenton nodded.

"My price will also be three hundred dollars."

Fenton looked at Joe with one eye closed. "You drive a hard bargain, but I accept. An even swap, my cure for your story. If one of the witches had put an exotic spell on you, like voodoo, it would be even more expensive."

"You can cure any kind of witchcraft?" Joe asked.

"Everything except curses. If I could, I'd have done that for myself. Most witches are likely to heal others, but there are black witches too. They're the ones that give me customers."

"What type of witches are in the Laughton coven?" Joe asked.

"It's mixed. Sayde Anderson and others are white witches, but some in that coven are very dangerous. The witch who put this spell on you would most definitely be a black witch. They try to control and manipulate others."

Meg is a black witch? "Let's get on with my antidote."

Fenton frowned. "Wait in the banquet room. I'll bring the ingredients there."

Joe and Brad sat at the long table where Nathon entertained his rowdy guests centuries ago. Soon Fenton entered the room followed by his employee. Both men's arms were laden with vials and bottles of potions. They laid the tubes down on the long table next to Joe.

With a wooden spoon, Fenton mixed some of the liquids and powders in a silver bowl. He dipped two fingers into the concoction and raised them to Joe's face. Reciting some words in Latin, he made the sign of the cross on Joe's forehead. Joe smelled garlic in the mixture.

Fenton said more words he didn't understand, then asked Joe to repeat them. While continuing his chant, Fenton picked up a small metal container, raised it over Joe's head and sprinkled what looked like water over him.

Holy water?

He set the container down and made the sign of the cross with his hand again. Fenton asked Joe to repeat more chants. Then the old man broke into a dance around Joe, flapping his arms up and down.

Joe stared at him in surprise. *This is the most ridiculous thing I've ever been involved in. These antics can't actually be breaking a spell.*

After a half hour, Fenton said, "Joe, I've done all I can for you. You must face the person who put the spell on you to be completely cured."

Joe's brow furrowed as he looked up at Fenton. "What if she puts another love spell on me?"

"With this powerful antidote, she will be unable to put a love spell on you, but another witch could. If I were you, I wouldn't let her know you're cured. Get her to break up with you somehow."

"When will I know if my feelings for her have changed?"

"How do you feel about her now?" Fenton raised his eyebrows.

Joe looked away and thought about Meg for a moment.

"Do you still feel like you're in love with her?"

The strong feeling of love is gone! Joe peered at Fenton. "No, I don't feel like I'm in love with her. And if her feelings for me were fake, why did she do this?"

Fenton shook his head. "I wish I knew, but your feelings for her will diminish even more after you've seen her. You may find you have contempt for her now."

Brad breathed a sigh of relief and laid his hand on Joe's shoulder. "For a while we thought we'd lost you."

"You were right, Brad. And I was so sure my feelings for Meg were real."

Brad gave Joe a stern look. "You've got to get out of that apartment."

"But how, if I have to pretend to be in love with her?"

Fenton blew out a breath. "Again, you have to do something that will make her want you to move out. If the decision isn't hers, she may cast another kind of spell on you."

While Brad drove them back to the warehouse, Joe said, "Something's bothering me. Fenton said when Medea cursed Nathon, she told him her avenger would bear her face."

"So?"

"I saw Medea's portrait. She's the spitting image of Meg."

Brad glanced at Joe. "But Meg doesn't have the ring, and Fenton isn't trying to get it from her. That was part of the curse."

"That's true, but I still have a bad feeling Meg is Medea's avenger."

"I hate to worry Fenton, but we'll have to let him know about Meg."

As Joe looked out the passenger window, he realized Brad was right.

"I'm going to leave for Chicago tomorrow afternoon. Please keep me posted."

"Do you think Ellen will believe what happened to me?"

"She's an understanding woman, but she is awfully upset right now. Give her some time. I'm sure she'll come around."

"How am I going to get out of Meg's apartment when I have to pretend I'm still under her spell? And what does she want from me?"

"She probably wants the information that Marcus was paying you for so she can gain coven power."

Joe shook his head. "I don't think that's it. She hasn't asked me a thing about my time-travel experience."

"Try to get on her nerves; make her angry with you, but don't let her know you're not infatuated with her."

"If she went to the trouble of using a love spell to keep me close, I don't know if anything I do will cause her to throw me out."

Brad dropped Joe off by his car then drove to Hillery mansion to fill Ellen in.

Heading to Meg's apartment, Joe grew angrier about what she'd done. Not only had she bent his will and destroyed his marriage, but everything he'd known about her was a lie. Joe had no idea who this phony woman was. His dream-like fantasy was over and his real world was falling apart. Thinking about Ellen, Joe realized he did still love her, but would she take him back? *Meg may have caused me to lose the love of my life.* Joe slammed the heel of his palm on the steering wheel. As he drove, he held back tears and tried to devise a plan to separate himself from Meg, if that was even possible.

At seven o'clock, Joe entered the apartment.

Sitting on the couch, Meg looked up from her book with a smile. "Hi, honey. Did you have supper yet?"

Gazing at her in her jeans and T-shirt with Shyebony on her lap, it was like seeing Meg for the first time. *I don't love her. "Hi, honey," what an actress!* "No, I haven't eaten." *If she can act, so can I.*

"Do you want to go to the club for a bite?" She rose from the couch and approached him.

"No, it's too expensive." *Maybe this is my chance to turn this into an argument.* "I'm going to lose my business soon. I don't need any help by going to the club every Friday and Saturday."

Meg stopped in her tracks with a frown. "I'm sorry I brought it up. I'll heat us something out of a can." She turned away and headed for the kitchen.

"Boy, that sounds delicious," he said sarcastically.

Meg stopped and turned toward him, squinting as if confused. *It isn't like Joe to be so disagreeable.* With a look of curiosity and anger on her face, Meg slowly crept toward him.

Gazing into the piercing brown eyes of Medea's avenger, Joe became nervous.

She stopped inches from him, still staring into his eyes. "There's something wrong with you, Joe."

Earlier that day, Joe felt lust for Meg and moments ago contempt but now he was feeling something else… fear.

"What are you talking about?" He took a step back.

Her eyes opened wider, gazing into his. "Where were you tonight?"

Could she actually know where I've been? "Now you sound like Ellen."

"Don't mention her name in my home." Pure anger flashed in her eyes.

I've got to pull myself together. "Boy, are you touchy. I told you I was with an old friend from Chicago. We had a couple of drinks and caught up on old times." *I feel like I'm lying to Ellen again.*

"You're not yourself. I trust my witch's instincts."

I overdid it. "Your senses are working overtime." Joe put his arms around her to give her a hug, but Meg pulled away with a glare then turned and headed into the kitchen. Joe swallowed hard, not knowing what action to take next. His argument didn't work, and she wasn't about to kiss and make up.

Joe sat down in the lounge chair. *Is this the real Meg? If I approach the subject of moving out, she'll know I had her spell removed, but if I continue to act like I'm in love with her, I'll never get out of here. And how much does she know? My pixie has turned monster.* Joe longed to be at home with Ellen and his kids. Again he fought back tears.

While they ate at the kitchen table, Joe knew he had to be more discreet about causing a problem. He had changed too much, too fast. Meg was cool toward him, but then she started to warm up as they watched television that evening.

As they got ready to retire, she lit an incense candle on the nightstand, sat on the bed in the lotus position, closed her eyes then hummed and chanted. Meg's weird customs bothered him now.

"May you be with us in all forms: the maiden, the mother and the crone." Finishing her prayer, Meg opened her eyes and slipped under the covers.

How am I going to get out of being with her without making her suspicious?

When Joe got into bed, Meg blew out the candle then snuggled against him with a smile.

"Do you want a quick massage?"

That was her code word for sex. "I'm kind of tired tonight, Meg." He rolled over.

"You're not even going to kiss me goodnight?"

Shit! How could I have been so stupid? He quickly turned over and kissed her. "I'm sorry. I'll be back to normal tomorrow." *Can I act well enough to keep that promise?* While he lay there, he wondered if Meg knew he wasn't under her spell. If so, he shuddered to think what spell she may use on him next. He still wondered why she wanted to keep him there if she wasn't in love with him.

Shortly after Joe fell asleep, he was awakened by Victoria's voice downstairs. It sounded like she was reciting something. He sat up listening, but he couldn't understand what she was saying. He looked at Meg. She was sound asleep.

As the old woman's voice grew louder, he felt certain she was using an incantation. The dramatic way she chanted unnerved him. He was going to wake Meg, but decided he'd ask her about this in the morning. Soon Victoria's voice faded and it was quiet again.

Joe finally fell asleep.

~ * ~

During breakfast, Joe questioned Meg about her grandmother's chanting.

"I didn't hear it." Meg casually took a sip of orange juice. "I know she does that sometimes. If it bothered you, I'll tell her it kept me awake and ask her to be more considerate."

"You're sure she's not upset about me living with you?"

"I'm sure." Meg smiled and patted the back of Joe's hand. "I have some errands to run this afternoon, then I'll stop by Grandma's. I'll be back here by five, okay?"

"That's fine." Joe smiled. *That'll give me time to call Brad and fill him in on my terrible progress.*

"Since the club is too expensive, there's a little diner that's reasonably priced that we can visit tonight."

Meg left the apartment, and Joe called Brad at the mansion.

"Joe, I told Ellen the whole story. She loves you but she's still very upset. Give her a little more time."

"Brad, you're still staying at the mansion?"

"Yes."

Joe was silent. "When are you leaving for Chicago?"

"I've decided to stay a couple more days. I'll probably go on Friday."

"I'll keep you informed about my situation here. Let's get together for lunch one day this week."

"Sounds good. Joe, it was twelve years ago today that we met Diehla Thorne's ghost."

"Don't remind me." Joe's heart pounded just thinking about the nightmare of his life.

That evening after Sunday dinner, while Ellen's kids played at a neighbor's house, Brad and Ellen sat on the couch with a glass of wine.

"You've got to give Joe a break, Ellen. This situation wasn't his fault."

"I know, but it's so hard when I think of him having sex with that woman. It's going to take some time wondering why his feelings for me didn't outweigh a love spell."

"I don't know as much about witches' spells as Fenton, but some are very powerful."

Ellen edged closer to him. "Do you realize twelve years ago we were also talking about Joe's witch problem? This is the anniversary of Diehla's burning and return three hundred years later."

"Yes, I mentioned that to Joe on the phone this morning."

"You were so brave that night." Ellen smiled at him. "I was a basket case. Even tried to do away with myself. Thanks to you, I'm still here."

"Anyone would have done the same as I did."

"You're too modest." She looked deeply into Brad's eyes. "Once again I'm grateful to you for what you're doing for me. I wish there was some way I could show my gratitude."

Brad leaned back. "Well, you're letting me stay here; free meals, room and board."

"But I'm taking you away from your work, and you've never complained once. There aren't very many men like you."

Brad smiled, but was afraid that Ellen, being in an emotional state, might start something foolish. He was right. She snuggled up beside him, put her head on his shoulder and kissed his cheek. Moving toward the front of his face, she kissed his lips. Brad's first reaction was to pull away, but to his own dismay he found himself kissing her back. Angry with himself, he gently ended the embrace.

"Ellen, I think you're a little confused right now."

"No. I'm finally seeing things clearly for the first time in my life."

"If I'm going to stay here, I have to be above board."

Looking into her big blue eyes, Brad found Ellen very desirable with her little nose and her light brown hair framing her narrow face.

"I'm sorry, Brad. I don't know what came over me." Ellen shifted her gaze downward and pulled a tissue out of her purse to wipe her eyes.

"There's nothing to be sorry about." Brad gave her a quick hug. "It's understandable with all you're going through. I'm flattered."

Brad smiled. "And if Joe weren't a friend, I wouldn't have stopped you."

~ * ~

That evening, while Joe and Meg ate at a local diner, Meg said, "When I mentioned the incantation to Grandma, she told me she'd be quieter from now on."

Joe gazed from Meg to the meat he was cutting. "Did you ask her what the incantation was?"

"No, I didn't think it was important."

Maybe I can do something with this. "I think the spell was to get me out of your apartment. I can see it in her eyes. She doesn't want me living with you. You said yourself you didn't want to tell her I'd moved in because it would upset her."

"But I've spoken with her about it." Meg's voice raised. "She's okay with it."

"She just doesn't want to upset you, Meg. She'd be happy if I left."

"Joe, she adores you. She's even knitting you a sweater."

Damn! Nothing I say can get me out of her apartment. Whatever she wants from me must be very important to her.

At the end of the meal, the waitress set the check on the table. Joe picked it up.

Meg snatched it out of his hand. "It's my treat."

Joe nodded. "I'll pay the tip." He put three singles on the table.

Meg glanced at the check. "We're going to have supper for free."

"And how are you going to arrange that?"

"You saw the bill was nine seventy-five?"

"Yeah, so?"

Meg leaned near and whispered. "I'm going to give the cashier ten dollars, but through psychic thought control, I'll put into her mind that I gave her a twenty."

"I've got to see this." Joe shook his head, then followed Meg to the register.

The young woman at the counter smiled. "Hi, that'll be nine seventy-five."

Meg gave her a ten. Meg's squinting eyes peered at the young woman in deep concentration.

The clerk put the ten in the drawer. "That's nine seventy-five from twenty."

Joe couldn't believe it, watching the woman hand Meg back a quarter and the ten she had just given her.

"Thank you," the clerk said. "And please come again."

Was that just a coincidence, or is Meg's mind really that powerful? Joe held the door for her as they left the diner. Outside, she turned and grinned at him as if to say "See!"

"I wouldn't have believed it if I hadn't seen it with my own eyes."

"Don't underestimate me, Joe. And don't ever betray me." She gave him a sharp glare that took his breath away.

Eleven

Revelations

The next night Joe went with Meg to the coven's full moon Mass. This was the first time Meg and Marcus had seen each other since Joe moved into her apartment. Feeling awkward about defecting from Marcus, Joe was surprised when the high priest gave Meg a warm greeting then shook his hand.

"Meg, I hope you and I can work things out. I don't want to split the coven up over our misunderstanding."

Meg squinted at him. "Are you willing to give in to my demands?"

Marcus gave her a sly smile. "We'll talk about that after the ritual."

The candles were lit, the lights in the room turned off and the ceremony began. Joe sat in the dark with the coven as they went through prayers to the goddess and meditation led by Circe for over an hour. Having been involved in several rituals now, Joe was more bored than frightened by them.

The lights came back on, Marcus approached Meg and whispered something to her.

She turned to Joe. "I'll just need a few minutes with Marcus and Luna in the office. Have some refreshments while you're waiting."

Joe nodded. "I'll be here."

Meg followed Marcus and Luna out of the ritual room. Joe helped himself to snacks with some of the others while he visited with Sayde and Barry.

Twenty minutes later, Luna strolled toward him in the now empty ritual room. "Meg said you should go ahead without her. Our meeting is going to take longer than we expected. One of us will drop her off at her apartment."

There's something wrong. "Is everything okay?" Joe asked.

Luna smiled. "Of course."

With that, she glided away toward the door in her long black robe. Meg had mentioned that Marcus and his followers were dangerous if crossed, and Fenton had warned him about Marcus as well. Joe remembered Trish was still missing because of their fearsome leader. And why didn't Meg come out to talk to him herself? They could be setting him up for her disappearance.

Joe left the building, but when he got into his car he decided to check things out. He hid his car so the coven would think he'd left then snuck back into the parish.

Luckily no one saw him enter as he crept down the hall, worrying he'd be spotted. He perspired, praying there was no one else in the building other than those in the office. There were muffled voices coming from inside the room, but Joe couldn't make out what was being said. He put his ear to the door but the voices were still faint. Circe was talking then Marcus said something and then Circe again. He put his ear against the keyhole and could hear the conversations more clearly.

"Do you want me to give her a post hypnotic suggestion then wake her?" Circe asked.

"No," Marcus said. "Take her back to her childhood."

They've hypnotized her.

Soon Joe heard Meg's voice softly answering questions. Then her speech became louder, more forceful.

"What age are you, Meg?" Circe asked.

"Who be Meg?" she questioned.

"Are you a child?" Circe asked.

"Nay. I am but twenty-seven."

"Marcus," Luna said, "that's older than she actually is."

"She must have gone back to a previous life," Circe said. "If you're not Megan, who are you?"

"Medea Laughton of Concord New Hampshire. Who from the spirit world questions me?"

"Marcus!" Circe gasped, "Do you realize what this means? Meg was Medea Laughton in a previous life."

"It's not possible," Luna said.

"It's true," Circe returned.

"Keep questioning her then," Marcus ordered.

Joe heard Meg's voice. "I ask again, who seeks knowledge from me?"

"Medea, my name is Circe, a witch spirit from ages to come. What is the date?"

"'Tis October first."

"And the year?"

"Seventeen hundred and six."

Joe swallowed hard, with his ear still against the keyhole. *This is unreal!*

"Where are you now?"

"I am in the town square, in the village of Suncook."

"What is your father's name?"

"Yves Laughton."

Joe heard Marcus say, "I think she's confused from all those stories she's heard."

"Should I probe her further?"

"Yes, continue."

"Is your mother living?"

"Nay. She was burned alive."

"She must be confused, Marcus," Circe said. "Her mother wasn't burned. Medea, what was your mother's name?"

"Diehla, Diehla Thorne."

Diehla! What the hell. I've been sleeping with the descendant of Diehla Thorne, the witch who cursed me and the Hillery family?

Everyone in the room was silent until Circe asked, "Medea, isn't your mother Gabrielle Lasaunt?"

"Nay, but she did raise me. With my mother's many enemies, Father thought for my safety, that my real mother's identity be kept secret."

"Incredible," Luna said. "No one ever knew Diehla had a child."

"If that's true," Marcus said, "Medea would have been at least two years older than we thought. That's why she's saying she's twenty-seven. Ask her something else."

"Medea, how old were you when your mother was burned?"

"One year."

"When were you born?"

"'Twas the summer of 1679."

"Bring her to," Marcus said. "We'll probe her further after I prepare some questions."

"She must have a lot of information being Diehla and Yves' daughter," Luna added.

"Ladies, do you know what this means to our coven? We have in Megan the mind of Medea Laughton. The irony is Meg will never know who she was. And I don't want anyone else besides Ken and Paula to know about this, understood?"

"Circe and I won't breathe a word of it, Marcus," Luna said.

Joe heard Circe bringing Meg out of the trance. He hustled down the hall, ran out of the parish to his car and drove back to Meg's apartment. While he waited there for her he debated what to do. *Should I tell her what Marcus and the others are up to or let her take her medicine for what she did to me? No, this is too big, and Marcus is dangerous. Maybe I should make her a deal for my knowledge that I go free?*

About twenty minutes later, Meg came in through the back door. Just seeing her face unnerved him now that he knew she was the soul of Diehla Thorne's daughter.

Joe baited her to see what she knew. "You told me you'd only be a few minutes. What took so long?"

Meg put a hand to her forehead. "I don't know. Marcus was telling me he wanted to share the coven leadership with me and the next thing I knew I was waking up. They told me I fainted, but I've never fainted before. Someone must have drugged me. And I'm worried because I don't know what they did to me while I was unconscious. How could I have been so naive? I should have had you in there with me."

Joe nodded. "Meg, sit down. I know what happened."

She frowned. "You do? How?"

"Just sit." Joe pointed to the couch.

Staring at him with a confused look, Meg sat.

"Marcus set you up. He had Circe hypnotize you."

"But she wasn't even there."

"She was. She must have erased that part of your memory with a post-hypnotic suggestion."

Meg nodded. "How do you know all this?"

"After I left the parish, I had a bad feeling, so I snuck back in and listened at the office keyhole. I heard almost everything."

Joe filled her in on the details.

"You're telling me I was Medea Laughton?"

Joe nodded.

She jumped off the couch and wrapped her arms around him. "Thank you so much for being there for me, Joe. I don't know how I can ever thank you."

Joe patted her arms.

"Knowing that I was Medea in another life is the greatest thing that's happened to me."
"Wait, there's more."
Nose to nose with Joe, she opened her eyes wide. "More?"
"Not only were you Medea Laughton, but your mother was... ready for this?"
Wide eyed, she nodded.
"You said your mother was...Diehla Thorne."
"Diehla? But we always heard Medea's mother was Gabrielle Lasaunt. If Medea was Diehla's daughter, why wasn't she living with her?" Before Joe could answer Meg said, "I'm Medea Laughton and a direct descendant of Diehla Thorne, too, and those rats were going to keep this to themselves?"
Joe nodded.
"Oh, I'll get them." Meg thought for a moment. "When Grandma hears all this, she'll flip." Looking at Joe, her smile faded. "Joe, this doesn't bother you, does it?"
Hoping this would give him an excuse to leave her apartment he said, "What do you think?"
She wrapped her wrists around the back of his neck and looked into his eyes. "Of course it bothers you."
Joe nodded. "It's a terrible omen. The descendant of Judge Hillery sleeping with a descendant and reincarnated daughter of Diehla Thorne."
"It was terrible for Judge Hillery to have burned Diehla alive."
"I think I should leave." Joe tried to pull away from her but she pulled him back.
"Let's not fight over something that happened centuries ago."
"Centuries ago? Diehla tried to kill me only twelve years ago."
Meg pulled away to look at him. "Think about what we have in common. We're the only two people alive today who have lived in the late seventeenth century. You, as the person you are now, and me in another life."

Joe shook his head in frustration. "Marcus told Circe he's planning on having you hypnotized again after he prepares some questions for you."

"I told you he was dangerous. Thanks to you, he won't get away with it. You did well tonight, Joe. You did really well!"

Is she finally being sincere? "Meg, if you're really thankful, I want the truth. Why did you seduce me?"

"You're irresistibly handsome." She smiled and kissed his nose.

Even after what he'd done for her, she still wouldn't admit she placed a love spell on him and he didn't know why.

Now I have a reason for being distant with her, so she won't suspect I'm not still under her love spell. This revelation may be my ticket out of here.

When they retired, Joe lay with his back to Meg. She leaned forward and blew out the rose scented candles. "Good night, Joe."

"Good night, Meg." Joe didn't turn over to kiss her this time, trying to gradually distance himself from her.

~ * ~

The following morning in his office, Joe was discussing business with his secretary when the phone rang.

"Carol's on break. I'll have to take this call." Joe picked up the phone. "Willstown Video Industries."

"Is this Joe Hillery?" came the sound of a young woman's voice.

"This is Joe. Can I help you?"

"This is Trish Spencer from the Laughton Coven. Joe, I'm in hiding."

He realized this was the missing girl. He waved his secretary away and she left the room. "Trish, what's going on? Where are you?"

"I can't tell you, but I'm in another state. I fear for my life."

"Who are you afraid of?"

"Marcus. I defected from him and his friends."

"Why?"

"He has a plan that I didn't want any part of."

Does this have something to do with Meg's love spell?

"Since you're the target of their plan, I felt I had to tell you about this. Marcus asked the women he hangs with to seduce you so he could stay in contact with you without paying you a fee."

Joe squeezed his eyes closed. "What does he want from me?"

"Luna had two psychic visions. She saw you holding Diehla's and Medea's magic ring in the palm of your hand. It was night and someone was shining a flashlight on it. She was certain you'd locate the jewel soon. That ring would give Marcus and his clique tremendous power."

"So that's the reason Marcus was paying me?" *And Meg was the lucky witch that succeeded with her love spell.*

"Yes, it wasn't for your time-travel stories. Please tell me none of his women succeeded."

"Meg's love spell worked."

"Oh no!"

"I'm not under her spell anymore. A friend of mine took me to see a witchcraft expert who removed it. But my marriage has been shattered because of Meg."

"I'm so sorry, Joe. Marcus was determined. If the seduction plan didn't work he was considering Circe's hypnotism. Joe, please keep me informed and let me know if they locate the ring."

"I'll keep you posted, Trish. Hopefully it'll be safe for you to return soon."

"Joe, please don't let Luna's vision come true. Don't help them find that ring. Marcus and his followers will be extremely dangerous if they get it. Here's my number, but don't let anyone else know that I called."

Joe scribbled down her number and they ended the call. He sat at his desk rubbing his forehead as he put the pieces together. *Meg used a spell on me so that when I located the ring, she'd be with me. I'll be damned if I'll help her or Marcus find it.* Although he knew the reason for Meg's actions, how could he use this knowledge to help his situation? He remembered Meg telling him Sunday night that he'd better never betray her. He couldn't concentrate on his work the rest of the day.

Joe called Brad and explained that Meg was Medea in a past life and Medea was Diehla's daughter.

Brad hung his head, then shook it. *This has to be Joe's worst nightmare.* "I can imagine how you feel about that. Reincarnation is more common than most people think," Brad said. "I should have thought of that when you told me Meg was Medea's twin."

"That's not all. Trish Spencer called me this afternoon."

"Trish Spencer?"

"The missing girl from the Laughton coven. She's in hiding and she told me that Meg put a love spell on me because Luna LaBrock had a vision that I was holding the ancient ring. Meg wanted to make sure I was close with her so she could claim the prize when I found it."

"That must have been the reason Marcus was paying you for your stories."

"It was, but Meg double-crossed him so she could have the ring for herself."

"It's going to be more difficult than we thought to get you away from her, but we'll think of something."

Later, when Joe picked Meg up at the book store, he decided to play cat and mouse with her to see if she'd finally be honest with him about her love spell.

As he drove to the apartment he asked, "Meg, does anyone know what happened to Medea's ring?"

She looked at him in surprise. "No, we don't know any more than Nathon, the man who killed her."

"What was his last name…Cyrus?"

"You were paying attention."

"What's your theory?" He glanced at her then back at the road.

"I don't have a theory." She turned to look at him. "Why are you asking?"

"Well, that was the same ring that put the curse on my family for three centuries and gave Diehla the power to return from the dead."

Meg gazed at him as if thinking.

Have I said enough to make her wonder if I know something, or should I say more?

"You're really freaked out that I was Medea Laughton." She stared straight ahead.

I'd better go with this. If I confront her about the love spell, she may put another kind of spell on me. "Yeah, Meg, I am freaked out."

They didn't say a word all the way to her apartment.

That evening Meg was standoffish, spending most of her time on the phone in the kitchen while Joe watched TV in the living room. When they went to bed, Meg kissed him goodnight and, as the night before, she didn't even hint about them getting together. Joe wondered what she was thinking. Had he overplayed his hand asking about the ring?

The following morning in Joe's office, the phone rang. As he laid his pen down to answer it, he wondered if it was Trish with more info.

"Joe," his receptionist said, "Ellen's on the phone."

Ellen! "Put her through, Carol." Joe was overjoyed to hear her voice on the other end.

"Joe, could we have lunch today?"

"Yes, Ellen, of course. I'm so happy to hear from you." Joe smiled and leaned back in his chair. "I'll pick you up."

"No. I've got some errands to run. I'll meet you at the office."

"Great. I'll take you to a nice coffee shop nearby."

"I'll see you in an hour."

Joe hung up the phone. "Yes!" He spun around in his chair with a laugh.

At the coffee shop, Ellen thought about her feelings for Brad but dismissed them for her desperate state of mind. She leaned forward and looked into Joe's eyes. "I'd like to start seeing you again. We'll take it slow."

Joe took her hand. "Of course. Honey, I really miss you." He felt like he was on his first date with Ellen.

Looking into her pale blue eyes, Joe felt guilty for having been with Meg, even though it was because of a spell.

"No promises," Ellen said. "But Brad did explain the love spell. I still find that hard to believe." She shook her head.

"My behavior was because of a spell, but it's broken, and I'm so sorry about what happened." Joe watched Ellen playing with her fork. *I can see she's a bit uneasy about this meeting.*

"The kids aren't the only ones who miss you." She smiled at him.

"Any time you want me back I'm ready." After Joe said that he remembered he couldn't keep the promise. What would Meg do to him if he told her he was moving out? Her comment about, "Don't ever betray me," went through his mind again. And with Marcus's plans against her, Meg seemed to be counting on him now. *How can I move back in with my family without making Meg angry?*

"Bev told me you moved out of her place. Did you find an apartment?"

"Yeah." Joe purposely took a bite of his sandwich to give him time to think of an answer for her next question.

"Where are you living?"

He continued to chew, trying to think of what to say. "It's a little dive in one of the apartments downtown. It's all I could afford."

"Maybe we should go to counseling before you move back in."

"What am I going to tell the counselor? That a witch put a love spell on me?"

"I guess you're right." She smiled and turned her face to the table. "Give me your phone number so I can keep in touch with you."

Joe swallowed hard. "My number?"

"You do have a phone, don't you? Brad mentioned he had called you." Ellen pulled out a pen and small tablet from her purse.

Joe had no choice but to give her Meg's number. He hoped she wouldn't call when Meg was home or when he was out.

After lunch, Joe drove Ellen back to the office. To his surprise she kissed him goodbye in the warehouse parking lot. As Ellen got into her car, Joe went into the warehouse office. When he got into the reception area he was surprised to see Meg sitting with her legs crossed reading a magazine. She smiled at him as he entered.

"Meg, what are you doing here?" Joe glanced toward the front door half expecting Ellen to return.

Meg rose and walked toward him. "I thought I'd surprise you and have lunch with you. I got the rest of the day off. Carol told me you already ate, so I guess I'm a little late." She leaned in and kissed him. "I should go so you can get back to work."

"I feel bad that you came all the way here for nothing."

"How sweet," came the sound of Ellen's voice.

Joe and Meg turned to see Ellen glaring at them from the doorway. Joe began to tremble.

Twelve

Ring of an Idea

"Let me guess. You're Meg, and Joe's living with you, right?"
Meg glanced at Joe then nodded.
Ellen glared at Joe. "No wonder you were so uncomfortable when I asked you for your phone number, you lying son of a bitch!"
"You must be Ellen," Meg said innocently.
"Very good. You're younger than I expected, but as long as you're out of high school I'm sure Joe doesn't mind. I didn't mean to interfere. I just came back for my hat."
As Ellen stomped passed them, Joe said, "Ellen, let me explain."
She turned back toward him. "You can explain to my lawyer."
When she returned to the lobby, Meg, in a mock tone said, "It was so nice to have finally met you, Mrs. Hillery, Joe has told me all about you."
Ellen glared at her. "Congratulations, you little slut. Joe is all yours now. I've decided to divorce him. He may not care about me, but he's also going to lose his children."
As Ellen turned to leave, Meg said, "You have a wonderful day now, Mrs. Hillery."
"Meg," Joe snapped.
Holding the front door open, Ellen turned, with tears in her eyes. "Screw you!"

"Oh, he does and he's great!" Meg returned with a smirk.

Ellen composed herself, holding back tears. "It's too bad they changed that law a few years back."

Meg squinted and blinked. "What law?"

"The one where they stopped burning witches." Ellen left the building in tears.

"Wow!" Meg looked at Joe with a frown. "Is she hostile or what?"

"What did you expect after what she saw and how you spoke to her?"

"Did you go to lunch with her?"

Joe nodded. "Yeah." *This bitch just destroyed my chances with Ellen. If only I could tell her what I really think of her.*

"I'd better go. I caused enough trouble."

Joe nodded. *That's an understatement, but I have to pretend to be under her spell.* "I'll give you a ride home."

She smiled. "Thank you."

Joe was too upset to concentrate on work. He told Carol, the receptionist, he was taking the rest of the day off and left the office with Meg.

On the way to Manchester Joe was silent. He was filled with grief wondering if he and Ellen were finished. *Thank God Ellen didn't mention Meg's love spell in front of her.*

Meg looked at him. "Joe, why did you find it necessary to have lunch with Ellen? I thought you and she were through."

Of all the damn nerve, but I'll have to be careful how I handle this. "We just got together to talk about the kids. You heard her. I won't be seeing much of them anymore."

"It was my fault that it happened, so I'll help you."

"If you try to help me, you'll just make Ellen angrier."

"Joe, I'm a witch, remember? I'll use witchcraft."

That afternoon in the apartment, Meg wore her black witch's robe and surrounded herself with a circle of green candles. Joe watched from the couch as she sat in a lotus position on the floor with Shyebony on her lap. She chanted in Latin while swaying and waving her arms in the air.

"*Alo Femoni*," she said repeatedly then, "I will Joseph Hillery to continue to have a relationship with his children, and may no obstacles get in his way, not even his wife, Ellen Hillery. *Alie Femoni.*"

While chanting in Latin, Meg rose and threw an herb into a candle flame then sat down again. With her arms and legs crossed, she closed her eyes and lowered her head. After sitting in silence for about five minutes, she opened her eyes and rose then blew out the candles.

"Well, Joe, you'll soon be seeing your children, and whenever you wish."

I don't want to see my kids because of witchcraft. "No harm is going to come to Ellen through your spell?"

Meg was silent.

Joe raised his voice. "Answer my question."

She looked at him with a grin. "The spell I put on Ellen is a doozy."

Horror registered on Joe's face. "What?"

Meg started to laugh. "Joe, you should have seen your face."

"You didn't put a spell on Ellen?"

"Of course not. I was joking."

He shook his head. "That wasn't funny."

Meg kissed his cheek. "I'm sorry."

After they went to bed, Meg started to rub Joe's shoulders. He knew this was a signal for sex. "Meg, I'm too tired for anything tonight."

"But we haven't been together for days. Is it because of who I was?"

"I don't know and I'm just not in the mood tonight." *I don't want to overdo this.* He turned over and kissed her.

Shortly after he fell asleep he was awakened by Victoria's voice again. It sounded like another chant or incantation. The dramatic way she spoke unnerved him. At first he was going to wake Meg, but then he decided to wait until morning to tell her.

The next thing Joe knew, Meg was shaking him. "Wake up, Joe." He looked at the clock on the stand next to his bed and saw it was just after six. "I'm awake. What's up?"

"I know how to find the ring! Medea's ring!"

Joe mumbled as if not comprehending.

She grabbed Joe's chin and forced his face toward her. "Joe, listen to me! I *was* Medea, so through my memory of the past I could retell my death and also where I hid the magic ring before I died. My subconscious has always held that knowledge."

Oh my God! This is my biggest nightmare. How can I stop her from finding the ring? "But how are you going to remember that?"

"Circe."

"Circe?" Joe raised his voice.

"Yes, she's a hypnotist. She can do a regression on me."

"You can't trust her. She's an ally of Marcus'."

"We were best friends before all my problems with Marcus. If she knew I could find the ring, she'd see things my way, trust me. After I put that ring on my finger nothing can stop me. Nothing!"

I hope I can stop her before she finds the ring. "Would Circe trust you?"

"I'll make her trust me."

After Joe dropped Meg off at work, he went back to Meg's apartment and called Ellen. As soon as she heard his voice, she handed the phone to Brad. Joe explained his version of what happened between Ellen and Meg.

"I'm sorry, Joe."

"Brad, that's not the reason I called. We've got a huge problem. Meg is going to have a coven hypnotist bring her back to the night when Medea was murdered. Meg's mind holds the answer to where Medea hid the ring. I'm afraid they're going to find their lost legacy."

"You have to stop her."

"How?"

"Joe, Meg will find the ring with or without you. I don't understand why she hasn't let you go, but with you still being with her, you'll also find the ring and know where she keeps it. If only you could find out where the ring is and get it before she does."

"You don't know Meg. That would be impossible."

"Then try to stall her until Fenton and I can come up with a plan," Brad said.

"I'll do my best, but we'll have to hatch a plan quickly."

"I'll talk to Fenton and call you right back to let you know what he thinks."

"You'd better warn him about the Cyrus curse and tell him who Meg is."

A half hour later Brad called Joe. "Fenton agrees with you that you won't be able to stop Meg from finding that ancient ring."

"What's his plan?"

"I'm getting to that. If you stay on Meg's good side, at least you'll know where the ring is; then Fenton or I can steal it."

"If Fenton goes for the ring and Meg catches him, he's playing right into Medea's prophecy. It would be like we're murdering him, Brad."

"Maybe I should be the one to steal it then."

"Now I feel like I'm being forced to stay in Meg's apartment even longer."

"Just until Meg finds the ring and we can get it from her."

"But I can't break up with her right after you steal the ring. She'll suspect I was involved."

"Fenton and I will think of some way to get you out of there. Meg finding the ring is big. You have to play along with her a bit longer."

Joe nodded. *I have to think of this as a mission. I'm acting for the good of mankind.* "I'll hang in there for you, but this has to end soon."

"Keep me informed so I know when and if they find the ring."

~ * ~

Joe picked Meg up at the book store. On the way back to the apartment she said, "I spoke with Circe and she's sure a regression will work."

Joe glanced at Meg. "I still don't trust her."

"We're going to do it this afternoon."

"This afternoon?" *She's not wasting any time.*

"Yes. I don't totally trust her either, so I'll need you to watch the session."

"How did you explain to her how you found out you were Medea?"

"I told her I had an informant among Marcus's allies. She's probably going crazy trying to figure out who it is."

Meg needs me as her ally. This is why she's not kicking me out of here.

~ * ~

At four o'clock Circe arrived at Meg's apartment.

"Joe knows?" was Circe's first reaction.

Meg nodded.

Circe grimaced. "But he's an outsider."

"I trust Joe implicitly. He is going to watch the regression."

Circe scowled at Meg. "He must take the oath then."

Meg stood with hands on her hips. "I'll take care of that. Let's get on with this."

"Very well. Lie down on the couch." Circe pointed.

Joe brought a chair out of the kitchen for Circe.

"Thank you." She sat in front of Meg. "I pray this works."

Meg opened her eyes and looked at the young Asian woman. "It has to."

Joe watched from the lounge chair as Circe started. *I hope Meg's mind doesn't have the answer, but if she does I can't think of one damn way to stop them.*

"Meg, I want you to look into my eyes." Circe raised her hands and opened her fingers as she drew her hands away from Meg's face. In a sing song tone she continued her hand motions as she relaxed Meg's body parts one by one. Joe struggled to keep from being influenced by her suggestions. He could see Meg growing sleepier by the moment.

"Your eyelids are heavy. You long for sleep. No matter how hard you try you cannot keep your eyes open."

Meg closed her eyes.

"You'll now hear nothing but my voice and you'll obey my commands. Can you still hear me, Meg?"

"Yes," Meg answered, "I hear you."

Being alone with this Gothic-looking young woman Joe feared she might do something unexpected. *Will she learn where the ring is then kill us both?*

Circe took Meg back to her childhood then back before her birth. "Take a deep breath. You're floating down, down through the ages on a red cloud. As you descend you can see the years reeling away. You see the early twentieth century, now the end of the nineteenth century. As the dates roll by, you see you are dropping through the beginning of the nineteenth century and into the end of the eighteenth century. Drifting lower still, you descend past the middle of the eighteenth century. You see the years: 1712, 1711, ten, nine, eight, and 1707. The cloud stops there. The date is October seventh. It is the evening. Are you alive?"

"I am."

"Who are you in this time?"

"I am Medea Laughton. Who is it that speaks to me that I cannot see?"

"I am Circe, a witch spirit from the future here to help you."

Joe was surprised to hear Meg speak in a different tone. Her voice was a bit deeper.

Circe turned to Joe. "I want to get some information from her before I continue." She looked back at Meg lying on the couch with closed eyes. "Medea, why didn't you live with your real mother, Diehla Thorne?"

"It was to protect me from those who would do my mother harm. I also learned later that my mother was not fond of small children. I was her only offspring."

"Do you now have possession of your mother's ring?"

"Ay. I am wearing it on my index finger." Meg raised her right hand as if the ring were there.

"It's beautiful," Circe replied.

This is my chance to find out how the witches got the ring back from Judge Hillery. "Circe, ask her how she got the ring," Joe said.

Circe nodded. "Medea, how did you obtain it?"

"'Twas given to me by my father."

"But how did he get it?" Joe prompted Circe again.

"Do you know how your father got the ring after it was taken from your mother at her trial?"

"Nay. But I assume it was when they murdered the judge that very night."

"So they did murder the judge in the fog," Joe said.

Circe turned toward him. "Let's get on with where she put the ring, okay?" She turned toward Meg. "Medea, where are you now?"

"I am being held prisoner in the home of Nathon Cyrus."

"Why?"

"Methinks for my ring. I fear for my life. He is a cruel man. I've examined the single window in this room. 'Tis blocked with iron bars." Meg wrung her hands and trembled. "I checked the walls and floor itself, but there is nowhere I might escape." Meg began to cry.

"Nathon does want your ring," Circe said. "I'm sorry, Medea, but history tells us that you are about to die."

Meg cried harder.

"Do not let them find the ring. Its power is meant only for us witches."

"But where shall I hide it?" Meg continued to wring her hands. "They'll search my body sure." She paused. "Aye, I know where they will never find it."

Thirteen

Search for the Ring

With Meg's eyes still closed, she said as Medea, "I shall swallow the ring!"

"Are you willing to do that?" Circe grimaced then turned to Joe with a smile.

"Ay," Meg said. "Tis the only way to keep them from obtaining it, but I fear I may choke to my death for I have no water to help it down. Wait, I see a cup that may contain some liquid." Meg was silent for a minute then said, "The cup contains a spot of wine. I pray 'tis enough to force the ring all the way down my throat." Meg's hand was bent as if she were holding a cup. "We lost the ring once to Judge Hillery. It shan't leave us again." She put her cupped hand to her mouth and went through the motions of drinking. She coughed, swallowing hard then took some deep breaths. "I have done it, sister spirit. They shan't find it now."

"Thank you, Medea."

Circe turned to Joe. Her black lips broke into a smile. "After all these years we know what happened to the ring!"

Joe faked a smile. *Damn, I hope they don't find Medea's body.*

Circe turned to Meg. "Medea, before Nathon comes for you, I'm going to bring you out of this place."

"But how, sister spirit?"

"Through witchcraft. I'm going to send you to your future life, to spare you the anguish that awaits you."

Meg gasped. "I shall live again?"

"Yes. Two hundred and eighty-five years hence."

Meg placed both hands to her heart. "Bless you, spirit sister of the future. Take me from this dreadful place."

"Medea, close your eyes. Feel yourself floating up, up upward on a cloud. Open your eyes to see that the cloud is blue."

"Blue it is, and I'm out of the Cyrus house."

"On this cloud you are floating through the years, the decades, as you continue to float upward. You continue through the ages until you see the year 1969 come into view. Glide into that year and you are born again. You are the descendant of your former self. I am in the year 1992. Glide up to this year and you are now twenty-three years old and in your apartment. When you wake you will remember what has just transpired in your former life, as Medea. Now on the count of three, you will wake up feeling refreshed."

I pray Meg doesn't know where Medea was buried.

"One, two, three. Open your eyes, Meg."

She opened her eyes and they darted around the room as if she were still in the Cyrus house.

"Are you all right?" Joe asked.

She took a deep breath. "I was afraid I was still locked in that terrible room."

Circe took her hand. "You're safe now, Meg. And we know what happened to the ring!"

Meg sat up. "Yes, I remember. I swallowed it. I feel the ring is still in my stomach."

"That's only in your subconscious mind," Circe said. "No wonder no one ever found the ring in that house. It was buried with Medea."

Meg placed a hand to her forehead, looking at Joe then Circe. "It's unbelievable, but I actually remember being Medea."

"Because of the regression I performed, you now remember the part of your past life just before you were murdered."

"Is it possible for you to let Meg remember her entire life as Medea?" Joe asked.

"No, only the selected times and places that I would designate through hypnosis."

Meg sat up on the couch. "We must find the ring as soon as possible."

"You're not up to that yet," Joe said.

"Of course not. But tomorrow night Jupiter will be in the constellation of Orion. It's as if that was the time ordained for this prophecy."

"But you don't know where Medea's body is buried," Joe said.

"I do."

Shit!

"We're going to have to dig it up after dark," Meg said. "We don't want to be seen."

This keeps getting worse. "Does it have to be tomorrow night?"

"Yes. What's with you, Joe?"

Circe looked at him. "Maybe he's squeamish about grave robbing."

"Of course I'll help you, but it's my first time being a ghoul."

Circe looked at Meg. "This is so wonderful. I feel the ring belongs to you."

I still don't trust Circe.

That night at the club, Meg seemed distant as if she were dwelling on the ring. On the ride home, she lay back on the armrest, using Joe's lap for a footrest. Most of the time, her eyes were closed. As Joe drove, he shuddered to think what she might do with a ring so powerful. When they arrived at the apartment, Meg went right to bed. She only gave Joe a goodnight kiss before she fell asleep.

Joe lay awake thinking. *Meg may have used me to find the ring but she's found where it is now and doesn't need me anymore, so why does she still want me with her? Because she has no other allies against Marcus and his friends? Either way, Luna was right. I will be there when they recover the ring.*

~ * ~

The next evening, Meg made dinner downstairs in her grandmother's apartment.

While the three ate, Victoria said to Joe, "Thank you for joining me for dinner tonight. With being confined to a wheel chair, Megan has to make some of my meals."

"You're lucky to have a granddaughter like Megan." Joe gave Meg a smile.

"It was my proudest moment when Megan told me she was actually Medea Laughton in her past life. And on top of that to learn we are both direct descendants of Diehla Thorne. We are truly blessed."

Or cursed. Joe shuddered as he looked at Meg and Victoria, realizing he was sharing a meal with Diehla's descendants.

"Now I see why I became so interested in witchcraft at a young age," the old woman continued. "I think Marcus should be thrown out of the coven for what he tried to do to Megan and that goes for his followers."

Joe nodded. *Is it my fault Meg is going to find the ring? But Marcus would find it if I hadn't told Meg what they were up to.*

The old woman smiled. "Megan, when you get back with the ring tonight, please wake me so I may see it."

"But Grandma, it'll be the middle of the night."

"Megan, please promise me."

Meg patted her withered hand. "Whatever you say."

"She knows about the ring?" Joe asked Meg.

Meg frowned at Joe. "Of course."

Victoria started to laugh. "What an irony to your relationship with Joe. You're the descendant of Diehla living with the descendant of Judge Hillery who burned her."

"But Grandma, Joe and I are different people."

The old woman continued to laugh, but her comment haunted Joe.

"Victoria, some nights I hear you chanting down here."

The old woman squinted at him. "Do you understand any of the words?"

"No." Joe shook his head.

She let out a breath then smiled at him. "I'll keep my voice down."

What is she up to?

At eleven o'clock, Joe drove as Meg directed him north to a neighboring town.

From the backseat Circe said, "Marcus called me last night and told me he wants me to put you under soon."

"When I produce the ring, won't he be surprised," Meg said. "Joe, didn't you tell me you saw Diehla raise a demon?"

"Yeah. They called him Abracax."

"Of course," Meg said. "He was one of the most powerful demons of the underworld. That is one of the main purposes for the ring."

"Where did that ring originate?" Joe asked.

"Victor Zabno got it from one of our gods to protect us against outsiders. That's why its owner could perform spells and curses so effectively."

Meg told Joe to exit right on Forest Street. He went about a mile before she told him to pull into a cemetery entrance on the left. Joe noticed there was a ground lying fog beginning to form.

"Medea's buried in a Christian cemetery?" Joe asked.

Meg sighed. "Just keep driving."

Soon Meg said, "Slow down. It's coming up on the left." When Joe was almost to the back gate she said, "Stop here."

They got out of the car and Joe opened the trunk. He handed shovels to Meg and Circe and took one for himself. Meg led them to the edge of the cemetery.

"Medea is buried inside the cemetery?" Joe asked again.

"Yes, but the edge is unconsecrated."

They walked only a few feet through the fog-shrouded grass when Meg stopped. Joe noticed on the other side of the fence were a couple of dead trees. Their branches looked like gnarled hands that were reaching toward him. With her eyes closed, Meg paced off a few steps. Joe was startled by the hoot of an owl from one of the nearby trees.

"How do you know where Medea's body was buried?" Joe asked.

Meg froze. "Shh!" She extended both arms straight out to her side then turned her face skyward to the moon.

"What's she doing?" Joe whispered to Circe.

"Drawing down the moon for assistance."

After a moment Meg relaxed and lowered her head. "We're going to dig here."

"How do you know this is the place?" Joe asked.

Meg gave him a piercing gaze. "Trust me."

"If you're wrong, not only will this be a lot of work for nothing, but we could be caught and arrested."

Meg forced her shovel into the ground with a sigh. "How about you, Circe, do you have any complaints?"

She shook her head. "No."

"Start digging then."

I pray she's wrong about where Medea's buried.

Circe stuck her shovel into the mist-covered grass followed by Meg.

I'd better help them before Meg senses my true feelings.

As they dug, the ground lying mist thickened. However, the full moon provided a hazy light.

After a few minutes Circe said, "Like Joe said, how do you know exactly where Medea's body was buried?"

Meg stopped digging and looked at Circe. "Do you think we'd be digging here if I had any doubt?"

After almost an hour of digging, Joe's shovel hit something hard.

"That's got to be the coffin," Meg whispered. "Joe, I'll let you have the honor of digging the casket out."

"Gee thanks," Joe said, as the girls climbed out of the hole and watched him dig. *What a grisly task this is going to be. I hope I have the stomach for it.*

Between the wisps of fog, they soon saw the top of some rotten wood. "Yeah, it looks like a casket," Joe said.

"Hurry." Meg peered down at him. "I want to get the ring and get the hell out of here."

"I'd still like to know how you found this," Joe said, going back to work.

"Shh! Just keep digging." Meg shined the light down on the casket.

As Joe dug dirt away from the rotten wood, he noticed there were several holes in it. When the lid was above the soil, Joe stuck his shovel below the top and forced away what was left of the coffin lid. *This is ghastly, but I have no choice but to check that skeleton for the ring.* He looked in and saw bones, but they were partially covered with dirt.

As he was mustering up his nerve to reach in, Meg shined the light on him and hissed, "What in the devil are you waiting for?"

"There's some dirt inside of the coffin. The skeleton is partially blocked."

"Well, do it then."

That bitch is really getting on my nerves.

Joe scooped out handfuls of dirt, throwing it up to the ground. Meg's light caught the bones of a musty looking skeleton. Joe swallowed with a grimace. *Maybe if I get the ring before Meg sees it, I could tell her it wasn't there. Forget it. She'll search me, and I'm not going to swallow it.*

"Joe, do you see the ring?" Meg whispered.

"No. Throw me the flash light. There's still some dirt here."

"I'm coming down." Meg lowered herself into the hole next to him. She leaned down and brushed more dirt away, then shined the light on the skeleton. A multi-glistening flash reflected back out of the box.

"There it is!" Meg shrieked.

"Yes! Yes!" Circe said looking down from ground level.

Joe peered in and saw a rainbow of colors just next to the skeleton's spine.

"It's been waiting here for me all these years." Meg knelt, reaching into the coffin.

Touching the bones of her former self doesn't faze her.

As Meg brought her hand out, Joe saw she had the ring in her palm. In awe, she shone the light on the ring. "It's more beautiful than I imagined. It's breathtakingly multi-colored." She looked at Joe, standing next to her. "This is the greatest moment of my life. Great things have happened to me since I met you, Joe." She looked down at the ring again. "No one has seen it since I had it in my past life. Say something, Joe."

Joe forced a smile. *I don't know if I can even fake being excited. I feel as if Medea and Diehla have possession of that evil ring again. Medea's dying prophecy is being fulfilled.* "I'm speechless," Joe said.

Meg held the jewel close to Joe's face. "This is Diehla's ring?"

He took a deep breath. "Yes, that's it."

She pressed it to her heart. "Then Medea did wear the same ring as Diehla."

"Meg, we'd better get out of here before someone comes," Circe warned.

Meg climbed out of the grave and Joe followed. Holding the ring over her head she looked up to the moon. She spun in circles laughing with joy while the mist swirled around her ankles like ghostly arms.

Meg stopped and Circe asked, "May I please see it?"

"Of course." Meg slipped it on her index finger, shined the light on it and lowered her hand.

"I can't believe that I'm actually looking at it," Circe said.

"Take it off my finger and look at it."

"Can I?" Circe asked.

Meg nodded. As soon as Circe touched the ring with her right hand, the darkness was lit up with sparks.

"Ouch!" Circe grabbed the fingers of her right hand. "The ring burned me."

Meg laughed. "It works for me the same as it did for Diehla and Medea. It won't let anyone touch it as long as I'm wearing it. But watch what happens when I remove it." Meg took the band off her index finger and handed it to Joe. She shined the flashlight on the ring. "Touch it now."

When Circe cautiously reached for the ring in Joe's hand, Meg realized this was the very psychic vision Luna had seen, Joe holding the ring in the dark with a flashlight shining on it.

Circe made contact and smiled at Meg. "Nothing. Let's fill in the hole and get out of here."

While Joe shoveled the dirt he asked, "Now that you found the ring, what are you going to do with it?"

"The first thing I'm going to do is make you a better lover." There was no expression on Meg's face.

Joe stopped shoveling and gave her a look. "You're so damn funny."

On their way back home, Meg looked at Circe in the backseat. "I'll need you to do more regressions to help me remember spells so I know how to use the ring."

"Of course." Circe smiled. "The ring isn't much good without knowledge."

Spells? This is getting worse. And I think Circe is pretending to be on Meg's side to help Marcus get the ring.

After they dropped Circe off, Meg lay back on the armrest with her dirty feet on Joe's lap. She held up the back of her hand to gaze at the ring on her finger.

It's nauseating to think where that ring has been.

Meg looked at Joe. "With me wearing the ring, sparks will fly when we kiss."

Not seeing any humor in that, Joe stared at the road without acknowledgment.

"Joe, I'm sorry if the ring bothers you. I know it was tied to your family curse and also your deadly test in 1680. I won't wear the ring when we're together."

If I hold her to that promise, it'll give Brad and Fenton a chance to steal it. Joe smiled at her with a nod.

When they arrived at the apartment it was three in the morning. After showering, Meg cleaned and polished the ring and placed it back on her finger. She lit rose scented candles all over the living room, then sat on the floor in her black nightgown holding Shyebony. For a half hour Meg hummed and chanted to the goddess.

Is Meg trying to freak me out?

When Meg finally rose, she set the cat on the couch and slowly, silently made her way toward Joe in her black flowing nightgown. By the piercing look in her dark squinting eyes, he wasn't sure if she was going to make love to him or kill him. Had she found out about his seeing Fenton and, now that she had the ring, dispose of him? After all, he was a descendant of the judge. When she reached him, she wrapped her slender arms around his neck. She gazed deeply into his eyes and kissed him. Now Joe knew where this was going. In the spiritual mood she was in, he was afraid to resist her.

After her kiss Joe said, "Meg, you're supposed to show the ring to your grandmother, remember?"

Without a word she strolled toward the bedroom, turned and motioned with her fingers for him to follow her. She opened the bedroom drapes. A flood of moonlight drenched the bed. She removed the ring and set it on her dresser, then stepped in front of the window gazing at Joe. With her back to the moonlight, she removed her nightgown. Her white shapely body seemed to glow as she stood there momentarily waiting for his reaction. Although Joe was exhausted, he did what she wanted him to and took her in his arms and kissed her.

As she made love to him on the bed in the moonlight, Joe wondered why this was happening now that she had the ring. *Is this to ensure I'm with her when Circe does her regressions or is Meg really feeling something for me?*

~ * ~

While Meg was downstairs showing the ring to her grandmother the next morning, Joe took the opportunity to call Brad and explain what had happened the previous night.

"As bad as this is, thank God you're still living with Meg. Had you moved we'd have no idea what she was doing with the ring. Could you talk her into taking the ring off to give us a chance to steal it?"

"She's not wearing it when we're together because she knows how I feel about it. But after Samhain, October 31st, she's not taking it off. Samhain is the witches' New Year and they believe whatever they wear on that day casts a spell for what they'll be in the coming year."

"That's a week from today. We don't have much time. I'll call Fenton and let you know what he thinks. In the meantime we need Meg to keep trusting you."

"I've been a great actor, but don't call me here on Meg's phone. I'll call you later from a phone booth around five."

At four-forty-five Joe told Meg he needed to pick up a couple of things at the store and left the apartment. He found a pay phone in front of the store and called Brad.

"Fenton said that without knowing what kind of magic the ring possesses he doesn't know if it can be deactivated. We both feel someone has to steal the ring. Besides you, who knows Meg has the ring?"

"Circe and Meg's grandmother. Circe did the regression and she was with us when we found it."

"Do you think you could frame her friend?"

"Maybe. Meg doesn't trust her, but Meg's so psychic she might know I was behind it."

"Fenton suggested he steal the ring since Meg doesn't know him."

"Brad, I told you I didn't want Fenton trying to steal the ring. It was in Medea's stomach when she placed her curse on Nathon Cyrus. That made her curse as effective as if she were wearing it."

"Can you meet us at Cliff's Diner tomorrow afternoon to discuss this with us?"

"No. Meg's planned a big dinner for us with her grandmother and one of her friends. It was difficult just getting away from her to make this call. How about Monday for lunch? Meg will be at work."

"Okay, meet us at Cliff's at one o'clock."

Joe remembered he had promised Trish Spencer he'd let her know if Meg found the ring. Joe found her phone number in his wallet and dialed. Trish answered. Joe filled her in on the graveyard hunt for the ring.

"I knew when Luna had that vision that they'd find the ring. And just like her vision, you were there holding the ring in the dark. You're still living with Meg?"

"Yeah." Joe sighed.

"I wonder why she hasn't asked you to leave, since she has the ring. It's probably because she needs your help against Marcus and his friends."

Should I trust her and let her know that we're planning to steal the ring from Meg? No, if she's not who she claims to be, I can't take the chance.

"Joe, please call me and let me know how Meg uses the ring and if I can be of any help to you, even by trying to steal it."

She's talking like us. "I'll be in touch."

Joe hung up the phone and headed for the grocery store.

When Joe entered the apartment with bags, Meg helped him put the groceries away. "Did you want to eat at the club tonight?"

Joe shook his head as he put the ketchup in the refrigerator. "We can't afford it."

"Maybe we can. I used a money spell to help your business prosper. I even wore the ring and used Shyebony."

Trying to stay on Meg's good side, he kissed her forehead. "Thank you, sweetheart. In that case, let's go to the club for dinner."

~ * ~

The next evening Brad took Ellen to the movies. When they returned home Ellen paid the sitter and made Brad a drink. They sat on the couch.

"Brad, how long are you planning to stay?"

"Only until we get that ring from Meg. If that's all right with you, of course."

She smiled at him. "It's my pleasure. I think I'd have gone crazy without you here to keep me company."

"With the danger of the ring being in the wrong hands, Joe is in a delicate situation."

"That might be true but I saw how he kissed her. And his love spell is supposed to be removed."

"He has to stay on Meg's good side. He's our informant."

"I could see that Joe enjoyed it. I'll never be able to get that picture out of my mind." A tear escaped as Ellen shook her head. "And he lied about living with her." Ellen's voice quivered. After several minutes of silence she turned to look at Brad. "How is it you never married?"

"I just never found the right woman."

"I'd like to know more about you."

"Well, I've told you most of what I do as a para—"

"I'm not talking about your work. Who are you and what are your hobbies? What drives and motivates you?"

Brad smiled as Ellen continued.

"I want to know all about this dynamic man who's staying in my home."

"Let's see I like to watch—"

Ellen shut her eyes and fell into Brad's arms.

"Are you feeling all right?" Brad knew full well what she was doing.

"I've never felt better. Continue, I'm listening."

Brad stammered as he began to speak again. Ellen softly kissed the side of his neck. Thrills ran down his arms.

"Ellen, Joe is my friend."

"Are you my friend too?" Ellen opened her eyes to gaze into his.

"I told you before, if these were different circumstances you wouldn't have to ask."

Ellen pressed her lips to his.

Fourteen

The Thief

Without wanting to, Brad found himself kissing Ellen back. He took her in his arms. He was uncharacteristically out of control even fumbling with the buttons on her blouse.

"Brad, I need you." Ellen's eyes seemed to be smiling as she gazed at him.

Brad didn't know if he could resist her as she removed her top and wrapped her arms around him, then kissed him again. They rolled off the couch and onto the floor. Brad couldn't stop his avalanche of desire as Ellen moaned with passion. He felt this was a special moment like he had never experienced before.

While Brad made love to Ellen, Joe never entered her mind.

~ * ~

At one o'clock the following afternoon, Joe, Brad and Fenton met at Cliff's diner in Willstown.

Just looking at Joe made Brad feel guilty. "I expressed my concern to Fenton about his safety," Brad said. "But he's a very stubborn man."

Joe looked at Fenton. "With Medea's curse, you're committing suicide."

"A witch's intuition will tell her who is responsible for a theft only if it's someone she knows." Fenton pushed his glasses up. "If one of us steals the ring, you'll be in the clear and you might be able to convince her that her friend is behind the theft since Meg already has doubts about her. I understand Meg isn't wearing the ring now?"

"No, but she never keeps it in the same place. It's hard to predict where it is at any given time. You'll have to steal it before their Samhain sabbat. After she shows the ring to all the witches who attend, she told me she's never going to remove it from her finger."

Fenton placed his hand to his forehead and looked down at the table. "That means we only have until Saturday to steal it, and this is Monday already."

Joe crunched on a nacho. "I've got an idea. This Friday night, the coven is holding a witches' ball at their parish and it's open to the public. There's a flier on the wall at the Occult book store where Meg works. Everyone is supposed to wear a costume. It's a witches' Halloween party."

Brad took a sip of water. "That might be a good time to steal the ring."

Fenton held up his hand. "But that's waiting until the last minute. I think we should try to get it as soon as possible."

"Where is the ring now?" Brad asked.

"In a jewelry box on her dresser."

"Why didn't you bring the ring with you?" Brad asked.

"Joe was wise not to have taken it. He'd be the first person she suspects and I told you a witch's instincts will confirm that he's guilty. Joe must be with Meg when the ring is stolen, so he has an alibi or he'll pay dire consequences."

Dire consequences?

"I don't see how we can get the ring in the evening with Meg at home," Brad said.

"You could," Fenton said. "If Joe left the apartment with Meg, but he'd have to convince her to leave the ring at home."

"She won't leave the ring at the apartment if no one's there. Saturday night when we went to the Chessie Cat Club, she put the ring in her purse and took it with her."

"I'd like to frame Marcus's group for stealing the ring, but I'm not sure how." Fenton took a bite of his sandwich.

"I'll try to come up with something myself," Joe said. "I'll phone Brad when I have a plan."

After supper that evening, Joe put a hand on the back of his neck. "This kink in my neck has been bothering me all day, Meg."

"Sit down." She pointed to a kitchen chair. "I'll get it out for you."

Joe sat and Meg started to work on his neck.

"Ooooh, you're right on it."

Meg continued rubbing and kneading. "I've been doing a lot of thinking today. If Circe is a traitor, I'm worried that one of Marcus's people may break in and steal the ring. We need a safer place to keep it."

We may be able to blame Marcus after all. "A bank vault?" Joe turned to glance at her.

"I was thinking of hiding it some place at your office, only until Samhain when I start wearing it."

My office? Is this good or bad? It seems too easy, and I don't want to be blamed for its disappearance. "Why there?"

"It's the last place Marcus would think to look and there are so many places to hide it."

Joe nodded. "Maybe you're right."

"It's settled. We're hiding the ring at your office."

"But where?"

"I'll go with you to work tomorrow and pick out a place."

What kind of plan can I come up with that won't make me a suspect?

Meg ended her massage. "How does your neck feel now?"

He turned his head side to side. "The tightness is completely gone."

"You still love me, don't you?" Coming around from the back of the chair, Meg searched his eyes, making him nervous.

"Of course I love you." He stood and put his arms around her.

"You haven't said it lately." She gave him a mock pout.

"All this business with the ring has me preoccupied." *With Meg already having the ring, can I get her to admit she put a love spell on me?* "Meg, are you in love with me? You haven't said it to me either."

"Guilty as charged. I'm sorry and I'll make it up to you tonight. I do love you." She kissed him.

"Meg, I want you to tell me the truth. When exactly did you fall in love with me?"

"It was love at first sight. I think I was infatuated with you because of your time-travel experience."

Will she ever tell me she used a love spell on me to get what she wanted? But that would be admitting she ruined my marriage.

~ * ~

Meg seemed nervous as she rode with Joe to his office the next morning. Since he didn't have a personal safe, she looked for a good hiding place for the ring. She went to his desk and opened every drawer. "You have locks for all the drawers?"

Joe nodded. "Yes."

She opened the second drawer. "We'll hide the ring here. Make certain this drawer is always locked." Meg slipped out a white envelope and slid the ring inside. "We can't leave anything to chance." She placed the envelope at the bottom of the drawer's contents and Joe locked it.

Meg smiled at him. "I feel much better." She kissed him on the cheek. "I'd better get on the bus to Manchester before I'm any later for work."

Joe walked her to the front door where she kissed him goodbye just as one of Joe's employees and friends approached the entrance of the building.

"See you tonight, lover," Meg said with a smirk, then turned and walked out of the building.

The man entered and Joe said, "Marty, you may as well know that Ellen and I have split up."

"No wonder you've been out of circulation lately. This girl's been keeping you busy. Did you trade Ellen in on a new model?"

"It's no joke. Ellen threw me out. It's a long story. I'll tell you about it some other time."

"Okay, chief. I gotta get to work anyway."

When Joe got back to his office, he sat behind his desk and glanced down at the second drawer. *Having that cursed ring here in my office gives me the creeps, not only because of where we found it, but because it was the instrument that cursed my family for three hundred years.*

Joe took a deep breath and phoned Fenton. "Guess where the ring is now. In a drawer here in my office. And it was Meg's idea."

"I'm not happy about the ring being in your desk. If the ring turns up missing, Meg will blame you."

"We may have to get the ring at the witches' ball like I suggested."

"Yes, she has to be with you when the ring is stolen and I assume she's not coming back to your office before Saturday."

"No, I'm supposed to bring the ring home on Friday."

~ * ~

That evening while Joe got ready for bed, Meg, wrapped in a towel, her hair soaking wet, ran into the bedroom. "Joe, I just had a bad vibe."

"Meg, you're dripping wet."

"Listen to me." Her hands tightened into fists on the towel. "Is there anyone working the night shift at your company?"

"Yeah, a couple of guys do maintenance and cleaning on weeknights."

She stuck her face closer to Joe. "Are they on duty now?"

"Yeah, they work until about five in the morning, why?"

"Call them now, please. Tell them to stay close to your office."

"That's ridiculous," Joe said.

"Joe, do it!"

"All right, if you feel that strongly about it."

Joe sat on the edge of the bed and dialed as Meg stood and rubbed her hair with the towel and watched him.

"Frank, this is Joe Hillery. I need one of you to keep an eye on my office. There's a chance someone may break in and try to steal something out of my desk." Joe paused. "Never mind how I know. Just watch my office. Talk to you later." He hung up the phone. *If Marcus does get the ring, the situation will get a whole lot worse.*

At three a.m., just as the two workmen went outside to throw away some trash, a tall, thin woman in black slipped in through the propped open front door. She crept into the reception area and down the dimly lit hallway looking for Joe's office. She was at the back of the building all the way to the large storage room before she realized she must have passed it. The young woman crept back up the hallway searching the doors again for Joe's name. When she was almost to the front reception area, she saw it. She tried the door knob but found it locked. The burglar pulled out a long piece of metal from under her clothes, stuck it into the lock and turned it. The door opened. As she entered she heard the men coming back into the building. She quickly closed the door and hid on the other side of Joe's desk. Soon the voices faded and she rose. The thief pulled out a pen light and searched Joe's desk.

Thanks to the psychic vision of Luna I know approximately where to look.

The woman opened the first drawer but didn't find what she was looking for. Trying the second drawer, she found it was locked. She sat on the floor with the light in her teeth while she jimmied the lock with a smaller tool. She finally forced the drawer open. Shinning the light inside, she removed a couple of papers before she found a small white envelope on the bottom. She snatched it and shined the light inside. A flood of rainbow colored light reflected back at her. She reached in with a smile and found the magical ring.

Thank you, Mother Goddess! This is the happiest moment of my life.

The burglar kissed the ring then slid it on her index finger. As she closed the drawer, there were voices in the hall. She pressed against the door to listen. The garbled voices grew silent. The woman slowly cracked the door open and peeked around the corner. Both of the men were outside. She locked Joe's door and started toward the front. From the night light she saw the men heading back into the building. Her heart pounded.

I locked Joe's office. Where can I hide?

She headed back down the hall to the open storeroom. It was well lit and all open space. *There's nowhere to hide!*

The men walked down the hall all the way into the storage room where the thief was.

"I'm telling you, Frank, the Blue Jays won the series because of their hitting. Why Joe Carter…" The short chubby man stopped and pointed. "Who's that?"

The tall thin man looked to where his companion pointed. "What do you mean who's that? It's a mannequin." He shook his head in disbelief.

"Why's Hillery storing a dummy in here?" the short man asked, walking closer to the woman posing next to the wall, both hands on her hips.

"How should I know? I just do my job and don't ask stupid questions."

"She looks real." He examined her dressed in a tight black leather suit and black nylon stockings. He looked into her icy gaze. "They must be making these clothes hangers out of new material. If I didn't know better, I'd swear she was alive."

I'll fool this dope with my mannequin training and witchcraft which not only lowers my body temperature to that of the room but also keeps me from blinking.

The chubby man touched her exposed wrist and hand.

This dope is making my breathing increase. Will it give me away?

"Dave, will you get away from that dummy and help me go through all this stuff?" Frank growled.

"She's cold but her skin feels real," Dave said.

"She's cold because she's a mannequin, you dummy."

Dave turned away slowly as if mesmerized by the life-like creature. He walked over to Frank and helped him sort through some junk. Paula's heart beat slowed again.

"I wonder why Hillery thinks someone is going to break in here tonight," Frank said. "And what are they after?"

"He didn't explain?" The short man frowned.

Frank put his hands on his hips. "And what are we supposed to do if we did catch the guy or guys? They could be dangerous. We're not security guards or cops."

Dave looked around. "All of this talk gives me the creeps."

"I wonder how Hillery got the tip," he repeated.

While the men talked, Dave occasionally glanced at the attractive statue-like figure.

Frank nudged him and pointed to the box of garbage. "Let's get this stuff out of here."

As the men carried the wooden boxes out of the room, the intruder stayed frozen until she heard their voices fade. She finally relaxed her tense body with a sigh of relief and rubbed her forehead. She kept her feet planted in case one of the men returned. Suddenly, she heard footsteps coming toward her. She placed her hands on her hips and froze again. Out of the corner of her eye she saw Frank walk into the room. She noticed he gave her a final glance before leaving. Paula relaxed again. She stood listening to them talking and joking in the front of the building, wondering if they would ever leave. At long last the door opened and closed. It was quiet.

I've done it. But can I get out past the men without being seen?

She crept down the hall until she was in the reception area. The men were standing outside just in front of the door, next to the dumpster. They were much too close for her to get past them unnoticed. She feared she'd have to run back to the storeroom and play possum again. Finally, the men strolled toward the left. Paula eased the door open and tip-toed out to the right. As she walked away through the darkness to her car down the street, she smiled.

Yes! I not only have the ring but I even heard Joe's men discussing his plans. Thanks to my special skills I tricked them without even having a place to hide. Marcus will applaud my performance.

~ * ~

While Meg made breakfast, Joe called Frank at his home. He assured Joe that nothing unusual happened at the warehouse and his office was locked all night. Joe gave Meg the good news at the table as they ate.

When Joe got to the office he checked his second drawer to see the ring. Panic gripped him when he discovered that the drawer was unlocked. He reached in and found the ring missing. He spotted the white envelope on the floor just under his desk.

Oh my God! Marcus has the ring and Meg will blame me. Joe's heart pounded as he dialed Frank's home number again. There was no answer.

He's probably in bed. I'll call him every hour. Even though Frank doesn't have keys to my office, could he and Dave have picked the locks and taken the ring?

Joe perspired, searching for a sign of a break-in but found nothing.

An hour later Joe called Frank again and finally he answered. "Someone was in my office last night and stole something valuable out of my desk. They had to have passed you to get in here. There are no windows in my office."

"Dave and I were around your office all night. We didn't see anybody."

"Did you leave the building?"

"Yeah, a couple of times to dump some boxes from the storage room into the garbage dump outside."

"One of you should have stayed in the building at all times."

"We didn't see anything suspicious. It was quiet."

"Well, someone got past both of you without you noticing."

Joe questioned the man again about their activities, becoming more suspicious as they spoke.

"Give me a break, Joe. We're not security guards, and its hard working with a slow guy like Dave. He wouldn't have noticed if the thief had been standing right in front of him. He spent too much time starring at that mannequin in the storeroom. I had a hard time getting him—"

Mannequin? "What mannequin are you talking about?"

"The dummy that's by the wall in the storeroom."

Joe was silent. The pieces were falling into place. "Frank, describe the mannequin to me."

"Well, it was taller than both of us, thin, with medium brown hair and bangs and it was wearing a tight black outfit. If she were real, she would have been a knockout."

Paula! Meg mentioned she had done some mannequin modeling.
"Why are you asking me about the dummy?"
"It wasn't a dummy. That was the thief, Frank."
"How could a mannequin steal anything?"
"It wasn't a mannequin. That was a woman posing as a mannequin. She freezes that way for department stores."
"You know who it is?"
"Yeah, her name is Paula Rulavich. She's a model."
"Wow! She sure fooled us. Sorry, chief."
Joe slammed the phone down then called Meg at work. He perspired as the phone rang. *At least I've got Paula and Marcus to blame.*
Meg answered the phone.
"Meg, sit down. I've got some bad news for you."
"I have nowhere to sit. I'm in the store. What is it, Joe?"
"Then go into the stockroom and sit."
"Just tell me." Meg's voice was raised.
Joe cringed then said, "The ring was stolen out of my desk last night."
"What!" Meg yelled in his ear.
"Meg, I know who has it. It's Marcus."
"How do you know that?"
"Paula went unnoticed playing mannequin in here last night."
"But how did Marcus know we even found the ring?"
Joe rubbed his forehead. "Isn't it obvious? Circe."
"Then how did they know where we hid it? We didn't tell her."
"I have no idea how Marcus knew where it was."
"Luna. She's a psychic, remember. You've used her services."

"Yeah. How can we get the ring back?" Joe asked.

"I've got a plan. I'll call you later." Meg hung up.

Joe called Fenton to fill him in on the theft.

"This is the worst thing that could have happened," Fenton said. "Now we don't have you on the inside to help us steal the ring, and Marcus is extremely dangerous. I'll call Brad and tell him what's happened."

"Meg told me she has a plan but hasn't explained it to me. Get back to me after you talk to Brad."

Shortly after lunchtime, Meg called Joe at his office. "I'm going to leave work now to get help from Grandma about this. When you get home, come to her apartment."

I'm with Meg one hundred percent until she gets the ring back.

~ * ~

Trish Spencer surrounded herself with white candles and lilies as she sat on the living room floor. Her cousin was at work so she thought this would be a good time for prayer. She prayed to the Mother Goddess that Meg would somehow lose possession of the ring. Just before her worship was finished, the phone rang. She didn't answer the call but played the message back five minutes later. It was Joe. "Trish, I wanted you to know that the ring has been stolen by Marcus's people. Call me back."

Trish put a hand to the side of her head. "My spell worked, but now the situation is even worse." She dialed Joe's office. When he answered she said, "Joe, this is terrible. How did Marcus get the ring?"

"If you have a little time, I'll fill you in."

When Joe was finished, Trish said, "If you need me for anything, just let me know."

"Believe me I will. I'll keep in touch."

~ * ~

At Hillery mansion, Ellen and Brad sat on the couch while the children played outside.

Ellen kissed Brad. "I should call Joe and tell him he can see the kids this week."

"Maybe I should call him," Brad said.

"Would you?"

He smiled at her. "Of course."

"Has Joe acted suspicious about you still being here?"

"No, he knows I need to stay until after Halloween, the witches' Samhain. That's when Meg will show all her fellow witches that she is Medea, the witch queen."

"I think my guilt is part of the reason I want Joe to see the kids." Ellen took Brad's hand and looked into his eyes. "Guilty, but very content."

Brad kissed her and pulled her close.

"When are we going to tell Joe what's happened between us?" Ellen asked.

"Let's wait until after Halloween when this ring business is over. Joe's got enough to deal with right now."

The phone rang and Ellen answered it. "Hello. Yes, he is." She handed the phone to Brad. "It's Fenton Cyrus."

Brad took the phone. "What's up, Fenton?" Horror slowly registered on his face. "My God, how did that happen?"

~ * ~

Joe walked into Victoria's apartment to find Meg and her grandmother eating dinner in the living room. The television was on and each sat behind a snack tray.

"Supper's in the kitchen," Meg said. "Help yourself."

He returned with a plate full of food and sat on the couch.

"Marcus admitted he has the ring," Meg said. "He's wearing it, in fact." She glared into space. "My ring." She gritted her teeth.

Joe shook his head, but was relieved that he was off the hook about the theft. "You talked to Marcus?"

Meg nodded. "Yeah, I called him."

"I'm surprised he admitted what he did."

"He's proud of the fact he was able to get the ring from us. It shows us that he's more powerful than we are."

Joe shook his head. "I don't have any powers, Meg."

"I was talking about me and Grandma."

Joe stopped short of taking a bite of his sandwich. "So what are we going to do?"

"After Grandma and I went over our options, we decided that I should call Marcus back and strike a compromise with him."

Joe gave her a blank stare as he chewed. "What's the compromise?"

"We can't get the ring while Marcus wears it, and he and his allies have more power than Grandma and me—"

"If he has the ring, what can you offer him?"

"Let me finish. There is no book that tells us how to use the ring. The only way to get that knowledge is through my mind of the past as Medea."

"So what deal did you make with him?"

"Marcus has agreed to be co-coven leader with me and we'll share the ring, starting on Samhain."

"I don't trust him," Victoria said.

"Neither do I," Joe added, as he took another bite of Polish sausage.

"Do you two think that I'm stupid?" Meg glanced from her grandmother to Joe. "I have a few tricks up my sleeve. I promise you both I'll make Marcus pay for this stunt."

Joe looked at Meg. "Marcus may have some tricks of his own."

Victoria raised her hand and pointed. "Megan, will you take the pumpkin pie out of the oven, please."

With all this talk about the ring, she wants pie now? I wonder if the old woman is becoming senile.

"Sure, Grandma." Meg left the room.

"I'm going to cast a spell on Marcus." The old woman laughed. "You'll see."

Joe was at a loss of what to say.

When Meg returned with the pie, Joe said, "Ellen's agreed to let me see my kids tomorrow."

Meg cut it into pieces. "That's great. You spoke with her?"

"No. We have a mutual friend who told me."

Meg grinned. "See, I told you my spell would work. Don't forget we're going to the witches' ball Friday night."

Joe nodded. "Yeah, the day after tomorrow."

"I need you to be with me when I meet with Marcus in the parish office, considering what happened the last time I met him alone."

"Of course." Joe continued to chew. *What could be more fun than a power struggle between two dangerous witches that have a deadly ring?*

Smiling at Joe, Meg took a bite of pie and rubbed the back of his hand. *Joe is more valuable to me now then when I needed him to find the ring. Besides Grandma, who can't leave this house, he's the only ally I have in this dangerous situation I'm in.*

Joe shook his head. "So after all we went through with Circe to find the ring, she still betrayed us."

Meg glared at him. "I'll deal with her when the time comes."

Joe nodded. *Circe's in trouble.*

~ * ~

When he arrived at work Joe called Fenton to keep him updated, then phoned Brad. He told Joe he'd drive the kids to his office at three.

That afternoon Joe took his children to the park for a cookout. It was a beautiful sunny day with a slight breeze, and the leaves were at peak color. While Joe roasted hot dogs on the grill, he tried to get reacquainted with his children. Amy hung on his arm and chattered away at him, but Tommy was unusually quiet. When they sat at the picnic table to eat, Joe watched his son, with dark bangs in his eyes, take a bite of his hot dog without a word.

"What's wrong, Tommy?" Joe asked.

The boy looked at Joe and shrugged.

"I thought maybe you were mad at me because I'm not living with you and Mommy anymore. I'll be back home soon."

Tommy gazed down to the ground and kicked at a leaf.

Joe rubbed his son's back. "What is it? You can tell me anything."

Tommy looked at him. "I didn't want to tell you, but I saw Uncle Brad kiss Mommy on the mouth."

Fifteen

Meeting for a Compromise

Joe's own son gave him the worst news he'd ever heard.

Tommy hung his head with a pout. "I'm mad at Mommy."

Still in shock, Joe swallowed hard. "Tommy, when did you see Uncle Brad kiss Mommy?"

"Last night. I heard them laughing, so I sneaked down to Mommy's room and saw Uncle Brad lying in bed with Mommy, and he kissed her on the mouth."

Joe could hardly speak, but forced himself to ask, "Does Uncle Brad always sleep with Mommy?"

The boy shrugged.

"Does your mom know you saw her and Uncle Brad together?"

Tommy shook his head.

Joe rested his hand on his son's shoulder. "Don't ever tell Mommy you saw what she did. It'll be our secret. Okay?"

"Okay, Daddy." Tommy looked at Joe and nodded.

Joe felt as if someone had driven a spike into his heart but he didn't want to traumatize his son any further by discussing the topic. Joe hung his head, feeling as if his life was over.

Amy tapped his arm, bringing him out of his stupor. "Daddy, can you buy me an ice cream cone?"

I don't know if I can pull myself together, but I have to try for my kids.

Joe looked at her and forced a smile. "Sure, honey. I'll buy you and Tommy an ice cream cone on the way home."

"Yay," Amy said clapping her little hands.

A tear came to Joe's eyes as he ruffled his daughter's hair, knowing his relationship with his children would never be the same.

On the way to the ice cream parlor, Joe picked up a pumpkin at a farm stand. It was dark when he arrived at Meg's apartment with the children. Meg wasn't home so Joe began carving a jack-o-lantern with the kids on the kitchen table. He pretended to be having fun, but his mind continued to dwell on his new problem. *I'm not going to yell, accuse and traumatize the kids for life. No, instead, when I get the kids home, I'll act as normal as possible. I won't let Brad and Ellen know that I'm aware of their affair.* "Stay with Meg," Brad had said. "Don't let her know her spell has been broken." *You bastard!*

Before they finished the jack-o-lantern, Meg entered the apartment through the back door.

"Hello, children," she said with a smile. "I'm Meg, a friend of your daddy's."

Tommy looked at her then back at the pumpkin without comment.

Amy glanced at her with a scowl. "Mommy told me you were a witch."

I'm surprised that Ellen mentioned that to the kids.

"How do you feel about that?" Meg asked.

"I'm afraid of witches." Amy looked back at the pumpkin as if uncomfortable.

"Why?"

Amy glanced at Meg. "Witches are ugly and they eat kids."

"Real witches don't eat kids, honey. That's just in fairy tales." Meg smiled. "Do you think I'm ugly?"

"No. You're pretty." Amy started to carve again.

Tommy frowned at his sister. "Amy, don't talk to her."

"Why?" Amy looked at Tommy. "She's nice."

Meg stepped closer. "I'd like to be Amy's friend, Tommy. Can I be your friend, too?"

Tommy didn't answer as he continued carving the pumpkin. Meg looked at Joe and twisted her mouth with a shrug.

Joe winked at her as if to say "Thanks for trying." *My living with Meg might be too much for Tommy to handle right now after what he's been through.*

Meg came up behind Joe and placed her arm around his waist. "Your kids are adorable."

Joe turned and smiled at her. *For the first time I'm actually happy Meg's in my life, or is she?*

On the drive back to Hillery Mansion, Joe became more angry than hurt. *With Brad and Ellen not knowing that I'm wise to them, it'll give me a chance for revenge. But it's going to be difficult to look them in the eyes and keep my cool. If I can do it, I'll get them where it hurts them the most and when they least expect it.*

Amy was asleep when Joe arrived. He carried her to the house followed by Tommy.

Brad answered the door and took Amy out of Joe's arms. "Joe, does Meg have a plan to retrieve the ring?"

Scumball. "You'd better put Amy to bed. We'll talk later."

Joe stuck his head in the door. "Thanks for letting me have the kids today, Ellen."

"I'll let you see them once a week, Joe," she said from the living room couch.

That comment just proves Ellen has no intentions of us ever being together, and she's only letting me see the kids out of guilt.

"Goodbye, Tommy." Joe gave his son a hug.

On the way to Meg's place, Joe went over one revenge scenario after another. When he pulled up in front of the apartment, Meg was sitting in a chair on the porch waiting for him. He got out of the car. She rose and pointed to the door. "Joe, come into Grandma's."

He shuddered to think what was up now. When he got inside, two other crones sat with Victoria around a card table in the center of the living room while incense spewed from several pots.

Joe looked around with a frown. "What's going on?"

"Grandma and her friends are going to put a spell on Marcus," Meg said. "These ladies used to be in her coven."

"Don't look at me for any help." Joe held up his palms.

Meg gave him a serious look. "Like it or not, Joe, you're involved."

Joe pointed at her. "I don't practice witchcraft, remember?"

Meg shook her head. "Sit on the couch and watch then."

"Why did you wait for me to arrive before doing this?"

One of the withered women asked, "Why is Meg seeing a non-wiccan?"

Victoria smiled. "Because he's a nice young man."

The woman frowned at her, while the other woman snickered.

I feel my being here will bring some bad karma to me.

Joe watched as Meg took a seat at the card table with the other three. They chanted some verses in unison. Joe didn't know what language they were speaking. They began waving their hands over their heads then bowed until their hands were parallel with the table. When they had repeated the phrases several times, the smoke from the candles swirled around, engulfing them in an incense haze. Finally, Victoria called for "Rossneth." God or demon, Joe wasn't sure.

"Spirit of justice, bring back the sacred ring to my granddaughter, Megan O'Leary," Victoria pleaded. "She is the rightful owner of its magic. Despair or death to anyone who would stand in her way! So let it be."

Joe's eyes widened when he saw the smoke swirl like a whirlwind around the table then tighten as it rose to the ceiling where it spun and dissipated.

Meg glanced at the three crones around her. "Sisters, the spell is cast."

"You'll have the ring back soon, my dear," one of the old witches said.

The other hag said, "Victoria hasn't lost her touch and Megan gets more powerful all the time."

"Thank you all for helping me," Meg graciously said. "You will be rewarded for this."

On the way up the stairs to Meg's apartment, Joe asked, "So what's going to happen to Marcus?"

"We don't know, only that he will meet with enough bad luck that I'll get the ring back. I don't want to talk about it now. What should we do tonight? There's nothing on television."

"Do you want to play a board game?"

"Oooh, Joe, you're saying you want to play with me?" She flashed him a coy smile.

Joe stopped her toward the top of the stairs and gave her a kiss.

"I like this game already." She smiled and kissed him. "But maybe we should wait until we're in the apartment to begin."

That night in bed, Joe couldn't shut his mind off. He wondered what kind of black magic the witches had used on Marcus. Even though Joe didn't like him, he wondered why they couldn't simply have used a spell to get the ring back. *Will their curse catch up with me when Meg and I meet with Marcus at the witches' ball tomorrow night?*

Suddenly, the picture of Ellen in bed with Brad went through Joe's mind. Were they making love even at this moment? He felt the ache in his heart again, then the rage of betrayal.

Joe's thoughts drifted to Meg. *Am I actually having some real feelings for her, or is it just a rebound? The thing that keeps my feelings from flourishing is that Meg won't come clean about her love spell and the game she's playing with me. Does she still believe I'm under her spell, or is she wise and just playing along because she needs me?*

The silence was interrupted by the faint sound of Victoria's voice below, as she recited another one of her incantations. *The old woman acts as if she approves of my living with Meg, but I've got an uneasy feeling about these spells she casts at night.* The old witch's voice grew louder. Joe could make out a few of the words this time. "Hear me," and "By the power of earth, water, fire and air, I curse him!"

Joe almost bolted up in bed. *Him? Who? Me? Or Marcus? Meg had already cast her spell on Marcus. So why the need for another? This had to be meant for someone else.* Joe began to tremble as the old woman's voice finally faded.

~ * ~

The following morning, Joe and his sales staff sold a new lucrative account. He wondered if this was because of Meg's spell that was supposed to help his business. By afternoon, Joe called Fenton to tell him about Meg's and Marcus's meeting that night for control of the coven and the ring. Joe was relieved that with Marcus having the ring, Fenton wouldn't be affected by Medea's curse.

Alone in his office, plans of revenge for Ellen and Brad's betrayal entered Joe's mind again. Soon it was replaced with fear of having to be involved with Meg's and Marcus's desperate meeting. He didn't trust Marcus or his friends.

When Joe got to the apartment, he and Meg changed into their costumes. Meg dressed as Medea, wearing a wig with long, dark, flowing hair and a gown. Joe also wore clothes of the early eighteenth century: a three cornered hat, vest and waist coat, with knickers and knee high white socks.

On the drive to the parish, the wind picked up and howled. Joe still had the feeling Marcus would double-cross them, but Meg wouldn't listen to him. She appeared calm as she sat in her usual position with her head resting on the door rest and her back against the passenger's door using Joe's lap for a footrest.

"Don't mention anything about the ring to Sayde or any of the others who aren't Marcus allies," Meg said. "They'll all find out about it with other witches of our area at our Samhain sabbat tomorrow night."

Joe glanced at her with a nod. *At least she's admitted that only half of the coven is aware of the ring.* "Again, why do you think you can trust Marcus?"

"Because he needs me to give him the ring's magic spells. I would never have agreed to meet with him if you weren't going to be with me." She smiled and rubbed Joe's ribs with her foot.

She does have a point, but if she's wrong, she's also putting me in danger.

"Don't worry, Joe. Our spell will help me get the ring back and seal Marcus's fate."

Joe gazed ahead at the road. "I'm still nervous."

"Since I've dragged you into this, I think I should place a protective spell around you." Meg took her feet off Joe's lap and sat close to him.

"Shouldn't I pull over or something?" Joe glanced at Meg.

"No, just relax." She mumbled something under her breath and with her right index finger made three circles over his head. "Now you're protected." She lay back on the passenger's door again.

"Just like that?"

She nodded with a smile. "Just like that."

I wonder if she really did put a protective spell on me, or was this just an act to calm me down.

"I don't know how I could have ever let myself become one of Marcus's whores."

"You actually had sex with him?"

Meg didn't answer, but stared at Joe from the other side of the seat. "Yes," she said slowly as she peered at him. "I didn't have to tell you that, but I want to always be honest with you."

She has a point. She didn't have to tell me.

"But Marcus is the past and being with you has been the happiest time of my life."

"Why were you and the other women so attracted to a man so dangerous?" Joe asked.

"Because Marcus has a great knowledge of magic and he's the high priest. It's a status symbol."

He glanced at her. "But wouldn't his dangerous nature be a deterrent?"

"No, that's a turn on for young witches, but having a kind guy like you who I can count on is so much better, and I owe you my life. Don't you ever let me forget it."

"I won't." *Now is this sincere?*

"I've got some good news for you, Joe."

He turned toward her. "I need some good news right about now."

"As of three weeks ago, I stopped taking the pill."

Joe frowned at her. "What?"

"I'm pregnant. You're going to be a daddy again." Meg flashed him a wide grin.

"Holy shit!" Joe jumped and almost swerved off the road.

"Gotcha." She laughed.

"Damn it, Meg. Don't do that." He frowned at her and shook his head. "You almost gave me a heart attack."

She clasped her hands together in front of her face with a giggle. "Oh, Joe, I wish you could have seen your face." She laughed again. "What a baby we'd have, a descendant of Judge Hillery and Diehla Thorn. Isn't that rich?"

They arrived at the witches' ball just after seven. As they entered the parish, they strolled past a few people in costumes. Guests bobbed for apples and played bean bag toss in the ritual room. In the corner, Joe spotted Luna dressed as a vampire sitting at a card table reading the palm of a man dressed as Frankenstein. Next to her a sign read: 'Fortunes $20.'

Sayde, dressed as a fairy princess, greeted them with a smile. "I like your costumes."

Meg smiled at her. "Thank you. When is the first ritual going to begin?"

"Eight o'clock sharp."

Meg glanced around the room. "Is Marcus here yet?"

"I haven't seen him, but he'll be along. There are refreshments in the parish hall: taffy apples, sandwiches, popcorn balls and, of course, witches' brew."

Joe frowned. "What's witches' brew?"

"Come on." Meg pulled his arm. "I'll show you."

With people helping themselves to food at the large table next to the wall, Meg picked up two plates and handed one to Joe.

Joe took a corned beef sandwich as he heard a woman say, "Hi, Meg."

He turned to see Circe dressed as a cat in a black leotard. She got in line behind Joe.

"There's going to be a band here after the first ritual," Circe said.

"Who?" Joe asked.

"It's a pagan band from Boston. They're called The Dark Tunes." When their plates were full, Circe said, "I see a spot in the back of the room."

"Who invited you to join us?" Meg snapped.

"Meg, I had nothing to do with your ring being stolen," Circe said.

Carrying her tray, Meg glanced at her. "Don't insult my intelligence."

"You look just like Medea Laughton in that costume," Circe said, trying to change the subject.

They walked to an empty table. When all three sat, Circe asked, "When are you meeting with Marcus?"

"After the ritual, I guess. I haven't seen him yet." Meg took a bite of her sandwich.

Joe took a sip of the witches' brew then raised his eyebrows. "Did any smoke come out of my ears?"

Meg laughed. "It's an ancient wiccan beverage. Good, isn't it?"

"If you like highly spiced apples."

Luna approached them holding a plate. "May I join you?"

"Be our guest, Vampira." Meg gave Joe a frown. "I hope you don't think I'm being rude, but Joe and I just finished eating." She jabbed Joe with her elbow to get him up.

As they rose from the table, Paula approached wearing a witch's costume. "Leaving so soon?" She set her plate on the table next to Circe's. Paula stayed standing and smiled at Meg. "Was it something I said?"

"What did you think of Joe's office when you were there the other night?"

"I don't know what you're talking about, Meg." Paula flashed her another smirk. "Joe, you've still got a lot of food on your plate. Are you sure you're finished?"

Joe gave her a frown. "Paula, are you still posing problems for people?"

Meg pulled on his arm and they walked away. "If you're still hungry, grab something from the sweets table over there."

Joe picked up a taffy apple. "We should have asked Luna or Paula where Marcus is."

"I wouldn't ask them the time of day."

Joe munched on his apple as they left the room. "Where are we going?" Joe asked as they squeezed passed people standing in the hall.

"To the ritual room for our ceremony."

Inside, a crowd of people stood in clouds of incense. Sayde walked to the center of the room. "I don't know how many of you here tonight have ever attended a wiccan ritual, but if you haven't, this will be an experience you shouldn't miss. Now I want everyone to form a circle around the altar table."

When everyone was in place, the lights dimmed, then went out, leaving only flickering flames from the small jack-o-lanterns on the altar table. Sayde led everyone through what Joe thought was a simple ritual. He assumed it was because of the curious non-wiccan guests in attendance. The usual cup was passed around, then Circe took everyone through relaxation breathing instead of her usual trance.

After the ritual, the circle was uncast and the lights went on. A band set up and started warming up for their first number. At the microphone the lead singer, who looked like a young Frank Sinatra, said, "Welcome fellow witches, warlocks and friends of wicca. We're here to entertain you tonight at the annual witches' ball. Is everyone having a good time?"

People yelled and shouted, "Yeah!"

"Great. The first number is one by old blue eyes called witchcraft. All right, guys, grab your sweetie. Somebody out there gave me one of these." He put two fingers together, making a cross. "Are you sure you're in the right place?"

Some people laughed. Then came the musical words "those fingers in my hair" as Meg took Joe's hand and led him into the dance area. While they danced, Joe got another vibe that something was going to go awfully wrong before the night was over.

"Hello." Meg snapped her fingers in Joe's face. "You're supposed to be gazing into my eyes. You look like you're somewhere else."

"I'm sorry." Joe smiled at her. Looking at Meg with her long brunette wig, large Gypsy earrings and flowing dress, he felt as if he were dancing with Medea herself.

"May I cut in?" a young heavy-set man dressed as a hunchback asked. Joe looked at Meg.

She shook her head. "I'm sorry. I only dance with my partner."

The man turned away.

After a few more minutes of dancing Meg said, "I have to visit the ladies' room." She headed away from the dance floor and Joe followed. "Wait here and behave yourself while I'm gone."

As soon as Meg left, a woman wearing a skeleton costume approached Joe. "Can I have this dance?" she asked, as "You Can Do Magic" began.

"I'm sorry. I'm waiting for someone."

"Joe, it's me, Trish. I saw Meg leave. I want to talk to you."

"Trish? What are you doing here?"

"Shhh," Trish glanced around the room. "I don't want anyone here to know it's me. Not yet. What's going on with the ring?"

"Meg and Marcus are going to have a meeting here soon. They're supposed to be compromising. He has the ring and Meg has the spells in her subconscious, but I'm worried."

"I've got to talk fast, before Meg returns. I have some important information to tell you about Marcus."

Joe spotted Meg walking toward them. "Meg's coming."

Trish slowly slipped away and tried to lose herself in the crowd.

"Who was that woman you were talking to?" Meg asked.

I hope Meg doesn't go looking for her and find out it's Trish. She'll know I was lying. "I didn't get her name."

"What did she say?" Meg cocked her head. "What did she want?"

"She asked me to dance, and I used the same line on her that you used."

Meg squinted. "I only dance with my partner?"

"Yeah, but she wouldn't take no for an answer."

"Are you sure it wasn't someone you know?"

Joe winked at her. "Forget about her. Let's dance."

They made their way back onto the dance floor and started to move to "Witchy Woman."

As they danced, Joe noticed a man on the stage in a red devil's costume. He was looking at Joe and motioning to him.

"Meg, look up there on the edge of the stage. It's Marcus, signaling to us."

Marcus got down from the stage and headed for the door. He turned and pointed out of the room.

"It's that time, Joe," Meg said.

As they walked toward the exit, Joe started to sweat. When they got to the office, there were no people in the area and the door was cracked. Meg peeked in.

Seeing Marcus and Circe inside, she asked them, "Who's going to be in this meeting?"

"Just the three of us."

"Joe's coming in as well."

Marcus scowled. "Okay, bring him in."

Joe entered behind Meg. Circe sat on a chair across from the desk as Marcus locked the door.

Meg turned toward Marcus. "Let me see the ring."

He raised his left hand displaying the ring on his finger. "As I said, I need you and you need me."

Meg glared at him. "You mean you need me."

"But I possess the ring, my dear."

"Yeah, you stole it. So what compromise are you willing to make?"

"None until I get a few of the ring spells."

"What?" Meg glared at him with hands on her hips. "I'm not giving you shit before we have an agreement."

Marcus looked at Circe and she rose.

"Obey," Circe said to Meg and snapped her fingers.

Joe watched in horror as Meg's eyes instantly closed.

Marcus laughed. "Joe, you look surprised. You see, Circe put a posthypnotic suggestion in Meg's mind that she would go under with the word 'obey' and a finger snap. That's something you missed the other night."

Marcus turned to Circe. "Send her back now. I need some spells for this ring."

Joe felt once again that this ring was playing into his possible demise. Feeling an adrenalin high, he was ready to rush Marcus, but with the danger of him wearing the ring Joe held back. He glanced at the door, then jumped up and tried to open it, but it was locked from the inside.

"Going so soon?" Marcus chuckled. "The fun is just beginning. Now Circe, bring Meg back to her former self."

Joe's breathing increased. *What in the hell do I do now?*

Circe stood face-to-face with Meg. "You'll hear my voice and only my voice." As Circe started to take Meg back, Joe yelled, "Meg, don't listen to her. Snap out of it!" Joe snapped his fingers, but nothing happened.

Circe continued her suggestions without breaking stride. Joe stepped in and tapped Meg's face. "Meg, come out of it, please!"

Marcus laughed. "Joe, Meg can't hear or feel you. Circe gave her the command, remember?"

"Medea," Circe said, "this is Circe, your sister spirit from the year 1992. Your reincarnated self and I need ring spells which will destroy our enemies. Can you help us, please?"

"Yes, sister spirit," Meg said softly.

Oh my God! What are they up to? Joe went to the door and pounded, hoping someone would hear him.

"This office is soundproof, Joe," Marcus said. "Save your strength."

Joe stopped and turned toward Meg and Circe when Circe said, "Medea, tell us how we can kill people with this ring?"

They are planning to kill us!

Meg said, "After a person dies, the ring can also make the body disappear."

Sixteen

Fulfillment of the Prophecy

"Medea," Circe said leaning closer, "how can we kill someone with the ring?"

"The ring is meant for casting spells, curses, and raising demons. You cannot directly kill a person using the ring, but when they are dead, the ring will make the body vanish, permanently."

Marcus pointed at Meg. "Get that spell from her, Circe."

Circe leaned near Meg again. "Medea, explain how we can make the bodies of our enemies vanish."

"You must spin counter clockwise three times, point the ring at the body and say the words Oma, Loma, Lepto, Nuero, Delisptous."

"Circe, get a pen and paper and write that down," Marcus said.

Oh my God! Meg's giving them the spell that will get rid of us for good. Listening to the wind howl, Joe's heart pounded as his mind raced through his options.

Circe picked up a pen and tablet off the desk and repeated the words back to Meg.

"Ay, that is the spell. Remember to point the ring at the body and say those words, 'tis all."

Joe closed his eyes and shook his head. *Let's make sure they've got it straight so they don't have any difficulty getting rid of us.*

Circe turned to Marcus with a smile. Joe felt Meg, as Medea, had sealed both their fates. He knew at least Marcus couldn't kill him with the ring, but did he have a knife or a gun somewhere in the office?

Joe started pounding on the door again, then slammed the door with his body a couple of times.

"Ask her for three or four of the ring's biggest spells and hurry before someone comes looking for us," Marcus said.

Meg gave Circe several spells, a curse, and finally, a demon-raising incantation which Marcus jotted down. While Joe yelled and pounded on the door, he wondered if Marcus was right as no one came to his aid.

"Bring Meg, too," Marcus said, standing next to his desk. "There's a very annoying pest I want to get rid of." He looked toward Joe at the door.

All Joe could do was tremble.

"Medea," Circe said, "it's time for you to go back to your future self."

As Circe started to bring Medea out of the trance, Joe felt he was going to die anyway, so he rushed Marcus with a swing. As if expecting it, Marcus blocked his punch with his left hand. Sparks flew when Joe made contact with the ring and the next thing he knew he was lying on the floor.

"Circe, keep going, bring her too. I want to dispose of them together."

Circe turned back to Meg. "On the count of three you'll wake up, feeling refreshed. One, two, three."

Joe picked himself up off the floor as Meg opened her eyes.

"Well, Meg," Marcus said, "you helped us out a lot while you were Medea. I know how to get rid of you and Joe without a trace."

Circe placed both hands on Marcus's shoulders. "But Marcus, if you kill Meg you won't be able to get any more ring spells."

"I'm afraid that's all the magic we're going to get from Meg. She and Victoria are too dangerous now that they know we double-crossed them. She and Joe both have to go now."

"I know not what you are saying." Meg's eyes searched the room. "Where am I?"

Joe took a deep breath. "Marcus is going to use those ring spells you gave Circe to kill us."

Meg stared at Marcus. "So you tricked me into giving you spells to destroy me? You are a Cyrus, are ye not?"

"Yes, I am a descendant of Nathon Cyrus, but how did you know?"

"Save for your beard, you are his twin."

"You're descended from Nathon?" Circe asked.

Joe noticed that without the beard, Marcus did resemble the man in the painting he saw in Fenton's home.

Marcus frowned. "After all the years that you've known me, why is it you just now noticed the resemblance?"

"I have ne'r seen you before, but I did meet Nathon. The night he did murder me."

Marcus looked at Circe. "Are you sure you brought Meg all the way out of the trance?"

"Meg is just having a little fun with us," Circe stammered.

Joe's heart pounded. *Is this an act to scare Marcus and Circe, or could Meg still be Medea?*

"When I did curse Nathon, I told him my deliverer would bear my face. Do you possess a looking glass?" Meg asked.

Marcus and Circe stared at her without a word.

"There's a mirror on the other side of that door." Joe pointed to the closet.

Marcus smiled as Meg opened the door. "This is becoming amusing."

Meg looked at her reflection with her long wig and eighteenth century clothes. She slowly smiled. "Ay, I have not changed from my former self."

Her head snapped to Marcus as if the pieces were coming together. She glared at Circe. "I know not what game you play with my soul, sister spirit, but I do know I have come to this time in 1992 for a purpose."

"Put her under again," Marcus ordered.

"Obey," Circe shouted and snapped her fingers, but Meg continued to stare at her. "It's not working, Marcus."

"That proves she is Medea," Joe said, hoping this would somehow thwart his and Meg's demise.

Circe grabbed Marcus's arm. "Joe's right. This is Medea."

Marcus turned to Circe. "How could she be?"

"When Joe attacked you, I was interrupted. I must have forgotten to bring Meg back to her present self. Instead, I brought her to as Medea." Circe looked at Medea. "We have no vendetta with you. You don't belong in this time. I'm going to send you back to your own time now."

"Don't let her do it," Joe said. "They tricked you once. You can't trust them. They want to kill us both so they can use the ring without opposition."

"'Tis madness!" Medea whispered, gazing at Circe. "Meeting my sister spirit is not a pleasant one. You keep poor company. 'Tis destiny that hath brought me here to see that my curse is fulfilled." Medea glared at Marcus and slowly approached him.

Fear registered on his face seeing the vengeful look of madness in Medea's dark eyes. He opened the desk drawer and pulled out a pistol. Medea stopped and peered at the weapon.

"You're going to force me to kill you as Medea. This will be the second time that you're killed by a Cyrus, but this time a Cyrus does have the ring."

Joe swallowed hard. *My God! This is the end of our lives.*

Medea said some words in Latin and the ring sparked. Marcus yelled then dropped the gun behind him and shook his hand.

Yes!

Medea said more words. Marcus screamed and threw the ring off, which landed under his desk.

Amazing.

Circe headed for the gun, but Joe grabbed her from behind, holding her in a bear hug.

As Joe held the squirming young woman, he remembered Meg had a strong grip from her massage training. "Medea, you have strength in your hands. Use your hands to stop him."

Marcus turned and headed for the gun. Medea went after him, squeezing her hands into fists. When Marcus bent down to pick up the gun, Medea wrapped her hands around his throat from behind. He began to gag. Marcus grabbed her hands trying desperately to release her grip. He tried pulling on her forearms, but with her standing behind him it was impossible to get free from her vise-like grip.

Suddenly, Circe stomped on Joe's foot. He let out a groan, then tightened his hold on her.

"Let me go!" Circe yelled. "She's going to kill him."

Medea whispered in Marcus's ear, "Just as I was strangled to death by your ancestor, now 'tis you who will succumb from strangulation."

Holding onto Medea's hands with a grimace, Marcus whipped his body hard to the right trying to throw her off balance. They both fell on the floor and Medea's grip was broken. As Marcus crawled to where the gun was laying, Medea whispered something then pointed at him as he reached for the gun. He froze in place. Joe could tell by the panic in Marcus's eyes that he couldn't move.

If Meg kills Marcus, I might be an accomplice, but if she doesn't, he'll shoot us both. I'd tell Meg to grab the gun, but with her being Medea she won't know how to use it.

Joe watched as Medea scurried to the desk, bent down and fished out the ring. She placed it on her index finger and stood glancing around the room at the others. "Yes, I have the ring once more." Marcus gazed up at her from the floor. Medea pointed at him and whispered more indecipherable words. Marcus slowly raised his hand and rubbed his throat with a cough. Circe stopped struggling and Joe let her go.

"It took me a quarter of a millennium to see my time of revenge." Medea turned to look at Marcus sitting on the floor, fear etched on his face. "My curse is on you Marcus, descendant of Nathon Cyrus."

Marcus picked up the nearby gun, turned and pointed it at Medea. The firearm had a silencer attached to it. "You should have gone after the gun instead of the ring, Medea. You're going to die before you can deliver your curse."

Medea pointed the ring at him.

Joe perspired profusely. *Now he's going to kill us both.*

The gun went off with a muffled sound. Joe waited for Meg to drop, but Marcus let out a moan instead and fell to his side on the floor. Blood from his chest soaked his red costume.

What the hell just happened?

"What did you do to him?" Circe screamed, holding her face with both hands.

Medea turned to face Joe and Circe. "I used the ring's magic. If you attempt to kill the person wearing this ring with it pointed at you, you suffer their fate. Marcus was wounded in the heart from his own gun. He will die shortly, if he is not dead already." Medea folded her arms. "My prophecy is fulfilled."

"No!" Circe yelled running to Marcus's lifeless body. She examined him and put her hands to her eyes and cried. She turned to Medea. "You will be executed for murdering him."

"Circe," Joe said, "she killed him in self-defense. Her fingerprints aren't even on the gun."

"There will be no body to prove that I killed him." Medea turned around three times then pointed the ring at Marcus's body. "Oma, Loma, Lepto, Nuero, Delisptous."

The body instantly vanished along with the blood that was on the rug. Although Joe was relieved that Marcus was gone, he wondered what Medea might do to him with the ring.

Medea looked at them. "You are surprised?"

"Yes," Joe said then froze.

"Who are you that hath befriended me?"

"I'm Joe or Joseph, a friend of Megan's, your reincarnated self in this time."

"Are we betrothed?"

"Well, yes. What should we do with this traitor?" Joe looked at Circe.

"He's not betrothed to Megan," Circe said. "Tell her your last name Joe. I'm sure she'll be interested."

She's going to tell Medea I'm a Hillery.

"Joe's ancestor is also an arch enemy of your family, Medea. His last name is Hillery. He's descended from the judge who burned your mother alive." Circe smiled at Joe.

"That's a lie, Medea. You can't trust this woman. She was on the side of Marcus."

"I'll prove it." Circe snatched the wallet out of Joe's pocket.

"Hey, give me my wallet!" Joe went for her, but Circe had Joe's driver's license out and showed it to Medea. "This is our identification in this time." She pointed to Joe's name. "See, *Joseph Hillery*."

Medea examined the name closely. "'Tis true." She turned and glared at Joe. "You are a Hillery."

Circe glanced at Joe. "You have to destroy him."

Joe held his hands up. "Okay, I'm a Hillery, but I'm in love with Megan. We both feel our pasts don't matter."

"But I have just killed a man because of the past. It doth matter." Medea cast a glare on Joe that made him shiver.

"You can put her under now, Circe, and bring Meg back."

"I have decided to kill you both." She glanced from Joe to Circe.

"But you can't kill with the ring, and we're not going to try and kill you," Joe said.

She picked up the gun. "I'll use this weapon and then use the ring to make you both disappear just like Marcus." Medea picked up the gun and examined it.

"Please have mercy on a fellow witch, Medea," Circe pleaded. "Don't kill me."

"I shall kill him first." Medea pointed the barrel of the pistol directly at Joe.

Our Father who art in Heaven...

Seventeen
Joe's Plan for Revenge

Joe waited for the bullet that would end his life. Instead, there was a knock on the office door.

If I could just open the door, Medea might not pull the trigger because there would be a witness.

No one in the room spoke or moved a muscle as Medea continued to point the gun barrel at Joe. Then came the sound of the door being unlocked. Trish walked in without her mask.

She froze when she saw the gun in Meg's hand. "Meg, what are you doing?"

"I am Medea. I am going to kill this Hillery descendant and this untrustworthy witch." Medea pointed the gun at Trish. "Close the door."

Trish's eyes widened. "You're going to kill me too?" Trish took a step toward the door.

"Yes. You should not have entered this room."

When Medea pointed the pistol at Joe again, Trish darted out of the room and ran around the corner yelling. "Help! Help! Someone is going to be murdered."

"Now people will come and you'll go to the gallows, Medea," Circe said.

Panic registered on Medea's face. She lowered the gun and headed for the door. Just as she went through, Joe tackled her legs as if he were playing football. As she fell to the floor, the gun dislodged from her hand. She turned and scratched Joe's face.

"Circe, get the gun!" Joe yelled.

The young witch picked the gun up off the floor while Joe held Medea in place.

Joe let her go. "Keep her covered. I'm going for Trish." He left the room and soon reentered with the red-head in tow.

"I yelled to make Medea panic, but there's no one around. Now what do we tell people if someone did hear me?"

"I'll think of something. Circe, give me the gun." She handed it over to him. Joe looked at Medea. "Give me the ring."

She peered into his eyes. "Shoot me if you must, but I shan't give you my ring."

"Joe, you'd better not shoot her; you saw what happened to Marcus," Circe said.

"What I want you two ladies to do is force her hand down so she can't point the ring at me."

"But you'll also be killing Megan," Trish said.

Medea smiled. "You won't shoot me then."

"Do you think you two girls could force the ring off her finger if I keep the gun on her? Then we'll have to get Meg back or we'll have to answer a lot more questions besides where Marcus is."

"Where is Marcus?" Trish asked.

"Medea killed him using the ring, then she made his body vanish."

Trish went for the ring on Medea's index finger.

"Don't do it by yourself!" Joe yelled.

Before Joe could finish, sparks flew and Trish lost her balance and landed on the floor. Medea laughed.

"I was trying to warn you about the ring's protective force. It's better if you and Circe do it together."

"I felt the burn of that ring the night we found it," Circe said. "But we have no choice."

"As bad as the pain might be, you both have to grab her finger at the same time and pull it off together."

Medea clenched her fingers closed, but both women slowly opened her hand. When they made contact with the ring they yelled and quickly let go.

"I see I'm going to have to help you," Joe said.

"But who's going to hold the gun?" Trish asked.

"Just grab her." The two women held the struggling Medea as Joe shoved the gun in his pocket and tried opening her hand again. Medea let out a shrill screech as all three pulled on the ring together. They yelled out in pain but were able to remove the ring. Medea cursed them as she made a break for the door. Joe had the gun out of his pocket and fired a warning shot just over her head. Medea stopped in her tracks then turned toward him wide-eyed.

Standing just out of the room, she looked at Joe. "Now you will send me to the gallows."

"No Medea," Joe said. "You're not going to the gallows."

Medea reentered the room. "Will I be spared?"

"To escape death, Circe is going to send you back to your own time."

"You must listen to me to save yourself," Circe whispered to her. "I have to put you back in a trance and bring your future self back into this body."

"Ay, my prophecy hath been fulfilled, but what will happen to Megan?"

"Because it was not Megan who killed Marcus and attempted to shoot Joe," Circe said, "we will not tell the authorities the truth of what happened here tonight."

"Are you ready to go back?" Trish asked.

"Ay, I have no choice in the matter."

"Medea, sit here." Circe pulled out a chair for her. She glanced at Joe. "When I'm finished, promise me you will protect me against Meg."

Joe closed the office door. "No promises after what you pulled, Circe. Take her back before someone comes to the door."

Circe put Medea under in a few seconds. "You see the year 1969. You enter it and are born. The next year you see is 1992. You stop there. You are now twenty-three. Do you know your name?"

"Megan O'Leary," Meg said softly.

"Good. Now on the count of three you will wake up and remember nothing of what has transpired. One, two, three."

Meg opened her eyes. "What happened? The last thing I remember I was talking to Marcus."

"Circe put you under," Joe said.

Meg looked around the room. "Trish, I'm so glad to see you, but what are you doing here? And where is Marcus?"

Joe shook his head. "It's a long story."

Explaining to her what had just taken place, Joe's mouth became dry. He closed his eyes and paused to take a deep breath as he told her how she had almost killed him. Meg touched his shoulder trying to calm him.

"After you killed Marcus, you made his body disappear over there." Joe pointed to the spot.

Her eyes widened. "After I killed him I made him disappear?"

"Not you. Medea. She pointed the ring at him and it made the gun backfire."

Meg looked to where the body had fallen. "I don't even see a single drop of blood."

"With the ring, Medea made everything disappear."

"I never knew you could kill someone with the ring."

"Only if the person is trying to kill you. It's like a defense mechanism."

"Where is the ring now?"

If Circe hadn't been a witness I could tell her the ring somehow disappeared with Marcus. Joe reached into his pocket. "Right here."

"What a relief." Meg fell into his arms.

Trish looked at her watch. "It's almost eleven-thirty. That means everyone is in the second ritual. That's why no one heard my screams."

Meg glared at Circe. "A word of advice. If you tell anyone what happened here tonight, zap! Do you understand me?"

"Yes, Meg," Circe gasped. "I swear I won't tell a soul what happened to Marcus."

Meg looked from Circe to Joe to Trish. "Our story is that Marcus and I had an agreement. He walked out that door and none of us have seen him since."

"The others won't believe you, Meg," Trish said. "Not with you having the ring."

"That is our story," Meg said firmly. "Unless anyone can think of a better explanation."

Joe shook his head, knowing how lame that story sounded, but what else could they say?

"One more thing." Joe looked at Circe. "Before we leave this room take off that post-hypnotic suggestion from Meg's mind."

Meg glanced at Joe. "What are you talking about?"

"When Circe snapped her fingers and said "obey," you immediately went under."

Meg glared at Circe.

"Fine, I'll remove it, but I'm going to have to put you under again to erase it, Meg."

Joe listened carefully to Circe's hypnotic instructions.

When Meg came to, Joe said, "Try the suggestion now."

"Obey," Circe said and snapped her fingers.

Meg didn't even blink this time.

"You're cured." Joe blew out a breath in relief then folded a piece of paper and placed it in his pocket. "We'd better keep this paper. It has the disappearing spell written on it."

"Now, Trish, what are you doing here?" Meg asked again.

"I called Joe to see what was going on. We've been communicating on the phone for a while. When he told me that you and he were going to meet Marcus, I felt I had to come out of hiding to see what I could do for you. Marcus is extremely dangerous. I'm actually glad he's gone." Trish looked at Circe. "Please don't tell the others in the coven that I was here. I'll reveal myself at the right time."

Joe glanced at Trish. "You can't trust Circe."

"If any of the others do find out that Trish was here, zap." Meg gave Circe another threatening gaze. "And don't think I won't. For betraying me, I feel you should be punished somehow."

Circe raised her hands as if surrendering. "I promise I won't tell anyone what happened here. I'll give them the story we agreed on, Meg."

Meg kept her eyes on Circe.

"Trish, I can't thank you enough for coming into this office." Joe gave her a hug. "You saved my life."

"I'm just happy my timing was right, Joe. You didn't deserve any of this." Trish shot Meg a look.

As they all left the office, Joe and Meg separated from the others.

"Let's go home," Meg said, putting her hand to her forehead.

Heading for the front door, they passed a few people lingering in the hall. Outside, strong winds buffeted the small crowd gathered near the porch. Joe grabbed his hat as a gust took Meg's wig and sent it soaring into the air.

"There goes my hair. Let's get to the car before the wind blows us away."

As soon as they were in, Meg said, "Joe, give me the ring."

He had no choice but to hand it to her.

On the drive back to Manchester, Meg lay back on the armrest facing him. "See, I told you grandma's spell would work." She gazed at the ring on her index finger. "Even if I were given a lie detector test about Marcus I'd pass, because I don't remember killing him. Medea did us a big favor."

Joe nodded. *I still can't get the picture out of my mind. Meg holding that gun on me, even though it wasn't actually her. And I didn't enjoy being a witness to a murder, no matter what kind of a person Marcus was.* "I'm worried about Circe spilling the beans to her friends. She was really upset when you, or Medea, killed Marcus."

"I think wearing the ring will keep her in check. And I'll know if she tells someone."

"How will you know?"

Meg took her feet off Joe's lap and sat up in the seat. "I'm going to level with you. I owe you that after all you've done for me tonight, including almost being murdered by Marcus and by me as Medea. Remember the night you came home late? As soon as I looked into your eyes I knew that you had my love spell removed."

Oh, my, God! She knew all the time. Joe took a deep breath and glanced at her not sure what to say.

"I only pretended not to know to keep you with me."

Joe turned to glare at her. "Wasn't that self-centered of you to destroy my marriage then put me in danger just because you needed someone?"

"Yes, and you can leave whenever you want."

"And go where? My personal life is in shambles. My son told me Ellen's having an affair with a friend of mine."

"Oh, Joe." Meg leaned near and took his hand. Joe pulled it away.

Neither said another word all the way back to Meg's apartment. When they got inside, Meg sat on the couch and Joe in the lounge chair across from her.

Joe gave her a sobering look. "Why did you put a love spell on me to begin with?"

She looked at him. "You haven't figured that out?"

Joe leaned forward in the chair with a frown. "I have, but I'd like to hear it from you."

She nervously twirled her thumbs. "I wanted to find the ring before Marcus did. Luna had a vision—"

"I know all about her damn vision of me."

Meg made a sad face. "You probably hate me."

I'm not answering that. Let her wonder.

Meg frowned. "So, what are you going to do now?"

"Do you want me to move out of your apartment?"

"No. I've grown rather fond of you."

"Gee, thanks," he said sarcastically. "I'll let you know what I'm doing tomorrow. I need some sleep so I can get the picture of Marcus's murder out of my head and you pointing that loaded pistol at me."

"It wasn't me, Joe. It was Medea. Circe is more responsible than I am since she's the one that put me under."

"Since we've stopped pretending, I'll sleep on the couch tonight."

Meg brought Joe a pillow and blanket. "I want to thank you for telling Circe to take that suggestion out of my mind."

"No problem." Joe lay back on the couch.

"She could have had the ring at any time if you hadn't thought of that. In fact if you hadn't been here, I'd be dead right now."

"You're welcome. Now let me get some sleep."

"I've decided that tomorrow night at the Samhain Sabbat I'm going to let everyone know about the ring and who I was. I'll probably be crowned queen of the witches."

"I know your ego is all that's important to you, but don't you think that's a little premature considering Marcus just went missing?"

Meg paused as if considering Joe's remark. "Goodnight, Joe." She left the room.

After a couple of hours, Joe was awaken with the sound of Victoria's chants again. She grew louder as she spoke. A passion grew in her speech, almost as if she were yelling. "I curse thee. I curse thee and thou shalt never be heard from again."

Marcus is already dead. Does the old woman know it? Or is this incantation meant for me?

~ * ~

At breakfast, Meg asked, "Joe, would you consider going with me to the Samhain Sabbat tonight?"

Joe's spoon stopped just in front of his mouth as he peered at her. "Why would I?"

"After all we've been through to get the ring, you're not curious to see the response of the entire witch community in New England?"

"No. And I hope I never see another witch." Joe took a bite of his cereal.

"So when are you leaving?" She squinted at him.

He looked up. "You're throwing me out?"

"No. I just assumed by your attitude that you were leaving."

"Give me a couple of days to find an apartment."

"Joe, I meant what I said last night."

"About being sorry for ruining my life?"

Meg cocked her head. "About staying here with me."

Avoiding her eyes, Joe toyed with his cereal.

"You're confused right now," Meg said. "Come with me to the sabbat and tomorrow we'll worry about whether you're staying or leaving."

Joe looked at Meg. "You're such a good actress. I never know when you're being sincere. You should have been on stage."

Meg raised her right hand.

"And don't give me that witches' honor stuff," Joe said. "I've had enough of that, too."

Meg's hand remained raised. "If you'd let me finish I was about to say I swear on my mother's grave I'm not acting." Meg turned her face away from him.

Is she actually going to cry? "I think I do deserve some credit for the ring being here."

Meg turned back with red eyes. "You deserve most of it."

"But it was your idea that led us to find the ring and you knew where Medea was buried."

"If you hadn't shown up to see Luna in the first place, or listened at the office door to find out I was Medea, no one would have looked for the ring. Last night you not only saved it, but both of our lives as well. You're my hero." Meg gave him a beautiful smile.

Looking into those brown eyes of hers I feel like I'm going under another one of her spells. Is it just because I've lost Ellen? Fenton said Meg would be unable to cast another love spell on me. "All right, I'll go with you tonight, but it's only because I'm curious to see what happens."

"Oh, Joe, thank you." Meg leaned across the table to give him a hug, but sat back down as if reconsidering. "Besides Grandma, you're the only person in the world that I can trust."

She seems sincere, but I can't let my guard down.

"It's hard to believe Marcus was Nathon's descendant," Meg said. "That means that through our descendants we were enemies the entire time I knew him."

Joe nodded, knowing his and Meg's ancestors were also enemies.

Joe dropped Meg off at the book store and drove to his office in Willstown. After taking care of some paperwork, he phoned Fenton.

"Did you know Marcus Phillips was also a descendant of Nathon Cyrus?"

"No," Fenton said. "I thought I was the last Cyrus. I guess Nathon's bloodline could continue through Marcus if he gets one of his lady friends pregnant."

"He won't." Joe explained what had transpired the night before.

"Being in the middle of a black witches' power struggle of that magnitude, you're lucky to be alive, Joe. I knew something like this would happen once the black witches found that ring. Murders and destruction will continue and even escalate as long as Meg or one of them owns it. Someone is going to have to steal the ring after all. And it'll have to be done today before every witch in the area sees it on Meg's finger."

"But who's going to steal it?" Joe asked.

"Does she take it off her finger?"

"Yes. She's wearing it on a necklace for now, but it's hidden under her top. She's going to put it on her finger in dramatic fashion in front of her witch peers tonight."

"We have to steal it today. Where is Meg now?"

"At the Bell, Book and Candle, the bookstore in Manchester where she works."

"How long will she be there?" Fenton asked.

"I'm picking her up at one."

"That only gives us about three hours to get to the store and steal the ring."

"But who's going to steal it?"

"I am, but I'll need Brad's help."

"Being a Cyrus, you're putting yourself in danger. I hoped you were finally safe when Marcus ended up being the wild card for the curse. Meg has incredible insight into things like this. She knew I had her spell removed."

"Good, then you don't have to stay with her. I'm sure Ellen will be happy to have you back."

Those words made Joe's blood flow with sadness then anger.

"It's worth the risk for me," Fenton said. "I'd rather lose my life than let the ring stay in the wrong hands and know I did nothing to stop it."

"I see I can't talk you out of this, but please be careful."

"I'll call Brad now. We'll hide in the bookstore stockroom. When Meg enters, one of us will grab her while the other lifts her necklace."

"The stockroom doors are locked on the outside. You'll either have to slip in from the front door of the store or go in through the window."

"I'll need you to be at the store yourself to make sure Meg goes into the stockroom alone."

"I'll head over there now." As Joe left his office, he told his receptionist he'd be out for the rest of the day.

Joe drove south to Manchester with his mind in turmoil. Was Meg sincere about him staying with her? Did he have real feelings for her, or was it only the trauma of losing his wife? Just having Meg with him to talk to the last couple of days kept him from breaking down, but could he trust her? Could there be any future with a witch?

Hey, this might be the perfect opportunity to fix that snake in the grass, Brad. If I don't get him now, I might never get the chance again. Just the thought of Brad having Ellen and Meg's ring, too, makes me furious.

However, Joe wasn't sure he should spoil their plan. Was it that Meg might connect him with the plot or that he wanted to protect Fenton? Or could it be that getting the ring from Meg was the right thing to do? *I don't care. I'm going to make sure Brad pays for what he did to me, but I've got to keep Fenton from danger.*

Eighteen

Samhain

Joe arrived at the Bell, Book and Candle bookstore just before eleven-thirty.

Meg spotted him and cocked her head with a smile as she approached him. "Joe, what are you doing here so early?"

"I want to check out a couple of books before we leave, then I'll buy you lunch."

"That's a pleasant change."

Joe forced a smile. "I know tonight's a big night for you and I wanted to show you my support."

Meg smiled, laying a hand on his arm. "I see a customer at the counter."

She left and Joe pretended to be looking at books, wondering if the dynamic duo was already in the stockroom.

I'll get Brad for what he did to me. When Meg goes in that storeroom, I'll foil their plan.

Meg walked over to Joe. "Look who's here."

He turned to see Circe looking at books along the wall. "What's she doing here?"

"I don't know, but she makes me nervous," Meg whispered.

Did Luna send her to steal the ring from Meg? Will she interfere with my plan?

"Is there somewhere we can talk in private?" Joe asked, hoping she'd take him into the stockroom.

She nodded. "Let's go into the stockroom."

Perfect. Joe followed her, lagging slightly behind so that Brad and Fenton would think she was going in alone.

As soon as Meg was through the swinging door, Brad sprang out and grabbed her. Fenton came at her from the side. The old man reached into her smock and lifted the necklace, trying to get it over her head, just as Joe entered.

Meg struggled with the two men. "Help, Joe!"

Joe grabbed Brad from behind and pulled him off as Meg jammed her elbow into Fenton's ribs. He let out a gasp. While Brad struggled to get free from Joe's hold, Meg sent a second elbow into the old man's side. Fenton went down to his knees with a cough, holding his mid-section. Meg opened the closet door as Brad threw Joe off.

"Joe, get him in here," Meg yelled as Brad bent down to help Fenton to his feet.

Joe and Meg together shoved Brad from the side. He fell halfway into the closet. They pushed his legs in and Meg tried to close the door, but Brad stuck his hand out to block it. The door closed on his wrist and Brad yelled in pain, pulling his hand back. Meg slammed the door shut and locked it.

Fenton tried to crawl out of the room, but Joe grabbed him and held him on the floor.

The manager, Sherman, entered the room. "What's going on in here?"

"A couple of thieves tried to steal a necklace from me," Meg said. "One is locked in the closet and Joe has the other one." Meg pointed at Fenton.

"Good heavens! I'll phone the police," Sherman said.

"No. I'll handle this my way."

"But Meg—"

Meg raised her voice. "Trust me, Sherman, and tell Circe to come in here."

"Meg, you are so stubborn." Sherman left shaking his head.

Meg looked at Joe. "Hold onto to that old man. I want to question him and the other guy one at a time."

The clicking sound of Brad trying to open the door could be heard amid the pounding.

Circe entered the stock room. "Where is that noise coming from?" She looked down at Joe holding Fenton. "What's he doing?"

"I was attacked by two men. My ring was almost stolen from me, again." Meg gave Circe a piercing gaze. "Surprised?"

"Meg, you don't think I had anything to do with this? I don't even know where you're keeping the ring."

Meg glanced at Joe. "Let him go, but block the entrance."

Joe got up and headed for the door. Fenton slowly stood.

Meg glared at him. "Just tell me who sent you and how you knew where my ring was and I'll let you go."

Fenton looked toward the floor without a word.

"If you want to play deaf and dumb, we'll do this the hard way." Meg turned toward Circe. "Are you going to deny that you sent these men to steal my ring?"

"Meg, I didn't. I'm as anxious to find out who they are as you."

"Then why did you just conveniently show up here today?"

"Think about it; Joe's the only one who knows where you're keeping the ring."

From the door Joe said, "Your friends didn't have any trouble finding the ring when it was in my office, did they?"

"Meg, the reason I came here was to let you know that Luna and Paula both asked me where Marcus was."

"And what did you tell them?"

"Exactly what you told us to say last night, that you and Marcus made a secret agreement. Marcus gave you the ring and left the room. I don't think Luna believes me. But even if they're not wise now, when Marcus doesn't show up for the sabbat tonight there will be more questions. They'll suspect foul play."

Meg stood staring at Circe as if considering her story, then turned her gaze to Fenton. "I'm going to make this old guy talk one way or another."

If Fenton talks, he'll tell them I'm involved. By the stockroom door, Joe nervously shifted his weight from one foot to the other as he watched Meg search Fenton's pants for some ID. "He doesn't even have a wallet on him. Very clever."

Joe breathed a sigh of relief. *How can I help Fenton escape and put Brad in the hot seat?*

Brad continued pounding on the door and yelling, "Let me out!"

With arms folded, Meg glanced at Circe. "Bring that chair over here."

Circe picked up the chair next to a small desk and set it behind Fenton.

Meg shoved him in. "Hold him while I persuade him to talk."

Joe watched Circe wrap her slender arms around Fenton from the side as Meg came up behind him. Brad kicked at the door as he continued to yell and pound.

Sherman returned. "Meg, I'm going to have to call the police. The man in the closet is making so much noise he's scaring our customers away."

"Sherman, just give me five minutes and I'll call the police. I have to find out who sent them here."

"Okay, Meg, five minutes, but then I'm calling the authorities." Sherman scurried out of the room.

Meg began to massage Fenton's shoulders then leaning near him, she said, "Have you ever had a massage?"

Meg's going to torture Fenton. What can I do to help him that won't give me away?

Fenton didn't answer, but looked toward the floor again.

"So much can be accomplished with a good massage and even more with a bad one." Meg raised her voice at the end of the sentence. "I'm going to do deep tissue work on you, Grandpa." Meg started to increase pressure and the old man cringed. "You tell me what I want to know and no more massage. You get stubborn and my massage becomes deeper." Meg increased pressure and Fenton gasped in pain.

This is not going the way I planned. I have to get Fenton out of this torture. He may even tell Meg I'm involved.

"I've only got four minutes left, old man. Now who sent you?" Meg squeezed Fenton's neck hard with both hands. He closed his eyes with a moan. Tears ran down his face.

Joe knew it was only a matter of time before Fenton would spill the beans.

As Meg continued, Fenton grimaced. "Stop, I'll talk."

Meg let up on the pressure. "You're finally becoming logical."

Oh, my God. Here it comes.

"Circe told me to come here to steal your ring."

Joe wiped his brow in relief.

Meg turned and glared at her. "I knew it was you."

Circe let Fenton go and backed away. "Meg, I swear I never saw this guy before."

Meg put pressure on Fenton's shoulders again. "If I find out you're lying to me, you'll wish you'd never been born." She let him go, and turned to Circe. "You'd better tell me everything, or zap."

"I'll say it again, I don't know this man. Witches' honor." She placed two fingers against her forehead.

Still sitting in the chair, Fenton rubbed his sore shoulders and squinted at Joe as if trying to figure out what his game was.

"I've got to keep both of these men locked up until I can question them, but this is the worst damn day this could have happened with having to get ready for Samhain tonight. Where can I keep them where they won't disturb the customers?"

"Sherman's going to be calling the police any time now," Joe said.

Meg pinched the bridge of her nose and closed her eyes.

"I've got it," Circe said. "I'll hypnotize the men. We can keep them both in that closet all night and neither will make a sound until you can question them in the morning. And with them being in a trance you'll also get the truth as to who they are and who sent them."

"I guess I have no choice," Meg said.

Joe's mouth went slack. *Oh shit!*

"Since tomorrow is Sunday, there'll be no one in the store. But can you hypnotize them both without their cooperation?"

"I'm the master of hypnosis. I've hypnotized people without their knowing." Circe bent down, putting her face near Fenton's and peering into his eyes as Meg tightened her grip on the old man's shoulders again. Fenton closed his eyes to keep from looking into Circe's dark, slanted, piercing eyes.

Brad stopped pounding momentarily. Joe didn't know if it was because he was listening to what was happening or was just worn out.

"You feel yourself growing sleepy. Your conscious mind is slipping away."

I've got to do something fast.

When Brad started banging on the door again, Joe ran to the closet and blocked that door with his body so the women couldn't see what he was really going to do. He quickly unfastened the latch.

"The guy in the closet is getting out," Joe yelled.

Meg and Circe turned to watch him, as Joe held the door closed with his body. Brad shoved the door hard and Joe let himself be pushed aside. Pretending to be overpowered, Joe flew backward and hit his head on a metal shelving unit then collapsed on the floor. From the floor, Joe watched Brad go to Fenton and pull him out of the chair as he pushed Circe away. When Meg went for his throat, Brad threw her off then put her in a headlock. Fenton tried to run, but Circe put a bear hug around the frail old man, forcing him to the floor. As he tried to pull the young woman off, Brad bent Meg's head down to his thigh.

"Joe, help me!" Meg yelled.

"I'm coming." Trying to avoid helping Meg, Joe pretended to be hurt, shaking his head as he slowly rose. Brad removed his left hand from his right arm to reach beneath Meg's top and pull out the ring. Joe limped toward them. With only Brad's right arm around Meg's throat, she was able to move more freely. She blindly reached up toward Brad's hands, grabbing for the ring. Joe reached Brad just as he had the necklace over Meg's head. Joe and everyone else froze when she jammed her pinky into the ring. Fear registered on Brad's face and a smile came to Meg's.

"Let's get out of here," Brad yelled, dropping his hold on Meg and running to Fenton to help him out of Circe's hold. Meg pointed the ring at them and started a chant. Brad ran through the door with Fenton behind him. Suddenly a bolt of lightning shot out of the ring and struck Fenton in the back. He yelled, arched his back then continued out the door.

Sherman entered the stock room again. "Those two men just ran out of the store. I told you to let me call the police. Are you all right?"

Meg frowned. "I'm just great. I guess I shouldn't have played detective."

"I think we should still call the police," Sherman said.

"No, I don't want the law involved. I'll explain it to you later."

Sherman left the room and Joe asked Meg, "What did you do to that old guy?"

"The ring put a spell on him."

Oh, my God! "What kind of spell?"

"Whatever physical ailment he already has will become worse until it kills him. If he's in good health, he may live for a while."

Joe frowned. "But he's an old man."

Meg smiled at him with a grimace. "Then he'll probably die soon."

"I thought you couldn't kill with the ring."

"Not directly, but you saw how Medea killed Marcus in self-defense, and this spell is also an indirect death sentence."

Fenton's words were coming true. Deaths were happening already. What other destruction would take place because of the ring?

Circe looked at Meg. "How do we know Joe didn't send those men here for your ring?"

Joe stared her down. "I had nothing to do with this."

Meg looked at Circe, then Joe. "I will get to the bottom of this. Joe, you took quite a fall. Are you all right?"

He rubbed the small of his back. "I think so. How about you? That big guy had you in a headlock."

Meg rubbed the back of her neck "Yeah, but I'm fine. If only that guy hadn't broken the door and gotten out we would have had them hypnotized and I could have found out who they were."

Circe walked over to the closet door and examined it. "Meg, there is nothing broken on this door. Maybe Joe let him out."

What do I say now?

Meg looked it over. "Nothing is broken, but he must have pushed it open somehow. Joe, how did you know he was getting out?"

Think fast. "Well, I could see the door moving every time he kicked it. By the time I got there the door flung open. I underestimated his strength. Maybe he's a martial artist."

"Well, he was bigger than you," Meg said.

Circe looked at the door again. "I still say there is no way he could have gotten this door open without breaking it."

"With hard kicks, latches can be sprung without actually breaking them," Joe said.

Meg looked at it again, then at Joe. He began to tremble. *Does she know the truth?*

"I'll see you tonight at the sabbat, Meg." Circe turned and left the room.

Joe took Meg to a drive-through hotdog stand and they ate as he drove. Listening to her talk about the attempted robbery, he wondered again if she suspected him of being involved in the plot.

Why couldn't Meg have cursed Brad with the ring instead of Fenton?

"Do you think that old guy was telling the truth about Circe sending them?" Joe asked, glancing at Meg.

"No. I think she was telling us the truth. It was probably Luna and Paula who are responsible."

Is Meg just saying that to throw me off?

"What time does your sabbat start tonight?"

"Promptly at midnight."

When they got to the apartment Meg said, "You didn't sleep too well last night after all that happened at the parish. Why don't you take a nap on the couch? I'll help you to sleep with a massage."

After watching her work on Fenton, I think I'll pass.

"Thanks, but I don't need a massage to fall asleep." Joe lay on the couch and was asleep in no time.

When he woke he didn't know where he was. It took him a minute to realize he was on Meg's couch. He sat and looked out the living room window noticing the sun was close to setting. The clock said four-thirty. He'd been asleep for over two hours. The apartment was quiet.

"Meg," Joe yelled, but no answer. He was upset for sleeping so long. With Meg gone this was his chance to phone Fenton to explain what happened and warn him about Meg's spell. Joe searched the apartment to make sure she wasn't there.

From the kitchen he called Fenton's home. His butler answered. Joe told him who he was and Fenton picked up the phone. "I wanted to explain what happened at the book store," Joe said.

"You owe both of us an explanation."

"I found out Brad is having an affair with my wife. I'm sorry you were the one they went after."

"Joe, by putting one of us in danger, you put both of us in danger."

"I realized the only way to help you escape was to let Brad out of the closet. But now Meg saw that the closet door wasn't broken, so I think she suspects I let Brad out."

"Your actions created a problem for all of us. If you want to rectify your mistake, you still have about seven hours before the sabbat meeting begins and Meg puts the ring on."

Joe lowered his head and let out a breath. "You're talking about me stealing it from her?"

"Yes. If you can take it from her before she starts wearing it, you'll still be a hero."

Joe placed his hand over one eye. "Yeah, but a dead hero."

"I'm sorry, but Brad and I can't help you now because Meg has seen us. Joe, it's the only way."

"I want to warn you. The lightning bolt that the ring sent after you was a spell."

"Did she tell you what kind of a spell?"

Joe closed his eyes. "Yes. Any health problems you have now will continue to get worse. I'm sure you must have a remedy for that with all the potions you have in your home."

Fenton was silent. "I'll do what I can."

There was a knock on the back door. "Again, I'm sorry for the way things turned out. I'll talk to you tomorrow and let you know what happens at the Samhain ritual tonight."

"Are you going to steal the ring?"

"I'll think about it." Joe hung up the phone and went to the door. *I'll be committing suicide if I do.*

When he opened it he found three costumed kids standing on the porch. "Trick or treat."

What in the hell are they doing here? Joe saw a bowl of candy on the bookcase next to the door. *Halloween. Meg must have left this here while I was asleep.* He placed candy into each bag.

"Someone told us real witches live here," a boy said.

"There are no such things as real witches." Joe smiled at him.

The kids made their way down the back porch stairs. Joe turned on the TV and sat on the couch, waiting for Meg. Soon she came through the front kitchen door.

"Where were you?" Joe asked.

"I was with my secret lover." Meg cocked her head and raised an eyebrow.

Joe frowned.

Meg laughed. "I was downstairs starting dinner. You fell asleep so fast I thought it would be a good time to see Grandma. Are you getting hungry?"

"We're eating at your grandmother's again?"

"Yes." Meg stepped near and squeezed his wrist. "This is our most important holiday, sacred Samhain."

There was another knock on the door. Meg opened it to find more trick-or-treaters. She put a handful of candy in each bag and closed the door. "I don't know why kids come up all these stairs for candy when there are so many other houses."

"I think it's because they know you're a witch."

Meg rolled her eyes. "I'm going down to finish dinner. Join us in about fifteen minutes."

"I heard your grandmother again last night. Her chanting was louder than ever."

"It's just part of being a witch." Meg winked at him and left the apartment.

As Joe sat alone in the living room, he wondered if Meg did know he was involved with the failed theft. *Are Meg and Victoria going to put a spell on me downstairs or maybe curse me?* With that ring, she could do just about anything to him. He wanted to flee the apartment and never return, but she'd probably find him anyway. *I just don't have the courage to steal that ring from Meg. She could have her subconscious tapped by someone at any time and learn all the ring spells. Look what happened to Marcus.*

When Joe entered the downstairs apartment, he found Victoria sitting at the table with the same two old women who helped her put the spell on Marcus.

Joe felt uneasy. "Happy Samhain, ladies."

"And happy Halloween to you, Joe," Victoria said.

Meg walked out of the kitchen carrying a baked pumpkin on a cookie sheet. "Have a seat at the table, Joe." She set the pumpkin in the middle of the table then placed corn on the cob and a baked potato on each plate. She removed the top of the pumpkin and steam rolled out.

Joe frowned. "What are we having for dinner?"

"Dinner in a pumpkin." Meg spooned out a large scoop of the concoction onto each plate.

Joe noticed bits of pumpkin mixed with ground beef, rice, vegetables and mushrooms.

Meg finally sat between Joe and her grandmother.

"Is this a witch's Thanksgiving?" Joe asked.

"Samhain is actually the witches' New Year," Meg said. "Our dinner is called the Samhain harvest feast."

Joe tasted some of the pumpkin filling. He was surprised at its pleasant spicy flavor. "This is delicious, Meg."

"Thank you. It's a very old recipe of Grandma's."

"What's in the sauce?"

"Soy and ginger, mainly. We also use special fresh mushrooms."

"Megan is going to put her ring on in front of everyone at the sabbat tonight," Victoria said with a smile. "She'll be queen of the witches. I would give anything if I could be there to see it for myself."

One of the crones stopped before gnawing on an ear of corn. "I wouldn't be surprised if Megan becomes the most powerful witch of all time, even greater than Diehla or Medea."

Meg smiled. "I'm going to spring it on everyone during the historical part of the ceremony as to who I was and show them the ring as proof. And as I promised I will reward both of you for helping me get the ring back from Marcus."

The other hag said, "I'm happy those two thieves didn't get your ring at the bookstore. When you find out who sent them, we'll help you and your grandmother cast a spell on them too."

Joe shuddered at their words.

Meg stood. "I hope everyone has room for a piece of my pumpkin pie?"

After supper when Joe and Meg were back upstairs, Meg put on soft music and snuggled against him on the couch.

"Hey, Joe." Meg put a finger on his cheek to turn his face toward her. "We don't have to leave for the sabbat for over three hours." She leaned near and kissed him.

"Meg, we're not pretending anymore, remember?" Joe looked into her piercing brown eyes. "Just because I agreed to go to the sabbat with you doesn't mean my feelings have changed since last night."

Without a word, Meg closed her eyes and met his lips. She kissed Joe passionately. At first he was going to pull away, but he suddenly became intoxicated by her.

He took Meg in his arms and started to make love to her when she breathlessly interrupted him. "Joe, let's go into the bedroom."

He followed her in. There were black candles all over the room. Meg lit each one then undressed and put on a sheer black negligee. She approached him, placed her arms around him and kissed him again. With a smile she slipped under the covers.

Joe got in bed and Meg said, "I'm so happy we can be ourselves now without playing games with each other. Did I convince you how much I care about you?"

Joe took her in his arms and kissed her. He made love to Meg like never before. This time she touched him softly and looked into his brown eyes the way Ellen used to.

After the lovemaking, Joe relaxed on the bed, Meg got up and put her black robe on. At the mirror she applied black eye make-up, lipstick and nail polish.

From the bed Joe asked, "Are you sure you look sinister enough?"

She turned to him with a grin. "Samhain is a very special occasion in addition to my presenting the long lost ring."

~ * ~

On the drive south toward Salem, Joe asked, "Where is the ring now?"

"In a secret compartment in my purse." Meg lay back against the door and placed her shiny black shoes on Joe's lap. "Why, are you planning to steal it from me?"

Joe gave her a look and she slowly smiled at him.

I hope she doesn't suspect that I actually was trying to steal it. How can I be worried about what she will do with such a powerful ring and still be attracted to her?

"The Samhain gathering we're attending in the Salem Woods is going to be the largest in the world," Meg said. "Not only will witches from New England be in attendance, but witches from other states, some even from other nations."

After a half-hour of driving, Meg directed Joe into a forest preserve. As he parked the car, another car pulled up beside them and three young women and two men wearing black robes got out. "Happy Samhain," one of the women said.

Meg retuned the greeting then took Joe's hand and led him into the woods and down a path to the sabbat grounds. Thick patches of fog gathered in the forest. When they entered the clearing, Joe saw over sixty people in black robes standing around a huge flaming cauldron and an altar table which was surrounded by several carved pumpkins. People continued to enter.

Circe approached them. "Meg! I can't wait until you show everyone the ring and tell them who you were."

Meg nodded. "Have you spoken to Luna recently?"

"No, not since last night."

"I wonder what she's thinking," Meg said.

"Ask her yourself." Circe looked up at Luna and Paula who were coming toward them.

"Hello, Meg," Luna said. "Circe told us Marcus gave you the ring last night?"

Meg smiled at her. "That's right."

"I've never known Marcus to be so generous," Luna returned. "He didn't ask for anything in return, just handed you the ring and left?"

"I'm not at liberty to tell you anything about our agreement. When you see him, ask him."

"If we ever see him," Paula added.

"He didn't tell you where he was going?" Luna asked.

"No, I assumed he was heading for the second ritual."

Luna shook her head. "No. He wasn't there. If he doesn't show up here tonight, Sayde's going to put out a missing person's report on him tomorrow. The police said we have to wait forty-eight hours."

"And I'm sure you'll be involved with the investigation," Paula said glaring at Meg.

I'm surprised that Meg doesn't look worried.

"Come on, Joe." Meg smiled at him and pulled on his arm.

"Bitch!" they heard Luna say as they walked away.

Soon there were over a hundred people in attendance. Joe noticed some of the other coven members, Sayde, Barry and Ken. The air was pleasantly cool without the hint of a breeze and the mist continued to thicken. Soon, a fiftyish looking woman wearing heavy black eye makeup with long dark hair walked to the altar.

"That's Deanna Corsette of Salem," Meg whispered to Joe. "She's the most famous witch in the country. I've got two of her books at home."

"Greetings fellow wiccans, on this sacred Samhain sabbat." Deanna smiled as she waved her right arm in a grand gesture. "We've got a beautiful night temperature-wise, although a little fog has settled in. Visitors, each of you must have a sponsor to participate. If you don't, you'll have to leave before we cast our magic circle."

Muttering with irritation, three men and two women left the group.

"Will the officers please form our magic circle now?"

When a young man and woman laid down a red robe behind all the participants, Joe noticed the altar table with white linen, had herbs, wheat and other grains on it, as well as several small, glass, candle-lit pots.

When the circle was cast, Deanna said, "It's now the bewitching hour on Samhain, when the veil is thin that divides the worlds of the living and the dead. It's the time when we remember our loved ones who have passed on but walk the earth tonight. It is our new year and also the time of the old year's death. We remember tonight that every ending is but a new beginning. This is the time of the harvest and Diana, the Mother Goddess, now casts her wintery blanket upon our land."

Deanna closed her eyes and said a prayer for loved ones who had departed during the year. Then there was a moment of silence. Sobs were mingled with the crackling flames of the cauldron. Next, Deanna filled a large silver cup from a keg next to the altar. It was passed around and everyone took a sip of wine as a middle-aged man played a flute. Joe took a sip as he watched three young women spring out of the crowd, run toward the altar and dance nude around the cauldron. When they had finished, one by one everyone in the circle jumped over the flaming cauldron. Meg took Joe's hand as they leaped up through the flames before taking their places back in the circle again.

I'm glad I didn't burn my britches. I feel like I'm in a bad horror movie.

Joe started to feel light-headed as everyone held hands and slowly moved in a circle while Deanna led them in a chant.

"We are the old people. We are the new people. We are the same people, better than before."

As they continued, the chant turned into a song and everyone raised their hands high in the air. Some closed their eyes.

When the singing was finished, Deanna took the broom that leaned against the cauldron and symbolically swept the ground. "We will now begin the historic part of our sabbat. Through our history, we suffered the persecution years or the burning times." Deanna's voice rose with emotion. "We were tortured, murdered, banished to caves and other secret dwellings and they called us witch!" She froze for a moment then raised her hands with a smile. "Yet we have overcome as we are here tonight. Would any of you like to add something to our historic portion?"

Meg was already standing before Deanna finished, making sure she would be heard first. "Deanna, my name is Megan O'Leary. I have something of great importance to share with my fellow wiccans tonight."

"I'm intrigued, Megan. Go ahead." Deanna smiled.

"I think most of you here know the name of Medea Laughton."

"I do," Deanna said. "For those of you who haven't heard the name, she lived in the early eighteenth century and was legendary for her magic. She was also the daughter of Diehla Thorne's lover, Ives Laughton. Now what news do you have for us, Megan?"

"Through hypnotic regression, I learned that I was Medea Laughton in a previous life."

Deanna frowned then blinked. "That's very interesting, Megan, but can you prove this?"

"I can. Through my mind of the past, I not only learned that Medea was actually the daughter of Diehla Thorne, but I found Diehla's ancient magic ring to prove my claim."

A murmur went through the crowd.

"You're telling us you actually have Diehla's magic ring?" Deanna's eyes widened.

Meg smiled. "Yes, and I have it with me here tonight to show you."

The murmur became more excited.

"If it's true, this will be the greatest thing that's ever happened to our Wiccan community." Deanna opened her hands and held them chest high.

Luna stood suddenly. "My name is Luna LaBrock. Deanna, may I interrupt here? Megan is lying. Although she is a descendant of Medea's, it was I who was Medea in another life and I have the ring to prove it." Luna smiled proudly and slowly held up her right hand, displaying the pentagram ring on her index finger.

Nineteen

Abracax

Meg frantically rummaged through her purse. In the firelight Joe saw panic on her face. She looked toward Deanna. "She stole my ring!"

Deanna frowned. "Do you two know each other?"

"Yes," Meg said. "We both belong to the Laughton Coven in Manchester."

"Luna, can you prove the ring belongs to you and not Megan?"

"I can." She pointed to Circe, who stood next to her. "This is Circe Tiiu. She's the hypnotist who did the regression for me. She can verify what I say. On the other side of me are two more witnesses from our coven." Luna pointed to Paula and Ken who also stood.

Meg interrupted. "Deanna, they're all lying. This is Joe Hillery, owner of Willstown Video Industries." Joe stood and she laid a hand on his shoulder. "He will verify that Circe actually did the regression for me and that I was Medea Laughton and the true owner of the ring."

"We'll take up the matter of who was Medea and whose ring it is later. I now want to verify that the ring is indeed the actual Diehla Thorne ring. Luna, bring it to me."

When Luna strolled to Deanna, Joe whispered, "How did Luna get the ring from your purse?"

"Paula must have lifted it when I was talking to Luna. She's not only a cat-burglar but a good pickpocket. Don't worry. Luna doesn't know any of the incantations. I'll get her for this."

"But Circe knows some of the spells. Maybe she helped Luna."

Deanna examined the ring carefully on Luna's finger. "Now for those of you who don't know, legend says the magic ring had a protective force. If someone was wearing it and another person touched it while it was on their hand it would give that person a shock or a burn of some kind. Luna, have you verified if this ring has a protective force?"

"Yes." Luna nodded. "It gave the person a stinging burn."

"Since I am leading our sabbat tonight, I suppose I should be the guinea pig."

Luna extended her hand toward the older woman.

Deanna raised her hand toward the ring. "I'm very nervous, not just because of what the ring might do to me, but I'm in awe of its power and history. Well, here goes." Deanna slowly lowered her hand and made contact with the ring on Luna's index finger. The darkness lit up with bright sparks. Deanna fell backward down to the ground. She sat up and rubbed her fingers then slowly rose as everyone watched in amazement.

Deanna took a couple of deep breaths then smiled. "Fellow wiccans, I'm proud to say that this truly is the ring of Diehla Thorne and Medea Laughton of colonial time. I think I need to discuss with Luna what should be done with something so ancient and powerful. Luna, could you demonstrate some of the ring's magic for us tonight?"

"Of course." Luna held up her hand so everyone could see the ring. "This ring was used for various spells and curses, but its true purpose was for raising demons to help the ancient witch and punishing her enemies."

Deanna peered at her. "Could you raise a demon for us here tonight?"

Luna frowned. "I've been studying an old book on ring spells since I found this. I'll try to summon Abracax, one of the great demons. The ring's first owner, Victor Zabno, raised him many times."

"I'm familiar with the great Zabno and with the demon Abracax," Deanna said. "We'll test the ring's power now." Deanna looked around. "If raising a demon is too intense for anyone here, I will permit you to leave the circle. Raise your hand if you wish to be excused."

About twenty people raised their hands.

Deanna shook her head. "I'm surprised that we have about a quarter of our people wanting to leave with such an exciting phenomenon. For the first time ever we will uncast the magic circle so some of you may leave then the circle will be recast so we can continue."

The red rope was taken up and over twenty people walked out of the clearing. The remaining seventy or so formed a smaller circle which was recast while the mist continued to thicken.

Deanna beamed at the group. "Those of you who have chosen to remain are in for a once-in-a-lifetime experience. I would not miss this opportunity for the world."

"Do you think Luna can do it?" Joe whispered.

Meg shook her head.

Meg has some kind of plan.

"Are you ready to raise Abracax, Luna?" Deanna asked.

"Yes, but what should I ask of the great demon?"

"Ask him to give us the wisdom of the ages and to protect us from those who wish to do us harm."

Standing next to Deanna, Luna pulled out a piece of paper from her purse. Reading it she said some words in Latin then stopped, as if expecting the demon to appear in front of her, but nothing came. She repeated the words, but still nothing.

Deanna frowned. "Is there a problem?"

Meg rose. "Deanna, since the ring is really mine, I can bring the great Abracax to you."

"Please come up here, Megan."

"Deanna," Luna said, "let me try once more. There must be some small thing I forgot to do."

Deanna took in a breath and shook her head.

Meg stood next to the other two by the altar. "Say the words again, but you have to be facing east while pointing the ring south. You had the ring pointing skyward."

Luna sheepishly nodded, then repeated the verse while facing east and pointing the ring to the south, but nothing appeared. "Now what's wrong?" Luna looked at Meg.

"You tell me. You claim to be the rightful owner of the ring, remember?"

Luna glared at Meg then turned to Deanna. "I'm sorry, but we may have to wait until Candlemas to raise Abracax after I become better acquainted with the ring's rules."

Deanna closed her eyes and sighed. "Megan, can you please help Luna with this?"

"Of course." Meg turned to Luna. "All you need now is the special charm."

"What charm?" Luna asked.

Meg glared at her.

"Please, Megan," Deanna said. "Help us with this, and we'll know who the ring's owner is."

"I'll do this for you and my fellow wiccans under one condition. After I raise Abracax, the ring is returned to me. Agreed?" Meg looked at Deanna.

Deanna let out a breath and nodded. "If you can bring Abracax to us, I agree."

Meg turned back to Luna. "You should have taken this small bag from my purse when you stole my ring." Meg held up a small green felt bag tied with leather draw strings at the top. Luna took the bag from her.

"The actual words are, Demous, Deyama, Demous, Deyama, Twutcha, Tin, Twutcha, Tin, Deabralose Cadabra. You were saying some of the words wrong. After those words you throw the bag into the cauldron and Abracax will come."

"Thank you, Megan," Deanna said. "What is in the bag, may I ask?"

"I'll tell you later in private."

Luna said the words while standing in the correct position, then tossed the bag into the large cauldron. As they watched, a red billowing smoky cloud rose from the cauldron. People gasped. The smoke didn't clear but continued to swirl and brew. After it billowed to about ten feet, two glowing lights appeared toward the top. Joe knew from his time-travel experience that this was Abracax.

"Why hast thou summoned me?" boomed the sound of a deep male voice.

Luna looked up at the thing and trembled. "We, we seek knowledge of magic from you to help witches of this time."

"Thou art the rightful owner of the ring?" Abracax bellowed.

"What – what do you mean, rightful owner?"

"I did not receive the sacred words of the ring's keeper."

Luna turned to Meg in desperation. "Meg! What's he talking about? Help me!"

Meg stood gazing at her without a word.

The deep voice continued. "By the law of the underworld I must destroy thee for blasphemy."

"No!" Luna screamed and looked at Meg. "It's going to kill me." Luna ran from the altar.

People moved out of her way as Luna passed them, trying to escape the witches' circle. A billowing tentacle from the demon raced toward her. People shrieked when the demonic red arm caught Luna and engulfed her in red smoke. She screamed as it lifted her just above the ground then spun her faster and faster like a top. The tentacle let her go and she fell to the fog covered ground just inside the magic circle. With that, the arm retracted into the demon. There was a round of gasps and moans. Luna lay motionless on the mist laden grass.

"I now descend to the underworld until I am summoned again by the ring," Abracax said.

The demon dissipated. Sayde, Paula, Circe and Ken went to Luna, followed by a middle-aged man.

The man checked the body for a pulse then shook his head. "I'm a medical doctor. I'm afraid she's gone."

Luna's four friends dissolved in tears.

"Does anyone here have a portable car phone so we can call the police?" Deanna asked.

"I do," the doctor said. "I'll go to my car and make the call."

"People," Deanna said, "as tragic as this is, none of you are responsible for what happened to poor Luna, so relax. I want all of you to back up my story when we say that Luna collapsed for reasons unknown. Her death will be blamed on natural causes. Please do not mention to the authorities that we have the ancient ring or that we raised a demon or there will be dire consequences."

"Deanna," Meg said. "You must know that I'm the rightful owner of the ring. None of this would have happened if I'd have brought Abracax to you. If we leave the ring on Luna's finger, the police will confiscate it and it will be lost to us for good."

"Yes, Megan. Remove the ring from Luna's finger if you can." Deanna stopped to take a breath. "This is all so unbelievable, but now that we finally have the ring we don't want to lose it again. I'll be in touch with you about the ring next week."

~ * ~

On the drive back to Manchester, Joe said, "We're lucky we didn't get into trouble over Luna's death. I was afraid the police would think we performed a ritual sacrifice."

"Everyone had the same story and most are respectable business leaders and educators in our community. Of course, we're still not off the hook. The officers have our names."

"I'm glad Deanna let you take the ring instead of keeping it herself."

Meg folded her arms behind her head on the passenger's door. "And because Luna was dead, I didn't get the ring's shock. I'll call Deanna if I don't hear from her first."

"Did you know the demon would kill Luna?" Joe glanced at her.

Meg nodded with a smile. "Yes, because she had everything I had given her to successfully bring Abracax except the sacred password."

"And you knew it?"

"I did." She smiled.

A chill ran down Joe's spine. *It doesn't faze her that she caused Luna's death.*

~ * ~

It was after three in the morning when Joe and Meg arrived at the apartment. Joe was surprised to see Victoria sitting on the porch at that hour.

"What's your grandmother doing out there?"

"She's probably curious to see how things went tonight, so she couldn't sleep."

They approached the porch and Meg said, "Grandma, you shouldn't have waited up for me."

"I had to find out what happened. Are you the witch queen now?" The old woman smiled.

"Not exactly. Not yet anyway. There was a problem. Luna stole the ring and claimed that *she* was Medea Laughton in another life."

Victoria's face dropped. "Of all the rotten tricks."

"Don't worry about her now. She's dead."

Victoria gasped. "What happened?"

"When she tried to raise Abracax, I helped her to a point, just to show Deanna Corsette that I was the rightful owner, but I didn't give her the sacred password."

"Megan, you're so very clever." The old woman clapped her hands in joy. "May I have the honor of holding the ring since it is still Samhain?"

"I'll let you have it this one time, then I'll never remove it from my finger."

Meg slipped the ring off and handed it to her. While Meg told her about taking the ring off Luna's finger, the old woman smiled as she put the ring on her index finger and gazed at it. Joe noticed that she whispered something but he couldn't hear because Meg was talking.

With a smile, her grandmother gave the ring back to Megan. "Thank you for letting me wear the ring, even if it was only for a few seconds. You've made your grandmother very happy, dear."

"Grandma, it looked like you were chanting. What were you saying?"

"I was praying thanks to the Mother Goddess." The old woman smiled and patted Meg's hand.

Meg gave her grandmother a hug and kiss before going upstairs.

In her bedroom, Meg put on a white nightgown. She placed her arms around Joe's neck and kissed him.

"Thank you for coming with me tonight."

"I couldn't have missed all that excitement."

Meg smiled and she and Joe climbed into bed together.

Meg lay in Joe's arms as they listened to the breeze rustle the leaves in the trees. The winds became increasingly stronger.

"It sounds like a storm's coming," Joe said.

Meg sat up. "My witch's instincts are telling me there's trouble brewing out there."

"You're kidding me again, right?"

"Not this time, Joe." Meg sprang from the bed to look out the window.

Joe followed after her. The manic wind blew the trees unmercifully and litter flew around the yard. Joe was afraid the whole building was going to come down.

He looked at Meg. "Do you know something you're not telling me?"

"Yes, but I don't know how to say this."

"Say what?"

Suddenly the wind stopped. Joe looked out the window in disbelief as the trees stood perfectly still, without even a rustle. The only proof that there had been a gale were the papers and branches that littered the yard.

"What in the hell is going on?"

"You just said it. Hell is going on. I fear Abracax or another demon is here."

"A demon? Did it follow us home?"

Meg put an arm around Joe. "Listen." She pulled away.

Joe heard Victoria's voice. She was reciting another incantation.

"Grandma!" Meg went to the other side of the bed and lay on the floor next to the heat register. "Grandma, what are you doing?"

A deep cackle that chilled Joe came up through the vent. "Abracax has come for Joe. So kiss him goodbye, dear."

"Grandma, I order you to stop this!"

Meg rose. "You were right about Grandma. She sent for Abracax. She must have summoned him when I gave her the ring."

"What am I going to do?" Joe's voice broke in emotion. He felt faint.

"Into the kitchen." Meg went around the corner and Joe scurried after her, unable to catch his breath.

Meg stared at the kitchen door. "He's here."

"Oh, my God!" *I'm going to end up like Luna.*

The sound of wind grew louder in the hallway on the other side of the door.

Joe put an arm around Meg. "You've got the ring on. Is there anything you can do for me?"

"I'll do what I can, Joe."

Suddenly, red smoke crept under the door into the kitchen. It swirled and brewed as it rose just in front of the stove. Two dim lights appeared again toward its top. They grew brighter.

"Abracax." Meg held her hand up and pointed the ring at the demon. "I am the rightful owner of the ring. Demous, Deyama, Demous, Deyama, Twutcha Tin, Twutcha Tin, Deabralose Cadabra! Omus Omid! That is the command that sent you here, but Victoria Sidedrop was not the rightful owner of the ring. The sacred words are Sabulabey Anterous!"

In a soft deep voice the demon said, "Yes, Sorceress, you are the rightful owner."

Keeping the ring pointed at Abracax, Meg said, "You must obey me now."

"No, I have been summoned by your ring to take someone and I cannot go back until it hath been fulfilled."

"Then take the one who sent you, for blasphemy."

"Nay, for the sender is not now wearing the ring. I must take the one I was sent for." A smoky tentacle headed directly for Joe.

Twenty

The Aftermath

Meg screamed, "No! You can't take him!" She whipped in front of Joe, wrapped her arms around him and closed her eyes just as the smoky arm reached him. It ripped Meg away and lifted her off the floor and up toward the ceiling. Inside the smoky red tentacle she spun slowly at first, but her spinning became faster.

"Let her go!" Joe yelled. "It's me you're after, not her."

In shock Joe watched Meg gaze down at him with an open mouth. He thought she was screaming or at least trying to scream, but he was unable to hear her. Joe picked up a knife off the table and threw it at the swirling body of the demon just under where Meg was spinning, but it had no effect. The tentacle slowly contracted Meg's body inside and she was gone. With the sound of the wind, it spun away from him toward the door then shrunk and squeezed under it, into the hallway.

In utter disbelief, Joe opened the door and watched the demon fade until it, and its cyclone-like sound, vanished. The building was as quiet now as it had been before Abracax appeared.

Joe closed the door and staggered to the kitchen table. He fell into a chair by the table with his hands over his face and sobbed in grief and disbelief. As nightmarish as the experience was, Joe knew it was all too real.

Why did she do it? Why did she sacrifice herself for me?

If Joe had any doubt about Meg's loyalty before, he didn't now. There was no sound from downstairs.

That old bitch was cursing me to die the entire time I've been living here. Well, she got her granddaughter instead. Does she even know what happened up here? Is she putting another spell on me now, or just listening and wondering? I don't hear any chanting. With all the yelling we were doing, Victoria must have realized Meg's fate.

Trying to pull himself together, Joe had to decide what to do next. How would he explain Meg's disappearance to the authorities? She was taken by a demon!

Joe felt Meg's cat brush against his leg.

Shyebony, poor cat. I wonder if she knows what happened.

"Come here, Shy." Still shaking, Joe picked up the cat and petted her, then glanced at the clock. It was after four-thirty. Besides the worry of being blamed for Meg's disappearance, something else troubled him. He missed her. But after what just happened, he didn't want to stay in that apartment another minute. He took the cat, and avoiding the place where the demon had just been, fled out the back door.

Driving toward his sister's home in Lowell, he decided he'd better stop at a payphone along the way to let her know he was coming.

~ * ~

Later that afternoon, Joe told Bev the whole story of what happened the day and night before.

She closed her eyes. "This all sounds unbelievable, but I do believe you. So, the ring went with her?"

"Yeah. The witches have lost the ring for the third time. Once after Diehla's death, then again after Medea was murdered, and now with Meg. I wonder why the demon left Luna's body but took Meg's. Maybe because she was the ring's owner?" Joe shivered, still in shock.

"I'm just thankful that you're all right. And I'm glad you called to tell us you were coming. A knock at five in the morning would have been more disturbing than a phone call that early."

Joe nodded. "Bev, please don't tell anyone else what I've just told you, not even Marty."

"Whatever you say." She took Joe's hand with a smile. "What are you going to tell the police?"

Joe let out a breath and shook his head. "That Meg wasn't in bed with me when I woke up this morning, and I have no idea where she is. I can't place a missing person's report for forty-eight hours. I'll call the police first thing Tuesday."

"The police are also going to be asking you about Luna LaBrock, since you're one of the witnesses."

"And don't forget about Marcus's disappearance." Joe lowered his head and put a hand to his forehead. "What a disaster this is, and each death was because of that ring."

Bev closed her eyes and sobbed. "Joe, I pray you can somehow get out of this mess. And, of course, Meg's grandmother will be contradicting your statements."

"I don't think the others in that coven will blame me for Meg's disappearance since they could be in trouble themselves over Luna's death. Maybe I should tell them what really happened to Meg since they know about Abracax."

"Joe, I'm so, so sorry to hear about Ellen and Brad."

Bev broke down, and Joe gave his sister a hug and cried with her.

~ * ~

At Hillery mansion that same afternoon, Ellen sat with Brad in the living room.

"Why do you think Joe double-crossed you and Fenton yesterday?" Ellen asked. "Could Meg have put him under another spell?"

Brad gave her a stern look. "No, but I have a feeling he found out about us."

Ellen closed her eyes. "Maybe Tommy knows. He's a smart kid."

"Joe called Fenton last night to warn him about the ring spell Meg put on him." Brad shook his head. "Whatever health problems Fenton has will soon kill him."

Ellen's mouth fell agape. "Oh, no! I hope he has an antidote for that."

"He doesn't, because he isn't familiar with the ring's magic. If we can get the ring, Fenton might be able to stop the spell, but how do we get it now that Meg's wearing it? If Joe doesn't help us get that ring, I'll hold him responsible for Fenton's death."

On the six o'clock news, the woman reporter said, "Police are looking into the mysterious death of Luna LaBrock, age thirty, of Manchester."

Ellen turned to Brad. "This is one of the top stories."

Brad turned the sound up.

"LaBrock died during a witches' Halloween Sabbath last night in the Highland Park Salem Woods just south of Salem. The coroner won't have his report for a couple more days. Some of those who attended the ceremony are being questioned further by police. This comes just twenty-four hours after Marcus Phillips, the leader of LaBrock's coven, was reported missing."

Ellen looked at Brad. "I wonder if Joe will get into trouble over all this since he was involved in both deaths."

"Maybe Luna's, but Marcus's body will never be found, thanks to the ring's magic."

~ * ~

Bev urged Joe not to go into the office the next day but he went anyway. On the drive he heard updated reports about Luna's death on the radio. Joe walked into his office in a daze and sat at his desk. He opened the morning paper that his receptionist always put on his desk. The front page showed a picture of Luna and a small one of Marcus. After Joe paged through the story, he wondered what Sherman was thinking now that Meg hadn't shown up for work.

Not only did Meg save my life, but I've become emotionally dependent on her.

With not having Meg around to help him forget about Ellen, his wife's betrayal seemed even more bitter.

Joe's thoughts were interrupted by the buzzing of his phone. He answered it.

His receptionist said, "Joe, there's a Sayde Anderson on the line."

"Put her through, Carol."

"Joe, the reason for my call is that Deanna Corsette just phoned me here at the parish to tell me she hasn't been able to reach Meg on the phone. She wants to know more about the ring."

"Sayde, I've got some terrible news."

"What happened?"

"You'd better sit down. The same demon that killed Luna also came to Meg's house Saturday night. It was after me, but Meg sacrificed herself for me."

"What happened to her?"

Joe explained the whole terrible event.

"Three of our members have been killed in just two days!" Sayde begin to cry. "What happened to the ring?"

"Meg was wearing it at the time. It went into the demon with her."

"We finally found it and we've lost it again? Joe, don't take this the wrong way, but it's difficult to believe that Meg would sacrifice herself for you after what Trish has told me."

"I know, but that's what happened." Joe closed his eyes.

"Trish filled me in on Marcus's demise and what the others were doing behind our backs. I'm sorry they used you for their pawn. I had no idea."

"I know, Sayde."

"I'm going to check on Victoria since she is in that house alone now."

"She deserves whatever happens to her," Joe said. "And tomorrow I'm going to have to make out a missing person's report on Meg. The papers will have a field day with that."

"Maybe it's better the ring is gone, with all the trouble it caused."

"Soon there'll be another death because of the ring," Joe said. "Meg used it on a friend of mine."

"Oh, no." Sayde was silent for a minute then said, "As far as Luna's death, Deanna told me she will use her powers to influence the coroner's report to cover up the truth, and Marcus's and Meg's bodies will never be found, so you won't be blamed."

Shortly after his phone conversation with Sayde, Joe got a call from the police telling him to be at the station by four o'clock. That afternoon police questioned Joe about Luna's death and also Marcus's disappearance. Joe dreaded telling them about Meg and adding that to his problems, but felt as long as he was at police headquarters, he'd better mention it.

"There's something else." Joe sighed.

The officer frowned. "What?"

"When I got up yesterday morning, my girlfriend, Meg, was gone. I haven't seen her since."

The officer looked at his list of suspects. "Is that Megan O'Leary?"

"Yes."

"We called her home today since she is one of the witnesses to the LaBrock death, but we didn't get an answer. Did you call to see if her friends and family members have seen her?"

Joe nodded. "Yes, but no one has."

"Do you think that Meg's disappearance could be connected to the fact she's mixed up with these other witches?"

Joe blew out a breath. "I wouldn't be surprised."

"How about you? Are you a witch, or pagan, too?"

"No. I'm a Christian."

"Then why were you at a witches' Halloween ceremony?"

"Because I'm living with Meg."

"So you like that free wiccan love, ha?"

Joe scowled. "That has nothing to do with the investigation."

"Why didn't you report her disappearance yesterday?"

"Because I know you have to wait forty-eight hours."

The officer sighed then called another policeman over to cross-examine Joe.

At eight that evening, Joe was finally released with the words "Don't think about leaving town."

On the drive back to his sister's house, Joe heard an updated report about Luna's death on the radio. Meg was now included. "The person of interest in Megan O'Leary's disappearance is her live-in boyfriend, Joe Hillery, owner of Willstown Video Industries. Hillery is being questioned by police at this hour. The coroner will have his report on Luna LaBrock's death by tomorrow."

On Joe's drive to work the following morning he heard the coroner's findings on the radio. "The coroner has concluded that LaBrock died from an allergic reaction to one of the herb drinks that was served at the witches' ceremony last Saturday night."

Deanna helped influence the report and she saved us.

"There are still no leads on the disappearances of Marcus Phillips and Megan O'Leary from the Manchester coven."

When Joe arrived at the office, he felt uncomfortable, as if his receptionist and other employees were watching him. He sat at his desk and read the latest story about the Halloween mysteries. There was a large photo of Luna with small pictures of Marcus and Meg under the word "MISSING." Glancing through the stories, Joe found his name in the section on Meg's disappearance.

Carol buzzed him. "Joe, you have a call from Brad Heins on line two."

"I'll take it, Carol." *I didn't think that snake would have the nerve to call me.* Holding the phone by his ear, Joe pushed the button.

"Joe, I just saw the report on the news. What happened to Meg and the ring?"

"Since Meg is gone, I guess it's time for me to come home to my wife and family, right, Brad?"

"Joe, I'm sorry. Let me explain. Ellen and I have fallen in love. We didn't mean for this to happen."

"You double-crossing son of a bitch!" Joe slammed down the phone.

Later that afternoon, Joe got a call from Trish. "Hi Joe, I wanted you to know that Sayde and Meg's uncle took Victoria to a nursing home today. I've got the key to Meg's apartment so you can get your belongings out of there."

"Thanks, Trish. I ran out so fast Saturday night that I left all my stuff there except Shyebony."

"Thanks for taking Meg's cat with you."

"I plan on keeping her. Did Victoria tell anyone anything about why she sent Abracax after me?"

"No, Sayde said she was incoherent. She's had a stroke or a breakdown, but she does know that Meg was taken."

"I figured that. Where do you want to meet?"

"Could you come over to my place tonight?"

"Are you back at your apartment in Manchester?"

"Yes, I'll give you my address."

~ * ~

Joe arrived at Trish's apartment at seven-thirty. Similar to Meg's place, there were candles and prayers to the goddess in the apartment. She asked him to sit on the couch in the living room then brought him a glass of wine and sat next to him.

"Trish, do all the coven members know what happened to Meg?"

Trish nodded. "Yes, Sayde told them. Joe, let me explain what happened on Saturday night. Victoria always wanted Megan to marry a wiccan, and with you being an outsider and a Hillery at that, she was determined to get rid of you herself. Sayde got that much out of her."

Joe squinted at her. "In the middle of the night, I heard her reciting incantations."

"She was casting a spell that she could find a way to destroy you, and her prayers were answered when she finally had possession of the ring and somehow knew the right words to conjure Abracax. She even had the charm she needed to throw into the fire of her small cauldron."

"Sounds like she had everything planned." Joe swirled the wine in his glass.

"Diehla's descendants will die out once Victoria passes."

"What about Meg's uncle?"

"He's from Meg's father's side and not related to Victoria. She only had one daughter."

Joe nodded. "The Cyrus line will die out soon as well, since Meg put a ring spell on Fenton."

"Why and when did she do that?"

He explained the fiasco in the bookstore stockroom.

Joe sipped his wine. "Medea's curse on the Cyrus line will be fulfilled once Fenton dies. It happened the way Medea told Nathon it would when a Cyrus descendant again tried to get her ring. Meg thought the prophecy was fulfilled when she killed Marcus as Medea. With her not knowing that one of the men who attacked her in the stockroom was also a Cyrus, the last in fact, she didn't know that the curse wasn't completed until she had cursed Fenton."

Trish raised her eyebrows. "That's interesting. And while I was in hiding I learned that Marcus was suspected of committing at least two murders. You and Meg would have been three and four, if Meg hadn't remained as Medea."

"Why am I not surprised?" Joe set his glass down on the coffee table. "Now I see why you went into hiding."

Trish nodded. "Now that I filled Sayde in on the details, she knows how dangerous Marcus's people are. As new coven leader, Sayde has asked Circe, Paula and Ken to leave."

"Trish, I want to thank you for saving my life. If you hadn't opened that office door at the parish when you did, Meg, as Medea, would have shot me."

Trish took Joe's hand. "I'm glad my timing was right. I was there because I knew something bad was going to happen with Meg and Marcus battling over that ring."

Joe nodded and smiled at her.

"Do you want another glass of wine?"

"No, I'd better be going." He rose from the couch. "I'll get my belongings tomorrow night from Meg's apartment."

Trish followed him to the front door. "Here's the key for the apartment. Are you going to be all right going back there?"

Joe shook his head. "I don't know."

"Do you want me to go with you?"

Joe smiled. "No, I'll get through it, but thanks anyway."

"I feel so bad about what your wife did to you." Trish touched his shoulder.

"Well, I was living with another woman at the time."

"But you were under a powerful love spell. I can't tell you how sorry I am that you lost two women in such a short period of time."

"I lost one. My wife, Ellen."

Trish leaned closer and looked into his eyes. "Joe, I'm not stupid. You don't sacrifice your life for someone if you don't have feelings for them."

Joe slowly nodded and looked to the floor, realizing she was right.

"If you ever need someone to talk to, just give me a call or stop by anytime." She smiled at him.

"Thanks. I'll remember that." He smiled back and gave her a hug before leaving.

~ * ~

Joe left the office the next evening and drove to Meg's apartment. It was dark when he arrived and seemed like a different season than when he had lived there just days before. It was cold and windy, and the trees had shed almost all of their colorful leaves.

If Joe hadn't needed his things, he never would have gone back inside that house. He carried several bags up the stairs and went in through the back door. He turned on the light by the entrance and a melancholy feeling pierced him as he entered the living room. Was it the terrible thing that happened to Meg and almost became his own fate, or was it some fond memories he had of her?

Meg's presence seemed to be all around him, even though she wasn't there. Her prayer to the goddess was still on the living room wall and incense candles were on the end tables.

Joe packed his things from the closet, but when he entered the bedroom, he tried not to look at anything that would bring back memories, especially the bed. Against his will, his eyes were drawn there, the place where he and Meg had made love. The bed was unmade with covers in the same position as they were on Halloween night when Meg jumped from the bed in fear to look out the window. It was as if the apartment were suspended in time.

When Joe went into the bathroom to get his prescriptions, he noticed Meg's hair brush sitting on the hamper. Still in the bristles were strands of her dark hair. A tear came to his eye and his lip quivered. He made his way back into the kitchen before remembering the sight of Meg being taken away by the demon just above the stove.

He strolled back into the living room as the cold wind moaned and howled against the window like ghosts from his past. Joe looked at the couch and remembered the first time he'd sat there after giving Meg a ride home from the parish. Meg had made him hot chocolate while she flirted with him.

Joe took one last look around the apartment. "Thank you for saving my life. I'll never forget you, Meg."

He breathed deeply then shut out the lights. Walking out of the apartment into the cold, he locked the back door behind him for the final time.

~ * ~

Two weeks later, in the car at the airport, Ellen sobbed.

Brad embraced her. "Don't cry, Ellen. We'll be together in Chicago soon."

"It's not just that you're leaving, but I feel terrible about Joe. Bev said he gets more depressed every day. She's worried about him, and so am I. Not only has he lost me and now his kids, but he's losing his business at the end of the year. And on top of that, you and I have put his ancestral home up for sale."

"It could be worse. If Sayde, Trish, you and I hadn't cleared him, he might be in jail right now."

"But what happened to Meg wasn't his fault. I believe he told Bev the truth."

"But if Joe hadn't betrayed Fenton and me, Meg wouldn't have had the ring on Halloween night for those things to have happened."

"The only reason he double-crossed you is that he was hurt. You told him he had to stay with Meg until you two got the ring from her."

Brad gave her a kiss. "The only reason I'm trying to help Joe is for your sake. I told his sister that I have the connections to get him a job at the Shnell Company here in New Hampshire, but she told me he doesn't want any favors from me, and he refused to speak to me. I'm just glad the ring is gone. That was our goal to begin with, except now we can't help Fenton and he grows weaker every day."

"It was Meg's grandmother that conquered the demon?" Ellen asked.

"Yes. Sayde told me Victoria had been casting the same spell on Joe every night since he moved in with Meg. And the spell finally worked when the old woman put the ring on and summoned the demon to kill him. That's why she's in the nursing home. She had a mental breakdown."

Ellen took in a breath. "Joe and Meg's relationship must have been more than just acting or she wouldn't have sacrificed herself for him."

"That makes me feel less guilty." Brad kissed Ellen goodbye. "I'll send for you right after Thanksgiving."

"I'm happy that we'll all be together for Christmas."

Brad smiled at her and got out of the car. Teary eyed, Ellen watched him walk away through the crisp air of the overcast afternoon.

~ * ~

Later that evening, Joe lay on his bed watching TV. Bev entered the room.

"Joe, Marty and I are going to bed now. Don't stay up too late. You've got a job interview in the morning."

"I know, Bev." Joe smiled at her. "Thanks."

"If you don't get this job, maybe you should reconsider taking Brad up on working for Shnell."

Joe turned down the sound on the TV and looked at her. "I don't want a damn thing from him, Bev."

Bev squinted. "I just meant you could work there until you found something else. At least you'd be making some money while you were searching."

"I promise if I don't have a job by the beginning of next year, I'll swallow my pride and look into that job. I'm not going to mooch off my sister."

"That isn't what I meant, Joe. I just don't want you to pass up this job and later wish you'd taken it."

"I've made so many mistakes that one more isn't going to make any difference." Joe looked into Bev's eyes. "I can't thank you enough for letting me stay here. If it weren't for you, I'd be living on the street right now."

"Joe, if you're on the street, I'll be sitting next to you."

Later that night Joe was awakened by Shyebony jumping up on his bed. When he opened his eyes, he saw a rainbow of tiny lights dancing around the room. A moonbeam was reflecting off something on the nightstand next to him. Joe turned on his lamp to see what was creating the colorful light show. To his amazement, he saw Meg's pentagram ring on his nightstand!

Meet

Ralph Horner

In August 2007, Ralph's short story, *Pandora Spoxx* was featured by Wild Cat Books in its monthly *Startling Stories* Anthology.

In June 2008, his short story, *Atalanta Alters The Tide Of Alida* was published in the *Heroes of Ancient Greece* anthology by Night to Dawn Books.

In March 2009, Ralph's first novel, *Tandem Tryst,* was published by Wings Press. His second novel, *Witch's Moon* was also published by Wings in December 2012. After Ralph's short story *Lucinda's Secret* was published in *Night to Dawn* magazine's October 2013 issue, his third novel, *Midnight Mist*, the sequel of *Tandem Tryst*, was published in December 2013.

Ralph is an active member of the Southland Scribes Writers Group in Oak Forest, IL

Ralph is also a professional entertainer, doing balloon art and magic since 1991.

VISIT OUR WEBSITE
FOR THE FULL INVENTORY
OF QUALITY BOOKS:

http://www.books-by-wings-epress.com/

*Quality trade paperbacks and downloads
in multiple formats,
in genres ranging from light romantic comedy
to general fiction and horror.
Wings has something for every reader's taste.
Visit the website, then bookmark it.
We add new titles each month!*

Made in the USA
Columbia, SC
14 July 2017